LIFE BEYOND BORDERS

LIFE BEYOND BORDERS

A NOVEL

JEAN-ERVÉ TONICO

FORWARD PRESS

Published by Forward Press
First Printing, 2008

Copyright @ 2008 by Jean-Ervé Tonico.

Please submit inquiries to: info@4wardpress.com.
This novel is based on a true story; most names have been changed. Some characters, places and incidents are used fictitiously.

Publisher's note: At times, the author has taken the short cut of referring to the United States of America as America.

Library of Congress Cataloging-in-Publication Data
Tonico, Jean-Ervé.
   Life beyond borders : a novel / Jean-Ervé Tonico.
   p. cm.
   LCCN 2007922025
   ISBN-13: 9780979135408
   ISBN-10: 0979135400
   1. Haitian Americans--Fiction. 2. Haiti--Social conditions--1970---Fiction. 3. New York (N.Y.)--Fiction. 4. Autobiographical fiction. I. Title.
   PS3620.O582L54 2008   813'.6
        QBI07-600222

Printed in the United States of America
First Edition

DEDICATION

*In loving memory of my brother,
Ronald Tonico, the man who taught me the
true meaning of unconditional love.
To his son and my nephew, Andrew Tonico.*

Contents

Acknowledgments ix

Author's Note xiii

A Beautiful Bird 1

Lesson in Discipline 7

A Teacher's Love 11

Micheline Gustave 16

Soul Train 24

Hope 36

Andy's Song 40

The Lady from Miami 62

A Family Vanishes 75

Dominique 78

Andy Revisited 96

Jeda's Decision 103

Detour 107

Jamaican Vacation. 121

Back to Haiti? 137

The Homecoming 148

Shame 163

Second Partings. 178

Connections. 189

Miami! 201

The American Dream 218

Jump or Die 230

Bits of Wood. 242

Looking Back. 251

Epilogue. 254

About the Author 256

Acknowledgments

I WANT TO thank first and foremost, my wife and publisher Dawn Moulton Tonico for her tireless, unwavering commitment to take a handwritten manuscript and turn it into a book. The daunting task of preparing this book for publication tested your limits. Your patience and resolve are magical. I love you.

I can't say enough about the love and support I received from my life's best rewards: my beautiful 25-year-old daughter Tatiana Joanne Tonico, my handsome 9-year-old boy Alexander Jean Tonico, and 5-year-old grandson Evans Bonilla-Tonico. You are my strengths and weaknesses.

I am indebted to my editors, S. Shange Amani and Anita Doreen Diggs. To think in one language and translate into a different one, while trying to maintain flow, substance and meaning, is not a picnic. I could not have done it without your complete understanding, insight and guidance. I offer a special thanks to my copy editor Katrice Grayson. Working with you over the years to complete this project has been a tremendous joy. Many thanks to all of you! Thank you for staying true to my voice.

I am grateful for my focus group members who gave so freely of their time in spite of their busy schedule: Marva Allen, Nicole Bazemore, Beth Caron, Marie Compas Polo, Albert

Dépas, Joya Fennell Meadows, Denise Lyttle, Tamaril Means, Karen Robinson-Salley, Cheryl Stevens, Frantz Tonico, and Tatiana Tonico. Your critique, feedback and encouragement were invaluable. I thank you from the depth of my heart.

I thank Janine Durand for going beyond the call of duty to ensure that my paperwork was always in order while I awaited my green card. You are a gift to the Haitian immigrant community. I thank my aunt, Rose Voltaire Thomas and uncle, Edward Thomas. I thank my brother Albert for initially sponsoring me for my green card and my former wife, Carline Tonico, for taking over the process. Many thanks are due to Mohamed Sylla, Soukeyna Diop, J. B. Armstrong, Ronald Gilbert, Matar Thiam and Shirley Faye Moulton. I thank my godfather and cousin, Frantz Portès, for helping me to secure my first job in Haiti. I love you! My cousin who lent me the money to escape Haiti, you gave me the best break of my life. My heartfelt thanks to all my brothers, sisters, nieces, nephews, in-laws, cousins and friends. You have played a pivotal role in my life. Much love! I thank those who allowed me use their names as characters in the book.

To all my crewmembers and friends (flight attendants, pilots, mechanics, in-flight service managers, ground and ramp agents) here and abroad at Delta Air Lines, ASA, Comair, my former Pan Amers, and buddies at other airlines your constant asking where is the book and how is the book kept me on the keyboard even when I was jetlagged. You have been terrific! Since I can't name all of you, I'll follow the simplest rule: thank you all! As you are spreading your wings traveling around the world, spread also some love and kindness. You have so much of it.

To my young Haitian brothers and sisters living in United States or wherever you may be, I want to leave you with one message: Weak minds destroy. Strong minds build. Build your minds so we can rebuild our beloved Haiti.

This acknowledgment is incomplete without paying due respect to my hero, my mother, Adrienne Tonico. I love you Mom and thank you for your guidance. To my father, Renel Portès, who is no longer with us, may your soul rest in peace Papa. I am sure you would have been proud.

Author's Note

IN APRIL of 1980, after reaching the shore of Miami with only the clothes on my back, I instantly became aware of the stigma associated with being a Haitian Boat Person. Unfortunately, many, including even some Haitians, have bought into the negative stereotype of a Haitian Boat Person as being very poor, illiterate or a mere economic refugee.

I became extremely passionate about the subject because I, too, am a Haitian Boat Person. Having survived the journey, I wanted you to have a glimpse of Haitian Boat People and share with you why some decide to leave their homeland, the intricacies of the journey, the agony, fear and frustration of it all.

Almost 28 years later, I often wonder, if I were to wake up in Haiti today in light of all the chaos that is still battling the country, would my decision be any different? After all, in the last 20 years or so, coup d'état has been the most lucrative business in the country. Sadly, it keeps building wealth for the same people—those who have orchestrated the coup. Meanwhile, young Haitian children keep dying of hunger, disease, and hopelessness. It's time to stop this man-made tragedy.

I thank you and would like to hear from you. E-mail your comments to: Jean@4wardpress.com.

A Beautiful Bird

MY GRANDMOTHER was going to see God. It was the summer of 1967. At the time, I believed that when someone was leaving for New York, that person was going to see God because that is where He lived. According to my father, once you were there, your life would take a new path, have a different meaning and become filled with joy because you would be living next to God. The airport was the place where the journey began for anyone who wished to see God.

I was a six-year-old boy and going to the airport would be more fun than anything I had ever done. I had seen airplanes way up in the sky, but never one on the ground. But here I was, about to go on my very first trip to the François Duvalier airport in Port-au-Prince, Haiti.

I remember waking up early that morning full of energy, wishing my grandma would hide me in her suitcase and take me along for the journey. But since that wasn't the plan, I gave her lots of messages to deliver to God. Every time my parents gave us something their lesson was always the same, "Thank God first because He gave us what we gave you." So I knew God was a good person. When He received my messages, I would be joining my grandmother, Grand Da, in New York.

The flight was to leave in the afternoon, but Grand Da had to be at the airport many hours before.

"Jacky," my mom yelled, "you need to get ready." With her help, I was dressed in my nicest clothes and my hair was neatly combed.

When it was time to leave the house, my father, Grand Da, two of my five brothers, a cousin, and I hopped into the Chevrolet that my dad drove as a cab driver.

My father was not as happy as the rest of us. He kept saying over and over again that his mother was going someplace he could never drive to see her.

The trip to the airport was exciting. There were big and small cars, trucks, old and new colorful *tap taps* (minibuses), bikes, and motorcycles cruising in the same or opposite direction at various speeds, on paved roads in some areas and dirt roads full of potholes in other places. Along the way, tall trees with long branches full of green leaves provided cover from the burning sun for people standing, sitting down, or simply walking on both sides of the road. Street vendors were everywhere, with everything from mixed vegetables and live chickens to candies, fresh fruits and roasted peanuts. There were women carrying piles of food on their head, calling out their names for greater attention.

All in all, I kept thinking what a special treat it was to go to the airport and how lucky Grandma was to be going to New York.

The airport was huge. People were moving at different speeds, some with suitcases and others without. I wondered if there was anyone inside those suitcases because some were very big. Everyone was cheerful, but those leaving were the happiest. It was going to take God a long time to see all those people and read all their messages.

While inside, I heard voices right above my head. But when I looked up, there was not a soul in sight. It felt somewhat strange, even frightening, especially when the person kept talking without showing a face.

The check-in area was a long desk with several people standing alongside each other, asking many questions of those leaving. I stepped closer to hear what was being said. If this was a test one must pass to see God, I needed to know the answers. About five to ten minutes later I figured out, "May I see your passport and ticket?" was the main question. But what was a passport or a ticket? I stayed silent, hoping sooner or later someone would call out the answers.

But then I noticed something else. Most people didn't even give an answer. What they did instead was hand over an envelope. What was the secret in the envelope? Unless I knew the answers or had an envelope to hand over, seeing God was not going to happen. But, if Grand Da passed the test, either she or my father must know the answers. Before long, one of them would have to share them with me.

About fifteen minutes later, my father, fighting back his tears, said softly, "Let's say goodbye to Grand Da. It is time for her to leave." She was in tears. My cousin Jean-René and my brother Ronald soon followed. I was crying too but nothing close to Jean-René. He was out of control. I mean, I could understand the crying, but not all that followed! One moment he was holding his head and the next rubbing his tummy or stomping his feet. Before you knew it, he was grabbing Grand Da's hand, yelling and jumping at the same time. One of the vendors was so moved by his tears he ended up giving him a free candy. I started to yell even louder, looking straight into the vendor's eyes, hoping for a free candy as well. Instead, he acted as if I scared him and walked away. I was angry.

We walked upstairs to see Grand Da get on the airplane. Since there was a crowd in front of us, I told my father I wanted to move closer so I could have a better look at the airplane. I asked everyone to excuse me while I pushed myself forward to get in front of the crowd. After a few dirty looks and a couple of pushes in return, I ended up exactly where I wanted to be.

I looked below and there it was.

I was shocked. If there had been any water on the ground, I would have said this was the biggest fish I had ever seen. But since it was dry and the airplane was standing still on the cleanest, longest paved road I had seen so far in Port-au-Prince, it looked more like a beautiful bird ready to flap its wings.

Why were the wings so wide? The tires? The tail? Why were they so big? What about the windows, why so many? How many people would have to push it to make it run? I had seen five, six and up to seven people pushing cars that wouldn't start. I thought a plane in the air with so many people sitting inside wouldn't get very far.

I lost track of everything else around me while looking at the airplane and all its parts until my father said, "Grand Da should be walking out soon." He then pointed downstairs to the people going to the airplane and told us to keep looking until we saw her. "When you do," he said, "call her name and wave goodbye."

It was hard to tell who would get to see God first, but I knew it was not going to be Grand Da because there were way too many people ahead of her. To me, Grand Da never walked, but traced her steps. When she moved, even the slowest cat could compete. She was short, pretty, and had a smile bright enough to cheer up even the meanest soul. But boy, oh boy, was she slow.

Finally, she made her way out. We did exactly what Dad asked us to do. We screamed "Grand Da, Grand Da!" and waved goodbye at the same time. From time to time, she would look back, stop and wave goodbye as well. As soon as she reached the airplane's stairs, she turned around and waved for the last time.

The entrance door was closed and the stairs moved away. I was about to watch what my eyes were ready to see, but my mind not yet ready to believe. The airplane started to move slowly. It took one turn, then a second; it started moving faster and became noisier. I kept wondering why no one opened a window to wave goodbye again.

Suddenly, the airplane stopped. I thought, "Oh no, maybe it's coming back to let some people off." I knew it! There were just too many people. I was nervous. I only hoped Grand Da was not one of them. But what happened next was really surprising. The airplane made a very big noise and started to run fast, very fast!

I screamed and yelled, "Faster airplane, faster!" About midway out, the head of the airplane left the ground. I was waiting for it to come back down, but in just a split second the whole airplane was off the ground, and yes, it was in the air all by itself.

"*Incroyable!*" shouted someone.

"Bravo, bravo," said another while clapping. The crowd joined in by clapping with even more excitement. With the wings jiggling from side to side, the airplane looked like a bird dancing in the sky.

I kept saying, "Bye airplane, bye airplane," but instead of saying bye back to me, it disappeared into the clouds with my grandmother in it.

On our way downstairs, I held my father's hand tightly and asked, "What is a ticket and a passport?"

As always, his answer was brief, "They are documents needed to get on the airplane." From the pain in his voice and the frown on his face, I knew I needed to be quiet. The sadness of never seeing Grand Da again began to sink in slowly.

As we were in the car heading back home, it seemed as if Dad was trying to catch the airplane. He sped like a mad man. I closed my eyes. My grandmother was gone and I would never get to see her again.

I cried.

Lesson in Discipline

WHEN I thought of my grandmother, the trip to the airport and the airplane taking off, the memory brought a smile to my face. But when I thought of how long it was taking God to answer my messages, my heart filled with sadness. It had been a year already!

From talking to my parents, I learned Grand Da went to New York to stay with my aunt Rose. I also found out God did not actually live in New York. Rather, for Haitians in my circle, New York was called *Péyi bon dyé,* "God's country," so whoever was going to New York would say they were going to visit God. In spite of this, I kept praying to go to New York.

But God was forever teaching me patience. Within two years we moved twice but not one of those moves lead me to New York. I spent much of those years getting used to my neighborhoods, so my prayers fell off a bit.

In October of 1971, my two older brothers, David, Ronald (whom we called Roro), and I started a new primary school. Our new school, *Coeur de Jésus,* "Jesus' Heart," was many blocks away from our rented apartment. The principal, Mr. Victor Baroulette, known as Maître Ba, had a reputation as a no-nonsense type of guy. To the *crétins,* as he would call the non-performers, he was merciless. I remember vividly his motivating speech during the very first day of school. It went something like this:

"You are here for one reason and one reason only—to learn—and don't you ever forget this. Your parents are making great sacrifices for you to be here, but they ask for only one thing in return and that is for you to do your best. Therefore, it is both my responsibility and duty to see to it that you deliver. Those of you who are thinking about doing less than your best, please be certain we will be very good friends. And those of you who are willing to work hard and deliver your very best, we, indeed, will be better friends. There is no such thing as the best school or the best teacher, there is only the best student. Your education begins in the classroom, but it does not end there. What you will learn is only a fraction of what you will need to survive where it matters most…outside. I'll see to it that everyone involved understands your education is their primary mission. But, let's be clear. Your role in this mission is vital." After a long pause, he finally said, "Your learning is your responsibility."

The school was one big enclosed room with over 200 students seated about five to six on a bench. There were always six classes being taught at the same time. Concentration was crucial.

Class began promptly at 8:00 A.M. If you were late, you had to have a valid reason. As soon as he saw a pattern, he would call your parents into his office and they would exchange a few words about being in school on time.

The day started with the pledge of allegiance to the flag, followed by a class prayer and ended with a class prayer. We were in school twice daily, from 8–11A.M. and again from 1–4 P.M. with fifteen minutes recess within each session.

He established a uniform and shoe inspection policy every

Monday and Wednesday. A part of the school uniform was a properly ironed white shirt, and he would accept no variations of that color or any visible winkles. If you were fortunate enough to own a pair of black shoes, which were also part of the uniform, when he looked at them he expected them to be shiny. If you couldn't afford leather shoes and had to wear plastic ones instead, we called these *boyo*, you still had to grease them so they too would be shiny. He would at times stand right behind us to see how we smelled. If deodorant was running low at home, which happened to be the case every now and then, we used a little soap with lime to work magic and save us a lot of insults from Maître Ba.

His emphasis on our appearance, he explained, was because he felt we reflect on the outside how we feel on the inside. Maître Ba exemplified what he preached. He was always impeccable. The teachers were no exception to the rules. He also had three sons in the school and they received no special treatment.

He would send us back home for sloppiness before turning us away for late tuition. If no improvements were made, he would call our parents to the school and at times curse them out in front of our peers. Luckily, I was blessed to have a mother who believed in proper attire, even when it meant staying up late at night and waking up early in the morning to make sure her kids presented themselves as expected.

On Sunday mornings, we were required to attend church also in uniform: white pants, white shirt tucked inside our pants, black belt and black shoes. He believed attending church was necessary to develop our spiritual growth.

Maître Ba was keen about discipline. He used any method to get our attention. At times, it involved copying a line many times and getting the paper signed by a parent before returning it to him. Other times, it was facing the wall for maybe ten to fifteen minutes in complete silence. And if we dared turn before the time was up, the process began anew. The last thing you wished for was a whipping. He did it with such passion, that when it was all over, you had but one choice—to become similarly passionate about your books.

My textbooks were my primary focus. I read them very fast, sometimes, two or three chapters ahead of the class. The more I read, the deeper my desire. Every book sparked my imagination. By the third month, I was first in my class by a wide margin.

Christmas vacation came and went with no major event. We started school again in January 1972. Since I was always reading ahead of the lesson plan, I had time to review almost every other day. At first, I was afraid it was pure luck, but by the end of January, I was once again first in the class.

Surprisingly, a few days later, my teacher chose me as the class monitor. Given that I was not the oldest student in the class, I shared my concern with the teacher. Growing up in an environment where the older ones had all the authority, with five older brothers, I was accustomed to following orders. He explained that his selection was not based on age, but solely on merit. Despite my hesitation, he encouraged me to give it a try.

The teacher then spelled out my responsibilities. As monitor, I was to ensure that the students behaved themselves and performed according to the class policy. If there was a problem, I would be held accountable. I learned a lot about leadership, discipline, responsibility, teamwork and the value of hard work.

A Teacher's Love

THE BORDE family had been our next-door neighbors for a while. Albert Borde was a cab driver like my father and they were very close friends. His wife, Nathalie, stayed at home and took care of their only child, Jeda, who was my age.

Although Roro was my best friend, Jeda definitely ran a close second.

In some ways, I didn't really think of Jeda as a girl. She could climb a tree or kick a soccer ball as well as Roro and I. And, although Mrs. Borde put ribbons in her hair for school and church, she didn't like them at all.

By 1972, we were both eleven years old and Jeda hoped that her mother would forget about the ribbons. She was wrong. I consoled her as best I could, reminding her that someday she would be a grown woman and could do as she pleased.

Some time in March of 1972, I became sick with a severe abdominal pain. When my parents took me to see a doctor, he immediately requested they take me to the hospital. I went into surgery in less than forty-eight hours for appendicitis.

All I remember from that event was my mom in tears and my dad kissing my forehead while saying good luck as they rolled me into the operating room.

I returned from the operating room many hours later with IV tubes and needles in my arm, a pile of cotton on my stomach and in excruciating pain.

It was the day before Good Friday.

If you missed any meal during the year, Good Friday was the day to make up for it. The menu was a lot of rice and beans, fish, beets, carrots, and watercress salad, fresh grapefruit juice—the best of Mom's cooking. Yummy! I was already starving.

When I asked how soon could I eat, the answer was far from my expectation.

"No food or drink anytime soon," said Mom and Dad in unison.

What? I was dying of hunger. To add to my misery, I found out a plastic tube had been inserted inside me and they removed something from my stomach. This meant no solid food for a few days. The sharp pain I was feeling was even more painful. No food; plastic tube? What went wrong? Just a few days ago, I was so healthy and all of a sudden my life was full of restrictions. This was insane!

I dozed off in mid-conversation and woke up later that night by the soft touch and caring smile of a beautiful nurse asking if I needed anything. I looked at her, smiled, and whispered back, "When do I get to leave?"

"As soon as we think you are well enough," she answered gently.

The bed was hard. I was starving. My back was killing me. I was surrounded by a bunch of sick people but I had no idea who they were or why they were there. The nurse's kindness, combined with her human touch, worked wonders in soothing my pain.

The next day, Mom showed up about six in the evening with Jeda and Roro.

Mom told me that she'd been in church all day, praying for my quick recovery. She showered me with her tender love, Jeda shyly wished me well and Roro gave me a quick hug. Then they all left.

I was discharged a few days later, with a long list of do's and don'ts, convinced that my survival was miraculous and due only to the daily prayers of Mom, friends and family members.

The surgery kept me out of school for almost two months. Besides, it left an ugly scar on the right side of my belly. While I enjoyed being at home and all the individual attention I received, I was eager to move on with my life. With roughly two months remaining before the final exam, if I missed any more time, I might have to repeat the year.

Usually, we received a report card at the end of each month, but every student and parent was concerned about the one from the final exam in June. What made the exam so challenging was that we were tested on everything from the first day of that school year. If you waited until the last minute to prepare, you were doomed.

If you failed, you would have one more chance to retake it in September. If by then no progress was made, you would have to repeat the year and it didn't matter how many times or how old you were.

If your parents had enough money, you could always go to another school and pay your way to the next class. Some opted to take that route, but Maître Ba cut no corners, big or small. For many schools, it was the money, then the students. But for him, it was the complete opposite. Money or no money, unless you performed, you didn't get promoted. It was that simple.

Mom was resolute. "Until the doctor clears you to go back, you will stay right here, even if you have to repeat the year." Nothing I said was good enough to change her mind. Her decision was final.

I was frustrated, angry, and miserable. I was praying but with no immediate result because, to my irrational self, my progress was too slow. I even argued with God for putting me through such misery. I thought He was upset with me for arguing with Him so I begged for forgiveness, but that didn't seem to make any difference.

First week of May, still no word from the doctor. I was getting nervous. I stopped by the school to share my concern with my teacher, Maître Vedette, and to find out what my options were. He calmed me down when he promised to tutor me for free during the summer recess if I had to retake the exam in September. He pointed out that repeating the year was not an option, if he had any say in it.

Like Maître Ba, he also understood the significance and diverse roles a teacher must play in building his students' confidence, self-esteem and a keen desire for learning.

Maître Vedette set very high expectations and always encouraged us to settle for nothing short of excellence. Therefore, even when we were not up to the task, we had very few choices but to perform. He was very gentle but firm, dedicated, enthusiastic, always smiling, and above all—a gift.

He taught me in his own special way the balance between work and fun, and the value of hard work and reward.

It was those simple little things that made him stand out from the rest of the pack. His kindness, dedication and love have been the invisible air beneath my wings. I salute and thank him again wherever he is.

In the meantime, Jeda kept me abreast of what was being taught in class. I was confident that if the doctor allowed me to return to school even by the end of May, I would have my work cut out for me, but I'd pass all my classes. Finally, my prayers were answered. I was released to go back to school by mid-May. I left the doctor's office with a great sense of relief and purpose.

I was happy to be back in school and ready to tackle any challenges waiting ahead. Maître Vedette kept his promise by helping me as best as he could to get up to speed with the rest of the class. After a few bumps and steadfast determination, with less than a week to spare, he agreed for me to take the May exam. I could often judge by the end of each exam what my score would be but this time I was clueless.

I don't know how I pulled it off, but by the time the report card came out, I managed to secure third place in the class. I was satisfied with the result, but there was still much work to be done. Maître Vedette was pleased and as a reward he gave me one *gourde,* which at the time was the equivalent of 20 U.S. cents.

I ran home to share the good news with my parents. No one was happier for me than Jeda.

Micheline Gustave

BY THE next school year, I was twelve. I had passed the final exam in June and life was even more enjoyable. There was a pretty new girl living in the apartment behind us and she was also in my class at school. Her name was Micheline Gustave.

Her beauty took a toll on my concentration. Her eyes were the size of bright stars, and when you looked at her, there was only one thing left to do—adore her—as you would a beautiful sky set ablaze by burning stars. Her lips were as red as rose petals, and when she smiled, my heartbeat raced three times faster than normal. It almost felt as if my heart was rushing up to meet her smile only to get disappointed or miss a beat halfway in between.

Whenever she realized that I was watching her, she would give me the sort of look that would send even the strongest heart searching for a new valve.

One day, when school was over, I finally worked up the nerve to approach her.

"Micheline, I would like to walk you home."

She looked me over from head to toe and then said icily, "Never. I can do much better."

She walked away before I could even think of an answer. I was more disappointed than I can describe and the first image that crossed my mind was to flee the scene. When I turned around to retrace my steps, I saw Jeda. I stood there motionless not knowing what to do or say. She had seen and heard everything. She looked surprised and hurt. How sweet of her to experience such pain on my behalf. It was quite an embarrassing moment.

Jeda opened her mouth to say something but I held up a hand. "I do not wish to discuss it."

"What is that supposed to mean?"

"Exactly what it means Jeda. I am in too much pain to talk."

She reached for my hand, threw her arm around my shoulder as if to lift the insult off my bent shoulder and gently said, "Let's go Jacky." I had almost been in tears but Jeda softened the blow and I recovered swiftly, but not for long.

We walked home in silence.

I kept asking myself, "How could she be so insensitive?" I loved Micheline and would never love anyone else. I was definitely crushed by her insult.

My rejection did not lead me to Roro. All night long, I thought about telling him what had happened to me. Yet I did not because he would tease me for a long time. But the main reason I did not tell Roro is because I was the leader of our duo. Even though he was the elder brother, I was always the one lecturing him. The fear of sobbing over a girl in front of Roro and thus losing his admiration triggered my silence.

The next day, Roro, Jeda and I went to take some homework to a classmate who lived in a different neighborhood. Since he was absent from school because of an illness, I felt it was the right thing to do not only as a friend but also as the class monitor. When we got there, Roro and I were beaten up with much passion by a group of almost thirty angry guys.

What caused the fight was a comment by another classmate that the only reason I was first in the class was because of my father's light complexion so Maître Vedette was sucking up to me. He also called me the teacher's pet. I was infuriated by his remark particularly against Maître Vedette, and wanted to get right back at him. So without thinking I replied, "If you study a little bit harder instead of making up excuses, you might end up securing a place for yourself in the intelligent students' club in the future." Well, as soon as I closed my mouth, the guy placed his index and pinky fingers in his mouth and whistled. The end result could have truly been avoided had I known he could not take a joke.

I didn't know how they all got there so quickly, but it appeared as if a ferocious tornado had opened a gate to some angry dogs and they were blown over in the blink of an eye. They did not bite; they chewed. In a flash, I was hit from every direction. It was like a downpour and no part of my body was spared. I was tossed in the air not once, but many times. It felt as if I was inflated, deflated and inflated again like a punctured balloon. They were as fast or even faster than lightening, which explained why I momentarily felt like a blind man.

They acted as reincarnated Haitian fighters who chased the almighty French army of Napoléon Bonaparte out of Haiti in 1804.

They whipped our behinds as Jeda screamed.

I was thinking to myself, "I am a nice guy. Can't you tell? I am the monitor. I was just trying to help." But the more I thought instead of fighting back, the more they whipped my butt.

By the time we managed to escape, there were bumps on my forehead, my eyes were swollen, my knees and neck ached. My shoulder felt like it had been dislocated and I had a serious headache.

Roro didn't look much better. "Why did you have to say that to him?" he asked.

"Why didn't you protect me?" I replied sarcastically.

"I was too busy wondering if they were going to let me out alive."

As bad as we felt, we all managed to laugh. This incident, painful as it was, taught me a valuable lesson: you think with your mind, feel with your heart and speak with your mouth. But when the mind and heart are not in agreement, it's best to keep the mouth shut. Nobody wants to be humiliated, especially in the presence of others. It took a nasty beating to understand this simple rule, but it has served me well.

When we reached home, Mom was furious. She had many questions and much to say. She was determined to meet their parents. But I had only one answer. I didn't want to go back. Even at 5'2", when Mom spoke, the house trembled and no one challenged her. Against my will, we did go back, but neither their parents nor any of them were anywhere to be found.

Hallelujah!

It is one thing to get beaten up in front of your friends, older brothers or even your lovely grandparents. But in front of your Mom or Dad, it's a total disgrace.

At school the next day, Micheline took one look at my battered face and sucked her teeth in disgust. For the next few weeks, she would not even look at me, stand near me or acknowledge my existence.

Micheline was not giving me the time of day no matter how many times I shined my shoes during the week or the additional fifteen minutes I spent in front of the mirror brushing my hair in the morning to make sure every strand would be right where it belonged when I reached school.

I thought of nothing but Micheline during my waking hours

and dreamed of her at night. I went as far as writing her name all over my notebooks hoping that the word would get to her and she would pay me some attention. But the harder I tried, the more she kept her distance. I was desperate.

My schoolwork began to suffer.

I moved from first place to third, sixth and then tenth. My mom could not understand what was happening.

Maître Vedette whipped me once, then twice. By the time he whipped me for the tenth time, my mother was complaining to me that it was all very embarrassing, painful and injurious to her pride.

I hit the books with a vengeance. After lots of hard work, total concentration and focus, I regained my first place position. That earned me a few smiles from Micheline, which sent my heart pumping at full speed again.

When I reached home that evening, I was stunned.

My grandmother was back from New York.

My father had known all along, but kept it as a surprise. It was indeed a wonderful surprise.

I was happy to see her. She looked prettier than when she had left.

Her presence brought back buried memories of the past. The passport, ticket, stamp, which I talked myself into believing was a secret, only to find out later on as I aged, it was common knowledge to many. I also remembered the ride to the airport, seeing the airplane take off, and mainly my longing to go along for the journey that day.

When I handed over my report card, everyone was pleased, including Grand Da. She grabbed me with both arms, squeezed me tightly against her chest and gave me a quiet kiss on my forehead. She went into one of her suitcases and pulled out a handful of pennies then said, "These are yours to keep."

I was excited! I went straight on the floor and counted exactly fifty-two pennies. Wow! Grand Da must be rich or else she would not have so much money to give away. I examined and re-examined those pennies, trying not to miss any detail. I mean front to back, top to bottom, side to side. My father had given me many pennies before, but there was something unique about those pennies. They were New York pennies. They were so shiny, I wondered if they had been polished before Grand Da brought them back.

She gave some to everyone who was there at the moment, so there was no need to share. I thanked her again and went to do my schoolwork.

As soon as I was done, I began to play with Grand Da.

Jokingly, I asked, "Did you give God all my messages?"

She laughed, "Yes I did and God sent you many toys and candies."

I was so eager to see the toys and candies I did not leave her sight for a minute or stop asking questions as they popped into my mind. I had many unanswered questions, but suddenly one in particular caught her full attention. I asked point blank whether she was rich?

She smiled, and after a short pause answered, "No, Jacky, your grandmother is not rich. There are many rich people in New York, but I am not one of them."

"But if you are not rich, where did you get so much money to give to everyone?"

"You're talking about those pennies? You don't have to be rich to have them. Sometimes, you find them all over the street. Most people don't bother with them, but me, when I see them I pick up every last one of them," she answered with a glow in her eyes.

My grandmother's comment about those pennies provoked

a chain reaction in my already spinning head. I was puzzled, but remained silent. Maybe, just maybe God does live in New York, but no one seems to know exactly where.

I felt Grand Da knew something, maybe not everything, but yet she was hiding it from me. I was dying to find out what it was, but I chose to leave her alone for a while. That did not last too long. As always, my curiosity got the best of me. So again, I went back to my grandma, only this time with a new set of questions.

"Tell me this Grand Da, have you ever met God in New York? Do you know or have you heard of anyone who has?"

She was laughing so hard; I could not get her to stop.

"No," she answered finally while still laughing, "but it almost feels as if God lives there. There is so much," she murmured.

She went on to explain how much clothing, food, and lots of other things go to waste in New York, and knowing how difficult things were in Haiti, it just ripped her heart apart. "I only wish I could bring many suitcases full of clothes for all of you," she concluded.

I cuddled every word coming from her small violet lips, but the sound of the pennies colliding with each other as they hit the floor was the single tune that kept playing in my mind.

I chose not to say anything else or ask any more questions.

I found a place all alone and started to think, "This time I am definitely going back with her. As soon as I get to New York, the first thing I'll do is find a pair of magnetic shoes and then, I'll need a magnifying lens." Armed with such tools, no penny would be safe. I'd become a penny picker.

The idea brought a smile to my face but reminded me of an incident I had observed many years earlier. One day, this car went cruising down the street and someone inside was throwing money out from a half open window. Some people were screaming and clapping with joy while others were fighting like cats and dogs to pick up whatever they could put their hands on. I was both intrigued and perplexed to say the least, so I rushed back inside to describe to Mom what I saw and wanted some clarification. All she offered as an explanation was, "It was Papa Doc, the president of Haiti." But I remember she frowned and harshly remarked, "Only dogs pick things up from the floor."

Well, would I then be considered a dog for picking pennies off the floor? I wrestled with the thought for a brief moment, trying to make sense of my mother's observation back then and wondered if I were to share my feelings with her today, would she have a different opinion. It was a painful reflection because, contrary to her traditional Haitian pride, I may eventually end up picking pennies off the floor. Slowly I said, "Penny, dog, dog, penny." Pause. "Penny, New York, New York dog." Hmm, a New York dog, a rich dog. I was beyond confused.

From that day forward, every time I saw a penny, I thought of nothing else, but New York and the ground. On occasion, I would close my eyes and visualize myself in New York doing nothing else but counting and polishing my pennies.

Sadly, when it was time for Grand Da to leave, I was once again disappointed; she left all alone. Still, I sent an internal message to God saying one day I'd pay him a visit.

Soul Train

THE NEXT school year, Maître Ba was my teacher. One day he pulled me aside and said he wanted to see my parents in his office right away. When he spoke this urgently, it meant the tuition was way overdue.

I had known him to be very patient and willing to do whatever it took to prevent the worst. And the worst was to send you back home until your parents could come up with at least partial payment.

What to do?

With December exams around the corner, I could only hope for the best.

The following week, both Mom and Dad showed up to see Maître Ba. He put my fear to rest by surprising my parents and me with what I felt was positive news. He told my parents I was too advanced for the class, so he would like them to consider not only the possibility of letting me jump to the next class, but also to take the official exam given by the Department of Education three years earlier than I would have taken it.

After kindergarten, the Haitian primary school system was divided into three cycles: preparatory, elementary and middle, with each cycle lasting two years. Since I had just started the second year of elementary, he basically wanted me to complete three years of schooling in one year. I liked the idea.

He explained to my parents that it was senseless holding me back because he was confident in my ability to pass the exam on the first try.

My father was all for it, but Mom rejected the idea.

Her reason was simple and fair: I had two older brothers in the same school. Ronald, older than me by two years, was in the same class. My other brother David, one year older, was behind by one class. No way would she accept such a leap. After listening to her reasons, I ended up agreeing with her because that would have been total disrespect to my older brothers. And in our family, that was a no-go.

Although Maître Ba pleaded and even spelled out the savings it would mean to them by eliminating two full years of tuition, Mom was immovable. My father protested, but she called the shots. Finally, it was settled that I would stay the course and finish the last three years as scheduled.

What was most remarkable about Maître Ba was his unconditional love for Haiti, his keen passion for Haitian history and his tireless devotion to the education of his children, as he sometimes referred to us. He had very little tolerance for mediocrity. It was excellence or nothing. When he started to recount the history of the country, especially the battles that led to our defining moment, our independence, he did it with such glory, it almost felt as if you were living the moment. I was inspired and ended up reading the history of Haiti with great intensity.

Some time during the year, we had a small talk and I asked him to explain what he meant by "your learning is your responsibility." He was surprised that I still remembered and answered, "All a teacher or a parent can ever do is to offer a foundation. Where you go from there is always a question of personal choice. The trick is to embrace what is offered and build from that foundation." I listened to his simple, yet powerful message, and wondered silently in which direction I wanted my life to go. Fortunately, by the time the official exam was over, Ronald and I succeeded on our first attempt.

My father was happy with the news and decided that he wanted me to go to *St-Louis de Gonzague,* which I understood was one of the finest schools in Haiti. This school had not only the best teachers and resources, but it was also where you would find the richest kids in the country. Its reputation was no secret. I believe the monthly tuition was between $20–$30, and to most Haitian parents like mine, that was a small fortune.

My father's wish was miles away from his reality. I say this because when I considered the financial burden to him and the strain to the rest of the family, *St-Louis de Gonzague* was not realistic. In addition, my two younger sisters were already going to a private catholic school, *Collège Marie-Anne*, also known as *Soeur Saint-Anne,* and it was more important to have them in a safer and more challenging environment. It was settled that Ronald and I would go to a public school, *Lycée Jean-Jacques Dessalines,* named after one of the key leaders who fought fearlessly and fiercely for Haiti's independence.

So, I started my secondary education at *Lycée Jean-Jacques.* There was no tuition, but we paid a small fee of $1.60 for an ID each year. The layout was nothing compared to what I left behind. There were two floors in the building with several classrooms on each floor. While some of the teachers were motivated, the crowded room reflected the price. My particular classroom was big enough for maybe fifteen students, but we were more than forty, packed like sardines in an undersized can, all with the hope of getting an education. The single window available for fresh air was at times forced by the teachers to remain closed because the one outhouse that was shared by more than 300 students was only a breath away. Given the tropical climate of Haiti especially in mid-afternoon, a simple fan in the classroom would have been luxury. Needless to say, we roasted like peanuts in a hot pan.

Despite the crowded rooms, the *lycées* were very popular, but unforgiving. It was hard to get in and even harder after you got in. It was a known fact that if you wanted to find the student with a quest for learning, look no further than the *lycées*. While they represented the classic example of mass education, by the time you came out, if you learned nothing else, you would at the very least master the true meaning of survival.

Can you imagine going to a school where competition was always at peak level, yet not have the books you needed to study? Well, this was all too common for many of us. But how we solved that problem was to exchange books with each other for a two-to-three day period. You meticulously copied the whole thing by hand into a notebook or two. Still, even after all that, many nights you found yourself studying by candlelight or kerosene lamp because of the constant blackouts in the country.

Books, as you now can envision, were precious commodities. Many were borrowed or disappeared for a few days or weeks until further explanation. However, some guys needed no explanation as to why their books were in your bag. It was a waste of precious time. They kicked your butt until they got their books back. Thanks to my big brother, Ronald, one of the borrowers learned to rush home when class was over. He never touched our books again without our permission.

As for the teachers, with the exception of a few, it seemed everyone shared the same opinion. We were privileged to be there and we must prove that we belonged or soon someone else would occupy our precious space. There were a few *lycées* in Port-au-Prince and they represented the best hope and only option for many of us if education was the end goal. Repeat one class too many, and your education might come to a drastic end; most of our parents could not afford to pay for private tuition.

The solidarity amongst the students was beyond comparison. Although we were faced with many challenges, getting promoted to the next class was everyone's top priority. The motto was: learn and move forward, don't and stay behind.

The interesting part about school in Haiti is that while French is the official language, it was secondary to most of us because Créole was what we spoke at home. This was the biggest challenge we faced, and what I believe was responsible for most academic failures. Some never managed to bridge the gap between the language spoken at home and that taught in school. But for others, myself included, what really helped was lots of reading and reviewing all the time. It was by no means a simple task. Moreover, we were required to learn English, Spanish, Latin and Greek.

I spent two years in *Lycée Jean-Jacques* and left the school in protest. What happened was that my brother Ronald flunked the grade while I was promoted with three stars on my report card.

Ronald was very playful and at times made fun of the teachers, but failing him with a very low score was uncalled for since he had been given no previous warning and he did very well throughout the school year. However, the principal claimed he and some other students were a great disturbance in the classroom and he had received too many complaints about them.

I too was part of the group who created the disturbance but, for some strange reason, I was spared any punishment.

The hardest part about this ordeal was how we were going to explain it to Mom.

There was no doubt in my mind Ronald was going to get it when she found out, but I might end up getting it as well because if I knew there was a problem, I should have said something. But what was there to say? It was a shock to both of us.

In any case, we agonized over our situation all the way home. Finally, by the time we reached the house, we agreed that our best choice was to tell Mom there would be a two-week delay before the report card came out.

She did not question us, but I could tell by the blank expression on her face she sensed something was not right. Was it maternal instinct, woman's intuition or just pure reflex? I am not sure.

Mom always gave us the impression she was operating on a sixth sense. She did acknowledge on more than one occasion, that her grandparents' spirits spoke to her in her dreams, as though there was an unspoken or invisible bond between her and the spirits. But this was one of those days I wished I could tell those spirits while she's awake, "To please mind their own spirit business."

I presumed the message was well received and the spirits were working in our favor. Unfortunately, a week later, Mom found Ronald's report card under the mattress. When she called us over and I saw the fire flickering from her round eyes, I knew we were in deep trouble. Please understand, under the mattress is a very special place reserved only to hide money. Although Mom felt money was not to be the driving force for our education, she was adamant that education was the engine to transcend poverty. Therefore, hiding report cards under the mattress was a clear indication to Mom that we were neglecting our education and the chance of finding money under our mattress would be slim.

While she was not formally educated, Mom used every tool at her disposal to nurture our drive for learning. She was disappointed, not only because we lied to her about something so meaningful, but, worse still, we went as far as covering it up for a week. Needless to say, she gave it to us with a delight.

As if that was not enough, when my father came home that evening, Mom shared with him what Ronald and I believed was such a fantastic plan. My father had one solution and it was for Ronald to go learn a trade instead of staying in school. Mom would not have it and they started to quarrel.

I had gotten a part-time job, and by then, I had already been working for over a year. I sold numbers. In Créole it is called *bolet*. The drawings were based on the Dominican and Haitian lottery for a total of six drawings per month. My salary was twelve U.S. dollars a month for the four Dominican drawings held every Sunday or eighteen dollars if I could manage to get up at four in the morning every other Friday and sell for a couple hours before I went to class. I had been using part of the money to buy used books as often as I could and gave the rest to my mother for whatever was needed in the house.

There was no way I was going to let Ronald get sent to a

trade school. I shared my concern with Mom and Dad and we all agreed I would use my salary to pay for Ronald's tuition and mine in a private school. There was one drawback. My mother insisted that Ronald and I would have to attend different schools. It was a very painful separation in my life because we were each other's best friend. Besides, we had been sitting next to each other in class for the last seven years. But under the circumstances, I chose what I believed would be in Ronald's best interest. And it worked out. From that point, his performance in school was outstanding. He maintained a single digit rank in a class of over thirty students all the way through the end of the school year.

We split up for sure, but it was only during class hours. My house was the place where we all met for fun, especially on Saturdays and holidays. Ronald and I were like the clowns in the neighborhood, so everyone knew where to come for a good laugh. At any given time, you could find between fifteen to twenty guys hanging out at our house doing nothing else but cracking jokes and laughing. Sometimes, we would be there from nine in the morning until about two or three in the afternoon when everybody went home to have a bite.

By the time they returned later in the day, everyone was fresh and clean. This was also a good occasion to present yourself in a different light if you were courting a young lady. In fact, one of the guys in the group, André, had a reputation for wearing clean clothes only when he was courting a woman. And we all knew very quickly whether he was successful. If things worked out in his favor, he was clean all day for as long as the romance lasted. But when he had a *refus*, a "denial," he would either disappear for a few days or go right back to being sloppy again.

I didn't see much of Jeda during those times. It would

have been unseemly for a young lady to hang out, joking and laughing, with a large group of guys.

What made this bunch so special was that we were all about the same age and very close to each other in class range. Our friendship was so strong we were like a big family, only with different parents. Sunday was also a fun day for all of us because that's when we got to put on our finest clothes to attend Sunday mass. By the way, this was also a good place to court a young woman, especially if her parents attended the same church. In that case, we had to be there.

I am not joking when I say this. If you were in school during the week and attended church on Sunday morning, you would score a huge bonus from most Haitian parents. And that went for both sexes. If nothing else, we wanted to make sure they saw us in line during communion. And when they looked at you from head to toe under those five-pound, double lens, black rim glasses, the message was loud and clear. "State your intention." The easiest way to handle this drama was to lock your fingers together, bow your head politely and whisper, *La paix de Jésus soit avec vous,* "May Jesus's peace be with you." This simple act of respect was a way to convey to them that you were not a sinner, and you posed no serious threat to their daughter's well being.

You see, Haitian parents don't play with their daughters when it comes to their education, at least for those who could have afforded such privilege. Their philosophy is plain and simple. Love and learning don't mix. And where the two cross paths, learning takes priority. For this reason, you dared not get in front of their house and start talking sweet to their daughters, especially during school days. If they didn't like the shape of your head or for some other crazy reason, the whole family would make even your shadow look like a leech anywhere near the house. They will scream, yell, curse or even use threats if nothing else worked. I knew this too well because Mom was one of those parents.

Apart from Mom, one of my older brothers was like a deadbolt lock when it came to my sisters. David was not very popular for that reason, but it worked. He had no mercy. He provided the necessary back-up system for my father since he was out of the house most of the time fighting a different battle in the street to provide for our survival.

Sunday afternoon was time for a movie, a soccer game, or a live concert. Since the movie or soccer game was a lot cheaper, they were the preferred choice. Our favorite movies were always the ones with Bruce Lee or anything else with Kung Fu in it. But what I really liked was the American TV show, Soul Train, and I was hooked.

Since we didn't own a TV, it would have been hard to keep up with Soul Train. Luckily, Jeda was as passionate as I was about Soul Train and she owned not just a TV, but a big colored one. So, my Sunday routine was attending 4 A.M. mass with Dad when feasible, selling numbers when mass was over, then rushing to Jeda's house to watch Soul Train. We glued ourselves in front of the TV studying all the moves and learning more English words as we moved along. The moment Soul Train was over, Jeda would put some music on her stereo system and we would start practicing while quizzing each other on our newly learned vocabulary words or phrases. One day we thought we were both so good, we decided to enter a dance contest at a movie theater.

The day of the contest Jeda and I rehearsed our moves to perfection for nearly six hours. By the time we got on the podium, we gave the audience a performance for their money. I don't know what had gotten into us, but we were on fire. I pulled out my handkerchief from my back pocket and pretended I was shining her shoes as we danced going up and down and side to side. There was a burst of applause. When Jeda hugged and kissed me on the lips, the audience went wild by giving us a standing ovation and we were declared the winners.

On the way home, Jeda casually said, "Micheline asked about you."

I was shocked. Although we no longer attended the same school, Micheline and I saw each other all the time. She would nod a hello to me if she were in a good mood and not even that, if she were having a bad day. And for a while she seemed to have had a succession of bad days.

"What did she say?"

"She asked how you were doing in school."

"And?" I prodded. "What did you tell her?"

"I told her that you were smart, quite charming and that some other girls were attracted to you."

"You did what?"

"You heard me."

"Why did you do that Jeda?"

"Why?"

"Yes, why?"

"She is very pretty; I must give her that. But, I am so angry when I see how she treats you sometimes Jacky. When she is around you behave and talk like she is a princess and she loves to play it to her advantage. I just don't want her to think she is all that."

I ruffled Jeda's hair. "Thank you. Someday, I will make a lot of money and Micheline and I will live in a big house. We will have you over for dinner."

Jeda smacked my hand off her head. "I can't wait," she said sarcastically.

She walked away in a flash of anger and didn't speak to me for a long, long time. I did not understand what I had done wrong but Jeda was having her moment so I stayed out of her way, even though I missed her terribly. I knew she would come around because she was not the type to hold grudges against anyone. She was usually outgoing and fun loving. Why she was acting like that? I had no clue.

I did not understand females at all.

Hope

I DID NOT think of Jeda's inexplicable coldness for very long. After running the whole conversation over and over in my head, I reached the conclusion that Micheline had sent me a message. She was willing to go out with me. Nothing else mattered.

So, I made my move on a Sunday at church. I approached her parents and asked their permission to take Micheline to a movie that same afternoon. Of course, they said she was busy. So, I asked if next week might be a better time. They agreed. There was something about their smiles that told me I would not be cursed, yelled at or subjected to any threat. I barely ate or slept that whole week. The way things had turned out, our first date would fall on my eighteenth birthday. What better birthday present could a young man ask for?

We watched the movie with our hands folded in our laps. Afterward, she allowed me to put an arm around her shoulders as we walked back toward our neighborhood. I knew some other guys might have been eyeing her with keen interest, so I pulled her closely under my arm just to show her off. I was walking on clouds.

"So, you are eighteen today," she smiled.

"Yes. How old are you?"

"I will be eighteen in another month. What presents did you get?"

I came very close to saying "you my gorgeous," but did not want to blow my chance for a second date or even worse make a fool of myself, especially after her first rejection.

"I am happy to be alive Micheline. What is a greater gift but life itself, especially in a country where many kids don't live long enough to celebrate their first birthday, much less their eighteenth. I am grateful and I am blessed."

I spoke the truth but, secretly, I was greatly concerned. At eighteen, you know your parents may be asking what to do with you, but it does not stop with them. You too start panicking and wondering what to do with yourself. You silently justify your anxiety by thinking, "This is a rite of passage." But on the other hand you also question where and when the passage ends. This day more than any other passing day of my life was the one I had been waiting for because my mother always said, "Only when you are eighteen can you make certain decisions on your own."

The situation in Haiti was not getting any better and my future was not looking any brighter. Thus far, in spite of my hard work in school, every time I opened my eyes to face reality or to look into the windows of opportunity, all I saw was a thick cloud hanging over my head obstructing my view. The more I focused, the more I realized how thick the layers were. It was evident that unless I made a move and moved quickly, I might find myself lost under this thick cloud, which from beginning to end seemed motionless.

She pushed her hair away from her beautiful face in a very seductive and provocative manner. The light breeze that brushed her hair to her sweet face was also working in my favor by lifting her flowered linen dress just above her knees revealing her sexy legs. She made no effort to fight nature's strength and I made every effort to look. Oh my, oh my, can someone please help me?

"So, what will you do now?" she asked, glancing from the corner of her eyes.

You don't want to know, I smiled to myself, rubbing gently on her bare shoulder. I wanted to kiss her, squeeze her close to me so she could feel and hear her thunder hammering down my soul. I wanted to cage her in my love, protect her so no other man would ever touch her again as long as I live.

Instantly, there was a spasm of desire rushing from my spine all the way to my knees. I shivered. When she caressed my face slightly with her fingertips as she moved her head closer to my shoulder, I almost collapsed. Just her presence had my blood boiling. She was *muy caliente* "very hot!" And I was burning.

"I have been thinking of going into the military," I answered calmly as if my head was no longer spinning.

"My father says that the military in Haiti is corrupt."

"Mine says the same thing," I agreed. "But if going into the military will increase my chances of getting into a university, which otherwise may prove to be an insurmountable challenge, I am not about to rule it out."

"I dream of going to the United States," she said.

Her eyes sparkled when she said those words and she said it with wonder, as though the streets there were paved with gold.

I, too, had thought of it. That would be a trophy to cherish forever, but with both my parents living in Haiti, the chance was almost zero to none unless a miracle happened. The miracle that I and other young Haitian students prayed for was a U.S. visa stamped in our passport and the ability to say, *Hasta la vista* Baby Doc. I realized so many young Haitians who came before me, despite their tremendous effort in school, their combative spirit in the face of adversity, and the many sacrifices made by their parents, had ended up nowhere.

The questions for me were, "Can I or anyone else close to me be next? And if so, where do I go from here?"

I led the conversation away to less troublesome ground and we talked and laughed like old friends until we reached her front door.

Kissing her was out of the question. So, I asked her to see me again and she agreed.

From that moment on, I considered Micheline Gustave my girlfriend. She was the woman who would someday be my wife and the mother of my children.

Andy's Song

I **WAS NO** longer a wide-eyed sheltered little boy. For the past several years, besides listening to some older friends commenting harshly, of course in private, on the political situation of the country, my father had been lecturing and telling us to get out of Haiti as fast as we possibly could. In addition, I had read several books on politics on my own and numerous articles from a weekly newspaper called *Le Petit Samedi Soir*. This led me to believe very soon there would be a major upheaval against the government and the gravity of its impact was unknown. Of course, the wisest choice was to get out of the country by any means.

On January 1, 1980, we celebrated 176 years of independence. One hundred and seventy-six years ago our ancestors fought a brilliant war against the once almighty French army for what they deeply believed was unjust, inhumane and unacceptable treatment of our people. And yet 176 years later, we were still subject to the same kind of unjust, inhumane and unacceptable treatment, but only this time it was from our own government and a few outsiders who had a firm grip on the country from behind the scenes. Even when the chain of slavery was broken, the invisible links were still scattered throughout the present. Buried so deeply and done so precisely, they were inconspicuous to the naked mind. Simply put, where physical slavery ended, mental slavery began. If revolution is the bedrock of evolution, our revolution certainly left us holding the rock. So heavy, this rock has left an imprint on the country, which no Haitian leader past or present has been able to wipe away. This to me was a cause for concern and one that has yet to be addressed.

During the last twenty-three years, or so, the country had been ruled by a small group of tyrants. As few as they may have been in numbers, they were powerful enough to dictate the course of our lives from one day to the next. What made this even more critical was that they showed no sign of weakness. If anything, they picked up more clout along the way, which could last another twenty-three years or more. Given this bit of insight, you found yourself asking one key question: How do you safely navigate through the mayhem? Asking that question usually led to a wall of silence.

No one in his right mind dared to answer unless willing to face the consequences, which at times involved jail time, torture, disappearance or death. Hence, you were left to either find your own answer or to create your own solution.

At about 11 o'clock one morning, the temperature was moving well beyond 70 degrees Fahrenheit but still I decided to wear a winter coat my grandmother left in the house on one of her recent visits to Haiti. I went around the neighborhood wishing all my friends Happy New Year, instead of the usual *Bonne-Année,* which is often followed by: *Santé, Paix, Joie, Prosperité et Longevité,* "Health, Peace, Joy, Prosperity and Longevity."

Every year we had the same wish, but as the years cruised by like speeding bullets killing both young and old, poor and poorer, we moved closer and closer to the grave. Health? Maybe, because I was still breathing. But the rest were potential dreams yet to be materialized. Peace was oppression in camouflage. Joy was sadness in silence. Prosperity was poverty in permanence except for the ruling few. And as for longevity itself, I refused to be fooled.

Thank God five days a week, twice daily, while I was attending *Lycée Jean-Jacques,* I traveled right in front of the main cemetery located on *Rue Oswald Durand.* My seeing the cemetery so often served as a constant reminder to give thanks and count my many blessings. Yes, I had to give thanks because many, even much younger than I, had lost their lives to an incurable disease commonly known as dictatorship that had plagued the country for a long period of time. That said, I had witnessed far too many funerals on a weekly basis which convinced me that this longevity business was a hoax.

Given time, we will all be nailed in a coffin on our way to the cemetery. It was a scary feeling.

In mid-January, Andy, one of my cousins who lived with us, came home from work and said he wanted to talk with me urgently. I asked why he was home so early.

He smiled, and then said, "From now on, I shall be early every day."

My first impression was he got into a fight with his boss and was fired from his electrician job or second, he got a young woman pregnant and the father was on a wild chase for his neck. Maybe he had decided to go into hiding until the dust settled.

I said, "Well, why don't we step outside, so we can have some privacy."

Leading the way, Andy said nervously, "I want nobody to know about this unless I say so myself."

Once outside, he called one of the kids who lived in the neighborhood, gave her a U.S. dollar and asked her to get us two sodas. I presumed, for someone who had just lost his job and with no future income in sight, he seemed rather calm and happy.

On the other hand, it was always hard to tell when Andy had or didn't have any money because he always acted like the richest man on the block. At 5'4" and no more than 140 pounds, he carried himself as if he were six-something and over 250 pounds, especially when his wallet was empty.

It was indeed a pleasure to ask him for money when he was in the company of others, just to teach him that saying no was not a sin.

He looked at me and smiled again. "You promise not to say anything?"

"Andy, you know I don't like surprises; if you have something to say, please say it and let's get on with life."

"What's the rush? We have all evening. Don't we?"

The young girl came back with the two sodas and handed them to Andy. He took the sodas, said thank you and told her to keep the change. He then pulled out his wallet and gave me 5 U.S. dollars. I looked around to see if anyone was observing, but the surrounding area was empty.

"Do you realize what you just did?"

"Yes, I just gave you $5."

Jokingly, I said, "Come here and let me take your pulse."

As I attempted to reach for his wallet, which I believed would have given me a better indication of how he was feeling, he pulled away, while asking me to keep quiet.

He was acting a bit strange, so I said, "If what you need to discuss is about money, I truly hope you put your head on your shoulder and decide what you want to do."

While rubbing his hands together, he looked left and right

as if trying to hide from something or somebody then said, "Jacky, we are rich."

"Cuz, when you say we are rich, are you referring to yourself or are you talking about the whole family?" I asked in a pleasant but nervous voice.

"Well, in that case, I am rich."

"Wait a second, didn't you just say we are rich?"

"Yes," he said smiling, "but I changed my mind."

"Oh no, before you can do that, let's go to the bank and put some in my name. Because next time you say 'we' again, I'll go to the bank to find out my balance. All right, Andy, enough joking. Let's get down to business. What's the deal?"

Again, he looked up and down the street and then pulled me close to him and whispered in my ear, "I won the lottery and I need your help."

Now, I knew Andy loved to take great risks. And I also knew he had won some money here and there on several occasions on Sunday's drawings, but to win the lottery was a once in a lifetime opportunity.

Pretending not to hear, I replied, "I heard you speak, but I didn't quite understand what you said."

This time, looking straight into my eyes, he said, "I won the lottery and I need your help."

I laughed, thinking he was losing his mind.

"Andy, to win the lottery, you have to be extremely lucky or, to say it in plain language, you have to be born under the right star. My friend, please correct me, but I don't think you were born under such a star," I said teasing. "I am asking you one more time. What is it you want to talk about?"

Without hesitation, he repeated this time very slowly, "I won the lottery and I am rich."

"Okay! I am under the impression you also understand

there are many coupons and to make some real money and claim yourself rich as you pretend to be, you must have all of them. Tell me, how many do you have?" I said, holding on to my composure.

"How many?"

"Yes, how many do you have?" I asked again.

"All," he answered, grinning from ear to ear.

I kept silent for a while, trying to digest what Andy had just revealed to me. If there was any truth to it, he was indeed a lucky, rich man.

"Jacky, are you all right?"

"Oh yes, yeah, Andy, I am. You won the lottery, you are rich and you need my help. Right?"

"Right," he answered still grinning.

"I was just processing what you said, Cuz. This is too big to swallow all at once." I finally took a deep breath and was able to collect my thoughts. "Andy, where are the coupons?"

"Why do you want to know?"

"I have two reasons, Cuz. One, I want to figure out how much you should be getting. Two, I want to verify that we are looking at the right coupons and the right date."

"That's all been done already," he answered, with lots of excitement in his voice.

"Excellent! So what is it exactly you want me to do, Andy?"

After a long pause, he blurted, "First, I want to know how much interest I should get on my money, and second, how best to use the money."

Still a bit confused or maybe just plain shocked, I said, "Andy, it is hard to say how much you will be getting unless I know first, how much money you have and second, which bank is currently holding the money."

"Are you telling me different banks give different interest? And by the way, what is interest anyway?"

"Let's deal with the first part of your question. Yes, it is possible to get a different interest rate from bank to bank. As to the second part of the question, think of it this way. Interest is like your money being married to time. Soon after the marriage, they start to procreate and make babies for you to enjoy. The longer the marriage lasts, the more babies you will have to enjoy. And they in turn will go on to produce grandbabies for even further enjoyment." I laughed and added, "Can you imagine having so many grandbabies calling you Grandpa?"

He laughed back, and then replied, "In this case, I'll have lots of grandbabies."

"Yes, that you will my friend and you must find ways to get them engaged in different things because they will keep adding up." I joked. "But on a serious note Andy, what you have is the principal and what the bank adds to it is interest for giving them access to your money to use at will. Where is the money?"

"In the bank."

"I know that, but which one? Cuz, if you want to stay rich, I strongly suggest you buy a mattress and hide the money under it until you can figure out all the details. Believe me, that is about the safest place for your money right now."

"But you just said earlier let's go to the bank to put some in your name."

"Yes, that is what I said, but I never said which bank."

"Are you saying you would choose one bank versus another?"

"Please tell me it's not *Banque Nationale*."

"Why?" Andy asked.

I sighed deeply. "Andy, given the political climate of this country, it is much easier to put your money in than to get it out. When dealing with a corrupt government such as Haiti, the banking system plays a major role in maintaining the corruption. Had it been mine, I'd have gotten a mattress and studied all the possibilities before deciding what to do, but it's your call." By the way, keeping money under the mattress was a method used by many Haitians who wanted to keep their money accessible and have peace of mind.

Andy looked puzzled and pensive all at once. "Do you really think they can steal the money?"

"My friend, anything is possible in Haiti. Can they steal it? I am not so sure. But why run the risk only to regret it later? Do you have any money on you right now?"

"Yes I do."

"Good! Let's get the mattress and you will sleep well at night. But until then, I'd check my balance first thing in the morning and once more right before they close."

Happily he said, "Jacky the money is in *Banque Royale du Canada.*"

We both looked at each other and burst into a roar of laughter.

"Well, in that case, I am happy for you, and thank you for sharing such big news with me. *Mes félicitations,* 'congrats!'"

"Do you think I made a good choice?" Andy asked.

"For now I think you did, but I'll still be restless so long as the bank is holding your money, whether the bank is foreign or local."

"I trust the bank, Jacky."

"Oh, I do too, Andy, but with someone else's money, not mine."

He laughed, stared at me for a second and said, "I am going to help you out. Think of what you want and let me know."

"If you really want to give me a valuable gift, I'll tell you what you can do for me. Please go back to school and try to educate yourself. So far, I have been helping you with both math and reading, but there is more to education than reading and math."

"Jacky, I heard everything you said and I will give it some consideration, but I still want to help you out. Why don't we go out to grab something to eat?"

"Yeah, let's do that. I'll change my clothes and we'll be on our way."

About an hour later, we were in downtown Port-au-Prince in a cozy little restaurant, sipping drinks. I had a soft drink while Andy happily enjoyed a cold Heineken, which was about three times more expensive than our local Prestige beer. While waiting for someone to take our order, I took a look at him as he smoothly lifted his Heineken to his lips and thought, "If he knows what to do, there is going to be a major change in his life for the better."

When it was time to order, I knew exactly what I wanted: some *griot,* a famous Haitian dish made out of fried pork, usually served with either rice and beans or just fried plantain along with a tongue-burning peppered spice locally known as *picklise*. I asked for the fried plantain, and a papaya juice mixed with carnation milk to ease the burning taste.

Andy was either too rich to be hungry or was just starting to develop a finer taste for the good life that comes along with money. He kept things on the lighter side by just ordering a small *griot* with slices of avocado on the side and another

Heineken. His voice reflected the sound of his bank account, deep and heavy.

Seeing how fast he was drinking his beer, I said, "Hey, mind your limit on alcohol." Andy took a small sip of his Heineken and licked his lips. "Jacky, when life wants to be good to you, you must also learn how to be good to yourself." He ordered yet another Heineken even before he was done with the last.

"So tell me this, Andy, when did you get to be a philosopher?"

"Since I won the lottery," he laughed loudly.

"I hear you, but I also think you can always be good to yourself even when life is not so good to you."

"Believe me, Jacky, money just makes it so much easier."

I kept quiet while reflecting on how money can change someone's life from one day to the next. For a brief moment, I looked back at my life trying to decide whether money would have made a difference. I was deeply lost in my thoughts when I caught him trying to order one more beer while flirting with the young woman who made it her business to entertain Andy. I took it upon myself to cancel the order, and asked the woman for the check. That would have been Andy's fourth beer since we had been there, and his slow speech coupled with his lax posture on the chair signaled to me if he was not drunk, he was hypnotized by the young lady stroking his ego.

In his half drunken voice, Andy shouted, "You heard what he said, the check please."

She handed him the check, he pulled his wallet out, handed it to me and said, "Here, you are in charge, Jacky."

His action confirmed that he had lost total control of the situation. To have him hand over his wallet when this young woman was only inches away observing his every move was unbelievable.

The bill was a bit more than six dollars. When I opened the wallet, I could not believe my eyes. Big money! Some were green, some were pink or purple, and others were blue. It was like a multi-colored festival. The greens were the U.S. dollars. The pinks, blues and purples were Haitian currencies in all different denominations.

In Haiti, even when you are the poorest man, if you have 5 U.S. dollars in your pocket all in one-dollar bills, it commands respect. Well, Andy had several tens and twenties. No more confusion. My cousin was indeed a rich man. I glanced back at the money and was very tempted to order him a full case of Heineken and say, "Here, enjoy the good life!" but instead I paid the bill, closed his wallet, handed it back to him, and we dashed out.

Since I left the woman a very big tip, she rushed behind us screaming, "Would you bring him back tomorrow?"

"No, we are going back to New York," I joked.

"Oh, you guys are from New York?" she shouted.

I said nothing and just kept moving.

Andy started to laugh and said loudly, "New York? I guess that's where you want to go. Well, for now Jacky, you can forget it because I need you in Haiti, not New York."

"New York? What are you talking about? Cuz, New York is for the future."

But deep inside I was thinking, "New York! When is the next plane leaving? Just tell me and I'll be there."

"You know Jacky," Andy said, "it would be nice to go just so I could see for myself why everybody is so crazy about it."

"Maybe we should go together someday," I answered. "Although I have heard some very strange things about it, so far everyone who left and returned for vacation always looked so happy. Some even refer to it as paradise. By the way, Andy, you still have not told me how much money you won."

"Let's get a cab and go home. We will discuss it tomorrow."

"Not tomorrow, I have a long day in school. My first class begins at 7:00 A.M. and I don't plan on being home until after 8:00 P.M."

"Why so late?"

"I have a date with Micheline."

"Can you take the day off from school tomorrow?"

"No. I have lots to do. Besides, I am trying very hard not to be absent from class."

Smiling, Andy said, "Even if you take the rest of the year off, I am confident you'll pass your exams with flying colors."

"I don't know about that."

"Why do you love school so much?"

"Andy, I don't know if I really love school that much, but I have to go. Sometimes I think the only reason I go there is to have fun with my friends. I can tell you for sure, I am crazy about books. I wish to write one someday."

"I'll pray for you and I also believe if anybody is going to make it, you will."

"That was a nice thing to say Andy, but you have made it already. You have lots of money now."

"Yes, Jacky but I don't have that much education," he said sadly.

"No one is born educated, Cuz. We all have to start somewhere. What locks the door of education to a great majority in Haiti is the money. But don't think for a second that's how it ought to be. No, it's a well-planned and thought out strategy so the starving cat can surrender without a meow."

We continued to walk slowly on *Boulevard Jean-Jacques Dessalines* and Andy was silent. He flagged down a cab stating he was too tired for a *tap tap* and was in no mood to deal with the frequent stops they made along the way dropping or picking up other passengers, especially at six in the evening.

Besides, we needed to head back home.

As soon as we were settled in the car, Andy spoke in a low voice saying that I gave him a lot to think about and he felt his life was moving in a new direction. I told the driver where we wanted to go and he stepped on the gas pedal.

Andy closed his eyes and in less than five minutes, he was in deep sleep.

In the meantime, I started seeing myself with Micheline in New York. I pictured anything that would intensify the vision. The big houses I have seen on television over my friends' house. Cars, coats, sweaters, nice suits, they were all going through my mind. I saw lots of libraries and tons of books. It was a great feeling to know that one day I might end up having my own private collection to treasure.

I kept thinking about the situation in Haiti and wondered if this was the best life had to offer or the best I was willing to accept. I can't say I was the best student, but I had managed to remain within the top five percent of my class at all times. But, what was the benefit of learning if it did not lead to any progress?

How far can a country progress when education is not at the top of its agenda? I mean seriously, if the past generation failed to identify the problem and the new generation does not even think there is a problem, where does that leave us in the future?

If I really had the chance to leave Haiti, could I say no? What would become of my family whom I love so much? What about Roro, could I leave without him? We were the most inseparable companions. I had a truckload of unanswered questions racing through my mind all at once, but I resolved to put them aside and focus on visualizing the beauty of New York.

The driver must have sped like crazy because it didn't take long for us to be right in front of the house. I woke up Andy, he paid the fare, and we went inside. Once inside the house, the atmosphere was quite different.

Mom started to ask all sort of questions. Where have you been? Did you eat and why did Andy smell like he had been drinking? Of course she had to smell my breath to see if I too had been drinking. Andy and I acted calm, as if everything were normal. I grabbed a book and walked outside to avoid any additional questions from Mom.

About half an hour later, I saw Roro walk in with a big smile on his face. I looked at him and placed my finger on my lips, asking him to be quiet. "Go inside and see if Andy is sleeping. If he is, come back out because I have some great news to share with you."

"What is it?"

"My friend, you are wasting precious time. Go on, you will like this one." I pulled out the five dollars Andy gave me earlier, smiled and said, "I bet you would like to have some of this. Wouldn't you?"

His face lit up instantly. "Where did you get that? Talk to your big brother."

"Would you like two dollars?"

"Let me go change it first, then I'll do whatever you want me to do."

"Roro, see if Andy is sleeping and come back to collect your money."

He ran inside and came right back out. "My job is done, so now pay me."

Just as I was getting ready to open my mouth, he stopped me by saying, "Yes, he's sleeping."

He reached into his pocket, pulled out some money and said. "This is not mine, but if you give me the five, I'll give you three back."

He gave me the three dollars and laughed, "Big brothers should always have more than little brothers."

I took my three dollars, cursed him out some, and we walked away from the house. When we reached what I considered a safe place for our conversation, I said, "Now tell me this, Ronald, can you keep a secret?"

"It depends on what the secret is, but if you ask me not to say anything you know I won't."

"Good. Well, Andy won the lottery and he asked me not to say anything to anybody."

He laughed and said, "So why are you telling me?"

"Listen, this is no joke. Keep this as quiet as you can because I am working on a major plan and if it works out, you will be a big part of it."

"What do you have in mind?" he said, sounding very excited.

"I don't even know if it will work, but I am determined to give it all I've got."

"Maybe, he can buy us a small car to go to school, Jacky. Did he say how much he won?"

"No, but I will get all the details tomorrow when we go to the bank together."

"Does anybody else know about this outside of us?"

"Yes."

"Who?"

"First, the one who paid him—the lottery department, and second, the one who is keeping it—the bank."

"Oh, so he's paid already," he yelled.

"Psst! Not so loud, remember this is supposed to be a secret."

"Wow! This is really exciting, Jacky."

"I told you. It's really huge."

"When did you find out?"

"Today."

"He is a lucky man, and I am happy for him," Ronald said.

"We should be, at least one of us is out of poverty. But I tell you what, so far he has very good intentions."

"What do you mean by he has good intentions?"

"He said to think of what I want and he would help me get it."

"Help you with what?"

"We didn't get into that yet. He simply said to decide, Roro."

"Maybe, he will pay for your school."

"Whatever he decides, I will be thankful."

"I hope he won't let a woman take it away from him Jacky."

"Roro, I have been doing a lot of reading about men and women and how this whole love thing operates."

"Why?"

"Never mind why."

"Micheline."

It was a one-word truth but I didn't want to talk about her.

"Roro, I have read that women don't just take your money. Most men believe that but it is a mistake to think that way. The reality is you give it to them in exchange for something else. My friend, to the path of a woman's heart, there is only one road—gentleness. If you learn how to be gentle to a woman, she will more often than not give you what you want without you ever showing your wallet. But when you are not gentle with her, she will empty your wallet so gently you won't even realize your money is gone until after there's none left. Anyway, in the case of Andy, if he does, that will be his choice. As they say, easy come, easy go."

Ronald shook his head and moaned, "What a lucky man."

"Yes, that he is indeed. Let's hope he buys Dad a *tap tap*. Or, maybe open a little grocery store for Mom. That would definitely change a few things. What do you think?"

After exchanging ideas about what we would like to happen, we decided it was best to leave it alone and carry on with life. We walked back home. Ronald went to talk to my cousin Zette and I went straight to bed.

The next morning, my dad asked why I wasn't going to school.

"I have something else planned for the day, and I need to stay home to get it done," I replied. He asked no more questions.

By then Mom was up fixing breakfast and ironing uniforms. Seeing how relaxed I was, she too wanted to know if I had class that morning and if so, why I was not getting ready for school. I also let her know I was taking the day off.

She smiled and walked away. As stern as she was, she knew when to leave us some breathing space.

I told her I was going back to bed, but to please wake me up by ten because Andy and I had something to do and we needed to leave the house no later than eleven o'clock. By the time I woke up, Andy was already dressed and waiting. He asked me to hurry up because we were going to be late. By eleven fifteen, we were in a cab heading toward the bank.

While in the cab, I joked with Andy about learning to drive and getting himself a car. "One thing at a time," he pleasantly answered.

When we pulled in front of the bank and got out of the taxi, Andy changed his mind and went in alone. He rushed out a few minutes later and only mentioned that it would take yet another day to share all the information with me. I started to protest about missing another day of school, but he was on a mission.

We got in a cab and Andy asked the driver to take us to a clothing store about ten minutes away from the bank.

He asked me to try on a few pairs of jeans, see how I liked them, and he would pick up the bill. I tried several and made up my mind about two. He picked up a couple jeans, T-shirts, paid the bill, and we left. We jumped in a *tap tap* and headed back toward the house. A few blocks short of reaching our stop, we got off and walked into a pawnshop.

Bank, clothing stores, and now a pawnshop? Was he about to pawn the clothes we just bought?

Andy asked the owner to see the stereo he had seen before.

Happily, I said, "Cuz, are you getting a stereo?"

"Let's see if it still works. If it does, then we'll buy it."

"Andy, for a stereo anything will do. Let's just take it and run, we'll try it in the house."

My philosophy was typically Haitian. What's in your belly is yours. If it's home and it doesn't play, we can always get the baby fixed for a dollar or two. But if it is in the pawnshop, it's not home. This was to be our first stereo ever, so I was really excited.

Seeing how eager I was, Andy said, "Jacky if you don't like it, we'll take the twenty dollars I gave him as a deposit and we'll go someplace else."

"No, no I like it already, so let's pay him whatever is left and carry it home." Finally, I would be able to have some loud sounds coming from the house instead of having to ask my neighbor to lower his volume because he was making too much noise. I was getting ready to compete to see who would have the best sound.

Wow! The stereo was plugged in, the light came on, and next thing you know music was booming. Turntable, cartridge, two speakers about one foot tall each. What else could one ask for when you are one of the last kids in the neighborhood to have a stereo? This was too good to be true. But there was one minor problem. With the stereo being so big and having limited space in the house, where would we put it? I knew Ronald and I wouldn't have a problem pushing the dining table to one side for more space to enjoy the latest hits from some of our favorites: Skah Shah, Tabou Combo, Scorpio, Frères de Jean, Carol Demesmin or a Roots, Rock, Reggae from the king of reggae, Mr. Bob Marley.

While I was trying to find a solution to my future problem, I heard Andy fuming, "It's too much money. It's not even brand new."

Not knowing the asking price, I came in very strong and said, "For that kind of money we can definitely buy a new stereo."

The owner came back with a very insulting remark, but quite appropriate. "What do you know about stereos?"

My audacity pushed me to say, "Enough not to pay you so much."

"You can't get this stereo anyplace else for less than the $150 that I am asking," he shouted. "I am actually taking a very small profit on it, but I need the money," he added.

Over the years, I spent lots of time shopping with my mother and learned to negotiate with street vendors to the last penny. A pawnshop owner was no different. When he mentioned the words "small profit," he left the field wide open for negotiation. I knew a loss meant a little less than double the price, break even was about three times the actual cost, and when they said a small profit, hold your wallet.

A pawnshop by all accounts was a lucrative business for two reasons. One, as long as your good was in the shop, the owner got to collect a sizeable return monthly, based on the interest rate charged. Sometimes this rate was 20 percent or higher depending on the value of the good pawned. And two, when you could no longer meet your monthly obligation, the owner would liquidate your good, usually at a substantial profit, to clear up his inventory and make room for the next victim. It worked more like loan sharking. However, it served its purpose when all other doors were closed or in a dire emergency. For most poor Haitian families including my own what we so freely called a dire emergency was a normal way of life. We just didn't want to accept the cruel reality and preferred to call it an emergency.

In any event, I looked at the man and said, "I heard you mention that you need the money. You being a businessman, I imagine cash is precious to you. What about making you an offer of $75. Do we have a deal?"

From the muscle contraction on his face, I could tell he was seriously considering the offer. I immediately added,

"Please think hard because you know that is way more than the stereo is worth. On top of everything else, you may have collected lots of interest on it already."

I had never bought a stereo and really didn't have any idea how much his stereo was worth, but by pointing out these two things to him, I felt he was more likely to conclude our offer was valid, so he could not afford to ignore it.

He was furious. "If you know so much about money and dealing, why don't you go tell the Haitian government to stop robbing the country?" he shouted.

I broke out laughing and replied calmly, "I can tell they are teaching you well." I looked at Andy and said in a very decisive voice, "Pay him $55 and let's get going."

I expected him to snap back, but he instead surprised me by saying, "You sure know how to talk someone into closing a deal. Now, pay me the $75 and get lost."

"I said $75 is what we are willing to pay, but $55 is what you will actually get because you already have $20 in your pocket."

"I was not counting the twenty."

"Why not? It's part of the deal. Isn't it?"

"Please take this thing and get him out of here now," he said to Andy.

Bingo!

Andy pulled out his fat wallet and paid him the money.

About half an hour later, I checked my friends out to see if they had any idea where the music was coming from. They did realize it, but as it turned out, no one wanted to compete because Mom did not allow the stereo to play at maximum volume. I spent the whole weekend playing with the stereo, trying to decode the mystery behind LPs, cartridges, and the speakers. By Sunday night, all the thrills about the stereo were already fading away. It was time again to face the real world.

A busy week with schoolwork, in addition to helping my two younger sisters and brother with their homework, left no time for leisure. The week went by very fast with the daily expectation of Andy bringing home a new gadget. By late Sunday evening, I was trying desperately to come up with a plan to present to Andy.

I had thought about several possibilities. A small business, but what if it failed? The money would be wasted. It was really confusing. Furthermore, at the rate he was spending the money and not knowing how much was left, made it hard to judge what was a fair request. I consulted with Ronald but he was as confused as I was.

On January 31st, which was almost two weeks from the time Andy made his offer, he showed up in the house about 6:30 P.M. looking all giddy. I pulled him aside and mentioned that I needed to speak with him urgently. I questioned him about the offer, to find out whether it was still valid.

To my great joy, he answered, "Because you had not said anything, I thought you were not interested."

I explained how difficult it was to build a plan regarding money when the amount that could be made available was unknown. He ignored my statement, but reminded me again, no matter the amount, he would try to work with it because he had initiated the offer.

We shook hands and ended our conversation with the expectation of having something more concrete to discuss next time we met. The pressure to come up with a proposal was intense; my mind was on overdrive, cruising at full speed.

The Lady from Miami

I RAN INTO my friend Yves.

We chatted for a while, and then he said quietly, "I have something to share with you."

"What is it?" I asked in a hurry.

"Well, Thony said to say goodbye and he will be contacting you guys once he gets settled."

"Goodbye? Goodbye for what? Where did he go?"

"Oh, he went to Miami."

"Miami? That's impossible. I saw Thony not too long ago and we spoke, but to the best of my recollection there was no word about leaving Haiti."

"He did not even know when he was leaving until the day before he left."

"Yves, why don't you stop?"

"I am serious, he left."

"Are you sure Thony is not hiding somewhere on the border of Santo Domingo and he has you going around telling everybody that he left for the United States? Now you tell me, how many Haitians do you know of who were leaving for the United States but knew nothing about it until the day before they left?"

"Look, you don't have to believe me, but I am telling you the truth. His aunt who lives in Miami came to Haiti recently and said she was taking him along. He had his passport done and a few days later, he was gone. She does this type of business a lot."

"That is incredible news, Yves."

At the time, one could purchase a hot U.S. tourist visa, a precious commodity indeed, for about 2,500 U.S. dollars. This selling of visas carried some distinctive names like racket, mafia, contraband, and monkey business, just to name a few. But why "monkey" not "donkey?" *Aucune idée!* "No idea!" After all, there were a fair number of donkeys doing business in the country. So much so that donkeys were the primary means of transportation and a great source of income for small farmers, vendors, and especially people in the mountains. The only thing I could think of was that maybe there were more monkeys riding on Haitians' backs rather than Haitians riding on donkeys' backs. Anyhow, if monkey was taking over the U.S. visa business in the country, I had to meet the monkey. You see, this visa was so precious, people would spend hours and hours waiting in line outside of the U.S. Embassy under the sun hoping to get inside just to try their luck.

"Yves, I am very curious about this. Do you know when she's coming back?"

"Why?"

"I just would like to know who is behind the deal and what price they are asking. If I could gather enough information, I may be able to come up with the cash." He laughed and began to walk away.

"Yves, stop! I am dead serious!" I screamed.

"Do you realize this is a well-organized business and it takes a lot of money to get into it?"

"Money is not the question. I just need to establish the contact."

"Wait a second now, have you come into a fortune lately and been keeping it a secret from the rest of us?"

"Tell me when I will hear from you Yves? Is it one day, two days or what?"

"Well, if it's that important to you, I'll see what I can do. But I am telling you this is well over 2,000 U.S. dollars!"

"Why are we still talking about money? All I need to know is when she is coming back and whether you can put me in touch with her. I can't tell you everything right now because I don't know everything. So far, I can only say the money is there and can be made available to me at a moment's notice. How much longer I can say this to you with the same level of confidence, I am not sure. But if you can get this information for me, it will be the key piece of this great puzzle I am desperately in need of solving. So please, help me solve it."

I was talking to Yves as if I already had the money under the mattress, and all I had to do was to lift it up, count the baby to make sure I had the right amount, and then say, "New York here I come."

Yves looked at me for a second, crossed his hands behind his neck, and remained silent for a few minutes. Finally, he said, "I'll get back to you."

"I know I asked this before, but do you have an idea approximately when?"

"That, I can't answer. I don't know when she will be back in Haiti. Sometimes, she flies to Florida and stays there for only forty-eight hours then back to Haiti or vice-versa. I can promise as soon as I find out she is here, I will see to it that you get an appointment to meet with her."

"So at least you know when she is in Haiti?"

"Well, not always. As I said, I can find out."

"Good! I am counting on you."

"OK, so let me go now," Yves said. "I will see you whenever I can."

"Oh, one more thing, Yves, if for some reason you come back and I am not home, do not leave a message with anyone regarding what we have discussed."

"Why? Don't you think your family needs to know about this?"

"They will, but I just don't think the timing is right. All I want you to say, if someone were to ask, is that you need to see me. No more, no less."

"I'll keep it in mind." We shook hands, hugged, and said good night.

I jumped into the air thinking that I had waited for this moment all my life and finally, here it was! I welcomed the news more like destiny, instead of pure coincidence.

I decided not to tell Micheline until I had actually spoken with Thony's aunt. What was the point of possibly disappointing her?

This latest development set my imagination on fire. My thoughts of leaving Haiti were increasing by the minute. Since it was a Saturday evening, I did not expect to hear anything from Yves until maybe a few days later.

To my sheer joy, by 9:30 P.M., he came back with incredible news. He said the lady would be back tomorrow and would stay in Haiti for at least three weeks before going back to Miami. I was thrilled. I thanked Yves and begged him to schedule an appointment for me right away.

"I'll get in touch with you when I get a date."

On that note, we wished each other good night and he left. Meanwhile, I was thinking two things: how I was going to approach my parents to give them the news and, whether Andy would be willing to lend me the money. If he said yes, how soon would I have to take it, before he changed his mind? My brain was racing ahead of me as the night wore on!

The next evening, Yves showed up at the house about 6:15. Before I had the chance to ask any question, he said, "I got you an appointment for tomorrow at 3:00 P.M."

"Well done, well done, Yves. You are a man of your word and I sincerely want to thank you. By the way, did you mention to her how old I am?"

"No, but why is it important?"

"I do not want her to know I am eighteen. You know how Haitian people are. They think because you are young, you are also senseless."

"Hey, don't you worry about that. She is a very cool woman. But on the other hand, who cares? You are paying your money. I don't think she will have a problem with your age." Yves gave me her address and stated for the first time, "Her name is Dominique."

We talked for an additional ten minutes, then he said, "I will meet you there at 3:00 P.M. tomorrow and please be on time."

"I will be ahead of schedule," I responded with lots of enthusiasm. "But remember, if you get there before I do, please do not reveal any more information about me."

"Are you bringing your Dad with you?" Yves asked.

"I was not planning to, but now that you mention it, I will think about it and decide later."

"Your choice. I will see you tomorrow," he replied.

"I will be there," I answered. "And, once again, I thank you for your help Yves. I am really excited about the whole thing."

I ran all over looking for Ronald, checking everywhere in

the neighborhood he could possibly be. To my dismay, he was nowhere to be found.

I had to talk to somebody.

What about Mom and Dad?

No, not until I knew for sure what to do.

With no firm decision, Mom would definitely try to talk me out of it. For now, they would have to wait.

The only person left was God. But how could I ask Him to help me with something I was not even sure about? I had learned from previous experiences that God only answers our prayers when we pray in faith. Thus far, there was no faith in my decision.

All of a sudden, there was a soft voice inside telling me not to worry, *"When the time comes, you will know exactly what to do."* I listened and reflected on the message.

As I was walking back home, I saw Ronald on our friend Evans' motorcycle with a girl sitting on the back. He was coming down the hill slowly and grinning as if to say, look at my prize.

He stopped, winked, flashed one of his big teasing smiles and said, "What do you think?"

"Can I see you at home? We need to talk and it is urgent, Ronald."

"Is it about the same thing we discussed the other night Jacky?"

"No, Roro, this is different. You may be in for a real surprise."

"Give me a few minutes, then we will talk."

"Hurry back! It is really exciting news. I can't wait to share it with you."

About fifteen to twenty minutes later, Ronald came back all impatient, this time being the passenger with Evans riding the motorcycle. He jumped off and asked what was so urgent.

"It is something we have to discuss in private," I answered. Evans got the message and said, "I will see you guys tomorrow."

"Ronald, let's walk away from the house where no one can see us, so we won't be disturbed."

"This must be deep, Jacky."

"Get ready for this my friend. I am about to unveil a master plan to you." We found a place where we could sit comfortably.

"Ronald, I need you to pay close attention to what I am about to say. But stop me if you have any questions."

He looked at me like I was crazy.

I said, "Do you remember that Andy asked me to let him know what I wanted and he would help me out?"

"Yes I do. But do you know what you want?"

"Roro, we may have to leave Haiti."

Ronald's face dropped. "What? Leave Haiti? Where did that come from? No, no, no, Jacky, why can't you choose something else? Besides, you know Mom is going to say no, especially when you are almost finished with school. Come on, do you understand how long it is going to take to get a visa? If this is your master plan I really think it is a bad idea. What about me? Are you ready to leave your brother behind? If you go, I am coming with you."

"Let me assure you, if you want to go, I am not going anywhere without you. Unless Andy has enough to cover both of us, he can keep everything. Concerning Mom and Dad, that is my biggest worry, but I will see to it they accept our decision."

After a brief silence, he said, "Jacky, I still don't think

leaving Haiti is the right thing to do. I would prefer that you finish high school and try getting into a university."

"Ronald, it is extremely difficult to get into a university. Dad has no contact in the government. Suppose I can't get into law school, then what? Mom suggested that I study to become a doctor, but I don't want to go to medical school. If my surgery did anything else, besides all the suffering it caused me, it also eliminated even the slightest possibility of my having anything to do with hospitals or blood. I am afraid of hospitals. I am afraid of blood. But even if I attended medical school, the sad thing is once I got done, I would only be making about 200 U.S. dollars per month. No way! When would I be able to help them? And you want to know something else, at the rate things are going now, there may not be any money left to pay a doctor in this country in ten years."

"You don't expect Haiti to stay as it is today, do you?"

"No I don't. But if you ask me how long it is going to take before any change occurs, I would answer, not today, not tomorrow and certainly not any time soon in the future. Ronald, to have any change in Haiti, you must first have a change in leadership and that is not likely to happen tomorrow. And by the way, when I say leader, I don't mean just any kind of leader. I am talking about someone with a vision, a purpose. I mean one who can redefine or rethink the meaning of our independence. The independence our ancestors have paid dearly with their blood, sweat and souls so we could be free, yet 176 years later we are still in chains. There is a pattern, a well established pattern and it is going to take someone with a mission, a passion, to break this pattern Ronald."

"But why do you feel that way, Jacky?"

"Roro, François Duvalier was president of Haiti for fourteen years and now Jean-Claude, his son, has been for the past nine years. That gives you a total of twenty-three years between father and son. What it means to me is that Jean-Claude Duvalier is more powerful today than his father was twenty-three years ago. Do you agree?"

"But Jacky, that does not mean he is going to stay in power forever."

"Certainly, but keep in mind, the Duvaliers are the roots, but after twenty-three years in power they have grown many trees, the trees many branches and the branches many leaves. Eliminating the roots, cutting out all the trees, cleaning out the branches, and sweeping away all the leaves will be the greatest challenge facing this country in the years to come. In my opinion, the roots are so deep underground, it might take years to dig them out, but many more to wash away the branches and leaves completely out of Haiti. This place is a ticking bomb. And yes, given time, it will explode without any warning."

"So, what do we do?"

"You know what Roro? Every time you take a small step towards the betterment of your life, the world will take a giant leap forward to celebrate your effort. My question to you today is very simple. Do you want to take this small step?"

Ronald looked at me and shook his head in disbelief. "Jacky, why do you want to throw everything away? You are in school, you are doing well and I would like to believe that sooner or later things will change for the better."

"Throw what away, Ronald? To use one's intelligence effectively, he or she must be placed in the right environment and that is socially, politically and economically. Unless you can find yourself in such a climate, your intelligence would just go to waste and serve no purpose. You say given time, things will change for the better? I agree, but the question is how much time we are talking about? Again, just last month we commemorated our independence, but what do we have to show for it? At what cost and to whose benefit?"

"Are you telling me if you wake up tomorrow and Jean-Claude is no longer the president of Haiti that you would not alter your decision to leave?"

I walked up to him and held his hand in mine very tightly and said, "I am not asking you to leave, I am begging you to do so. Please, Ronald, please. Haiti is not for us. We have no business being here if we can get away. Yes, you are right. There will be change, but I am afraid to say things will get worse before they start getting better. What is it going to be?"

He gave me a hug and whispered, "Jacky, we are leaving."

I could not believe my ears. I did not want to leave him behind, but had he refused to come along, I was determined to go solo.

By the time I let go of him, Ronald hit me with the very next question, "Who is getting us the visa?"

"Do you know Thony is already in Miami?"

"That's not true; I saw Thony two weeks ago. Who told you this, Jacky?"

"I said the same thing when Yves told me. But he claimed one of Thony's aunts, Dominique, who lives in Miami, came back recently and decided to take him along with her before she left. He had his passport done and a few days later, he was gone."

"Yves lies so much, why do you listen to him? That's why he is so short." Yves was well in his mid-twenties and was about 5'3" or 5'4." We all used to call him Ti Yves, Little Yves, because of his height.

"Jacky, don't let anyone fool you. There are a lot of fake visas floating around. You don't want to be a part of this. Again, you are doing well in school, so consider your choices."

"I hear you Ronald, but tell me this, do you really think doing well in school has done anything for me in this country? Really, other than a couple of stars on my report card, what else has it done for me so far?"

"Jacky, how do you know if this woman is for real?"

"I have an appointment to see her tomorrow at three. I am sure once we meet and talk to her, we will make the decision whether to proceed or withdraw."

"You waste no time, do you?"

"Well, the money is not mine, but time is on our side. So we might as well jump on it."

"Is she the one who is getting us the visa?"

"Ronald, to tell you the truth, I don't know. Yves did not elaborate, but maybe, by this time tomorrow, we will have this question answered as well."

"Do you know how much we will have to pay?"

"Not at the moment. But whatever the price, if Andy has enough to cover both of us, I will take it without any hesitation."

"What about pocket money? Have you thought of that?"

"No. But why not discuss that when we get to it? For now, let's concentrate on getting the money for the visa."

"Will we take Dad with us?"

"No. Getting Dad and Mom to go along with our plan is not going to be that simple. But, if we can prove to them we have the cash for the visa, passport and our pocket money, it will be a little hard for them to say no. Basically, all we are trying to do is stack the odds in our favor."

"But don't you think if we bring Dad along this lady will be more careful, if she chooses to fool us?"

"If she chooses to do so, what we say or even Dad being there will have no bearing on her decision. For now, let's give her the benefit of the doubt, until she proves us wrong."

"I am guessing you want me to go with you, don't you, Jacky?"

"I would love you to, Ronald. But if you are not comfortable with the idea, I will respect your decision and go alone."

"No, I will go with you."

"Good. Then meet me at school tomorrow at 2:00 P.M. Do not mention anything to anybody." We hugged each other tightly for about a minute and started to walk back home.

"Tell me, what do you think of Micheline?"

"I think she is too arrogant."

"Did you mean too elegant?"

"No, arrogant," he said. "Just hearing her name annoys me," Ronald shouted.

"Come on Roro, you're just jealous."

"Jealous? I don't know what you see in her, but personally I would not waste a single breath talking to her. Jeda told me about the incident in school. You kept it a secret. Why?"

"I was too ashamed to talk about it back then," I replied feeling betrayed by Jeda. "What else did she have to say with her big mouth?"

"That was a good thing you kept it a secret because I would have put Micheline into her proper place. That witch. What was she thinking? Anyway, Jacky, do you seriously think the government is that bad?"

"What government Ronald? This is not a government.

It is a family-owned business and a very lucrative one at that. It was created by the father and inherited by the son. Instead of a government, I would rather call it an enterprise. In any government, when public interest is ignored and private interest is embraced, you would be a fool to think you have a government. A serious government doesn't abuse its people; it protects them instead. It doesn't neglect its people. It embraces them. It doesn't keep them in the dark. It illuminates their pathway. Anything short of that, the best government is self-government. They are looking out for themselves, so we need to look out for ourselves."

"Forget the government for now. About Jeda."

"What about Jeda, Ronald?"

"What are you planning to do with her? She is looking mighty good lately. I saw her leaving Chez Tati's restaurant last week wearing a mini skirt. Her hips were talking to me."

"Keep you hands off her Ronald, she is my buddy." I said laughing, "You hear me Ronald?"

"I think she is very fond of you Jacky, but you know your brother likes a well-padded woman, so hands off? I am not too sure. Get her or I will. As I said, she is looking mighty good."

"Mighty good? I have been thinking she is a volcano ready to erupt at any time. And when she does, she will set some hearts in flame."

"Yeah, that's it Jacky. A volcano! And you want to be right there when she explodes," Ronald said with much excitement. He crossed his hands over his chest yelling, "Burn me, burn me Jeda."

We laughed loudly as we walked inside the house.

A Family Vanishes

I DECIDED TO tell Micheline. It was either that or burst from excitement.

No one answered the door at the Gustave's apartment. The front door was slightly ajar.

I pushed the door and it swung open. All of the lights were on. Something didn't feel right. I walked in and called out their names. No one answered. There was nothing else to do but go home, so I turned around and went back out, trying to figure out why I felt so spooked.

On an impulse I went to Jeda's house. We made small talk in the living room. I sat on the sofa, while she stood ironing some blouses.

"That shirt looks pretty fancy," I teased. "Do you have a hot date?"

She stared at me in a very odd way. "Yes I do. What do you think of that?"

"I think it is wonderful. But, if he is not worthy of you, I will beat him to a pulp. Jeda, do you mind trying that blouse on so I can see it on you?"

"Are you trying to see me naked?"

"I will keep using my imagination. How is that?"

I chuckled and waited for her to laugh too. She didn't. Instead, her mouth pursed up until it was little bigger than an infant's.

"Maybe if I were as thin as Micheline I would have gotten a different answer. I need to lose some weight," she remarked harshly.

"Why this concern about your weight all of a sudden? You are very pretty. Do not underestimate yourself."

"I'm surprised to see you looking so cheery," she observed.

"Why shouldn't I be cheery? I'm young, strong and healthy. Why should I be unhappy?"

Jeda turned the blouse over on the ironing board and whispered. "So, you're not in love with Micheline anymore?"

"You must look like a knock out in that blouse."

"Why are you changing the subject? I asked if you are still in love with Micheline."

"Who said I was in love with Micheline?"

"Oh come on, Jacky. You've thought of little else since she moved into the neighborhood all those years ago. You are always showering her with all kinds of attention. I think you are in love and you don't even know it."

"Stop it. You are exaggerating."

"Not by much. Anyway, no need to explain yourself, it's none of my business."

"That is true. Believe what you want, but maybe there is a part of me you don't know. Right now, my focus is on my future." I answered tersely. "Shouldn't you be worried about this fella you're going out with? Micheline and I will be fine."

"Is that so?"

Did a smirk cross her face? Jeda seemed to be growing into a quarrelsome busybody and I didn't like it one bit.

"Yes. That is so. Someday we are going to America and start a new life together."

I didn't mention Dominique or just how fast it all might

happen. There was a strange vibe between Jeda and me. I wasn't sure if we could still trust each other with our secrets.

"Oh. So, that's it. You sent Micheline ahead of you to prepare a home. Why did she take her parents with her?"

My heart began to thunder in my chest. "What are you talking about?"

Her eyes widened. "You don't know?"

I jumped off the couch. "Know what?"

"Micheline and her family left."

"Left? Where did they go?"

"To New York."

I went over and gently pulled her by the shoulders. "Jeda, stop talking nonsense."

"Your girlfriend went to New York," she answered coldly.

"She wouldn't have left without telling me."

We stared at each other for a long moment because that is exactly what Micheline had done and I finally knew it.

I didn't sleep that night. I sat up and let the suffering consume me. It was not that I was angry with Micheline. I did not know what means she and her family were using to escape Haiti. Perhaps, she had been told to keep her mouth shut. What bothered me was the idea that deep down inside her soul, Micheline would not miss me the way that I would miss her. I felt that I had not had enough time to really capture her heart. To make her love me. If she really loved me, I could expect to receive a letter from her someday. The way things were now, I had no such hope, just memories of her wide smile and sparkling eyes. It is said, out of sight, out of mind. But even when Micheline was not in sight, she was heavy on my mind. I knew if I did not get to America soon, some other man would claim her as his own.

Dominique

AT DAYBREAK, I washed myself, dressed in my uniform, and hit the road. I made it to school in time for my French literature class with Professor Matar, a very intelligent man by all accounts. He was from Senegal and while studying in France, he fell in love with a beautiful Haitian woman in Paris and followed her back to Haiti, a few months after he completed his courses. They got married, had a few kids and since then he made Haiti his refuge. He was quite an hospitable man by nature. I always liked to participate in his class by asking many questions, but that day, the word New York kept buzzing in my mind over and over again. I was so focused on New York, I didn't know when Professor Matar left or the next one came in.

By 2:00 P.M., I packed my bag and headed outside. Within the next few hours, I had to start making some critical decisions in my life. How they would turn out, God only knew.

I had mixed emotions about the meeting. If I cancelled at the last minute, I would no longer have to think about it. The idea of leaving Haiti and being away from my loved ones was heart wrenching. On the other hand, if I didn't go, I might let my biggest opportunity slip by without taking advantage of it.

All of that was behind me. Micheline was in America. I was going to America and find her. It was as simple as that.

I stood in front of the school looking for Roro, but he was

nowhere in sight. In the meantime, I started to think about the people who would be left behind and the impact they have had on my life.

My mother, without a doubt, had been the most influential person in my life. Although she was at times too strict, deep down I knew her strictness was responsible for the person I was. Sometimes I drove her insane and she never failed to punish me when she felt it was necessary. Yet, her tender and constant love, ceaseless words of encouragement, kind, noble and selfless acts to put our needs ahead of hers were by far unparalleled to her temporary punishments. Frankly, given what she had to work with and under the circumstance she had to raise all seven of us, it is remarkable how she always managed to handle herself so gracefully even in the face of dire adversity. I treasured her invisible strength.

My father spent much time out of the house. Not by choice. He was always working…fighting for the next meal. He had taught me some valuable lessons from his actions rather than his words. He worked very hard. His reward was small. This fact kept the fire burning inside me and propelled my drive to steer my life into a new path.

My brothers, sisters, cousins, aunts, and uncles, I ached from the pain of leaving the secure and loving environment they created for me. I hoped that they would understand my facing the unknown was not in any way a lack of love for them, but rather a necessary step toward a better future for myself and theirs as well in the long-term.

I would miss my friends, especially Jeda. I don't think she was even aware how much I valued our friendship.

My neighbors, on countless occasions, had to step in to play the role of a parent when mine were absent. It was a great blessing to know you had another set of eyes looking out for you to ensure that you stayed on the right path.

As for Haiti itself, what could I say? Despite the misery and poverty of our land, the country overflowed with a wealth of kind, compassionate and goodhearted people who were never afraid to welcome a stranger, yet deeply proud of our own heritage. When we became the first black nation to fight for our freedom from a colonial empire, and the second nation to be independent in the western hemisphere, we set the tone for what was to become a model for others to emulate in the pursuit and struggle for their own freedom, not only in the Caribbean where slavery was rampant, but also across other borders, rivers and oceans.

If the revolution of Haiti was a spark in the eyes of many, it was without question a catastrophic inferno in the minds of a few. For that, the country has been punished severely.

How?

In 1806, only two years after the country's independence, Haiti was hit with a huge trade embargo from France, Spain, the United States and other foreign nations that lasted several decades. In 1825, Haiti had to borrow 150 million French francs from a French bank to pay France to recognize the independence they fought for and won. Plus, there was an additional thirty percent in loan fee and six percent in interest that Haiti had to repay. Furthermore, as part of the package, France also insisted on a 50 percent reduction of import duties for every French vessel destined for Haiti, which gave them a monopoly of the country's commerce.

Those sequential blows fastened by almost a century of widespread corruption and brutality from Haitian government officials brought the country down on its knees. Haiti is still struggling to loosen the grip from its neck.

Also, let's not forget the United States occupation that lasted nineteen years, from 1915–1934, which resulted in a change of the Haitian Constitution that granted foreigners from various nations, some with no other intention but the exploitation of the country, the right to own land in Haiti.

Since then, a small elite controls the wealth of the country. Shamefully, many choose to deal with this small elite with little if any regard for the progress of Haiti, so long as the monetary benefits are mutual.

Once in the past, our country with its crystal blue sea, warm sandy beaches, green mountains tops, which at times melted right into the clouds, was so beautiful it was dubbed the "Pearl of the Antilles." So productive and prosperous, it was considered the jewel of the French empire. But now, we cuddled our glorious past, mourned our present and dreamt of our future. To many of us—rich or poor, educated or not, young or old—Haiti is and will forever remain our cherished treasure, our uncut diamond waiting for the right hand to carve it to its finest cut so the world can experience its true brilliance. But until that happens, I must focus on my future.

Where was Ronald? It was already after two but I told him 2 o'clock. If by 2:30 he didn't show up, I was gone.

Only moments later I heard from a distance, "Jacky, Jacky, let's go."

When I turned in the direction of the voice, my brother looked awesome. Boy was he handsome. Ronald was always a jeans, t-shirt and sneakers type. To see him in slacks, long-sleeved shirt tucked inside his pants, well polished shoes and socks, it had to be a very special event. At 5'10", he was very slim and had a set of long legs, which helped him to move very fast. I joked and asked if he just flew back from New York.

He slapped me on my head and shouted, "Let's make it quick, so we won't be late."

I kept on laughing and said, "Look who is talking about being late. Do you realize you are almost twenty-five minutes late?"

I smiled then said, "Roro, since you are so dressed up, how about if you do all the talking?"

He laughed then explained that he had left school around twelve o'clock to go change into civilian clothes so Dominique would not think we were just students, pay us no mind or decide to treat us as if we had no money.

From our location to her house it was a half an hour walk. So we moved as fast as we could, while holding each other's hand. We had to cross a few red lights along the way but, as usual, most of the lights were not working. We ignored the lights that did work, dodging our way through traffic, past the madness and swearing of some angry drivers and a crowd of pedestrians. Before long, we were two blocks away from Dominique's house with a few minutes to spare. We stopped to catch our breath, got a drink and worked out a plan to deal with Dominique.

"I will discuss the price, conditions, and her obligation to fulfill her promise. And you Ronald, if you realize I am sweating bullets with a question or answer, jump in and take over."

Ronald smiled and answered mockingly, "The way you sound, I don't think I will have much to say."

"I am nervous as hell Ronald, and I suppose you must be feeling the same way. But let's walk in there pretending we have it under control and give it all we've got."

Three o'clock sharp we were in front of the house, not knowing what to expect. We could no longer back out. Yves was already waiting on us all dressed up in his white pants and shirt like he was about to go to Sunday mass or attend a funeral.

Yves led the way and walked straight to a lady standing in the backyard next to three chairs. In a very sweet and loving voice, she said, "I am Dominique."

"My name is Jacky and this is my older brother Ronald. Pleased to meet you Dominique."

"Have a seat," she said kindly.

Once the introduction was over, Yves mentioned he had someplace else to go and would check back with us later to see how the meeting went.

Meanwhile, I was studying Dominique like a book, trying to establish a connection between the image I had in my mind and the person standing in front of me. Dominique was a beautiful woman. She was about 5'8" and weighed no more than 120 lbs. She had a long face and combed her hair in a ponytail, which made her look much younger than what I estimated to be between thirty-five to forty years old. Her café au lait complexion, sparkling, slanted, brown eyes under a set of beautiful eyebrows revealed a sense of self-confidence and audacity. Her mouth was somewhat small, but when she smiled it was clear she had nothing to hide. Beautiful teeth! She wore her skirt below her knees as if to say, I am from the old school, but the perfect coordination between her blouse, sandals, along with the silver earrings, necklace and bracelet she was wearing spoke volumes about her fashion taste. She was a true Haitian beauty.

She again invited us to take a seat and proceeded by asking if we cared for anything to drink. I requested a glass of water and Ronald decided to pass and had a cigarette instead. Deep inside I felt my protector, my big brother, was really getting nervous. Dominique called her niece out and ordered her to bring some food and a glass of water. Ronald was in his own world puffing his lungs out. I looked at him and smiled gently to reassure him that everything was going to be just fine.

Dominique's niece came outside carrying a tray with a full plate of rice, beans and some sort of vegetables, along with the water. She took the tray, said thank you to her niece, and handed me the water. She started eating while I took a sip. My heart was pounding faster and faster. I knew it was time to start asking questions, but I wanted Dominique to make the first move. After a few spoonfuls, she asked if our parents were coming to meet us.

I took a second sip of the water and answered fearlessly, "No."

She kept eating and finally said, "Where are you getting the money to pay for this?"

I felt a bit disturbed by her bluntness but also knew she asked a valid question. I took a different approach and without hesitation, I asked her, "Money for what?"

She took a full spoon of rice and beans and asked, "If you don't know money for what, why are you here?"

I took a look at her face, trying to penetrate the blank stare in her eyes, but again she left no clue. "Dominique, Yves told me you came here a few weeks ago, asked Thony to get his passport done and a few days later he was in Miami. I have many questions, but I will start with two."

"Go ahead," she said. "I am listening."

"My first question is, how did you do it and could you do the same thing for my brother and me? My second question is how much do you charge, what are the conditions involved, and how soon would we have to come up with the money?"

Dominique took a couple sips of her drink, put aside her food, and asked me, "How old are you?"

"Eighteen," I answered.

"Eighteen?"

"Yes, eighteen," I said in a very nervous voice.

"What about your brother?"

"He is twenty."

"What grade are you in?"

"If everything goes well, we hope to finish school very soon."

"Do you have any family in Miami?"

"No, we don't and we are not actually staying in Miami. New York will be our final destination."

"Well Miami is as far as I would take you. You have to find your own way to New York," Dominique said with a smile.

I smiled back.

Dominique carried on with her interrogation by asking some more questions and we did the best we could to answer them all. Finally, she insulted us by saying we were too young, therefore she would need to speak to our parents.

I looked at Ronald with the expectation that he would take over as planned, but his facial expression clearly stated, *"Don't look at me pal. I told you we needed to come with Dad."*

I said, "Dominique, you will get to meet our parents when the time is right, for now pretend we have none and deal with us as two responsible adults."

Suddenly, my brother began to be very talkative.

"Dominique," he said, "why don't you explain the process involved, give us the price then we will discuss it with our parents when we get home."

With a bit of more confidence, I said, "Dominique, you see this guy and me? We are like twins. As he said, we chose to see you alone because we want to have a clear picture of the whole deal."

She remained silent.

For a moment, all I could see was a puzzled face and no counter strategy. She broke her silence by saying, "Since you are so young, there are some decisions you can't make by yourselves." Then she added, "That's the difference between America and Haiti."

She looked straight into my eyes, the first time since we had been talking, and questioned, "If you guys are so close to finishing school, why not get it done and then leave right afterward?"

"Does that mean you can get us the visa?" I replied.

"Only your money will stop you."

"We would love to stay and finish school," I said. "That seems to be the ideal thing to do. But we think it is far more important to leave now or else the money might be gone by then. That would mean passing up one of the best opportunities life ever presented to us and we might live to regret our decision."

She got up, took the tray and everything else, and started to walk inside. I asked for more water and that ended our conversation for the time being.

Ronald lit another cigarette and asked why I was being so positive.

"Roro, there is no other way to be."

"Suppose Andy says no, then what?"

"For now, keep him out of the picture. Let's focus on getting all the details. If she can get us the visa, we will get the money." We ended the conversation when we saw Dominique coming back out.

Dominique sat down, placing her chair at an angle. This gave her a full view of us.

Very gently, she began, "I really don't like to do business with young people, but since you want to leave, let me see what I can do to help you. You are very well-mannered and seem to have no doubt about what you want to do, especially the little one."

Dominique addressed herself directly to Ronald. She handed him a sheet of paper and a pen then ordered him to write down our full names, address, and dates of birth. As Ronald started writing down the information, I asked him to wait because things were not clear to me.

I said, "Dominique, could you tell me why you need that information?"

"It is information needed to get your passports done. Once I have that, we'll proceed to the next stage. Do you have any more questions?"

"Yes I do," I answered calmly. "How much are the passports going to cost?"

Yves was right. She was a very cool woman. Why did she refuse to discuss the passport deal?

I took a new approach and said "Dominique, when do we pay you for the passports?"

With no delay she answered, "It's included in the price."

"Great! Is there anything else besides the passports?"

"Your roundtrip ticket to Miami and three days at my home until you can contact your family in New York, or be on your own."

I said, "Roundtrip ticket? Dominique, why do we need a roundtrip ticket?"

"It is required as long as you have a tourist visa in your

passport. It is an indication you have a firm intention to return. The U.S. Embassy makes no exception."

Hmm, that made sense. "So how much do we pay for all that?"

"Not much." She got up and started to walk inside again.

"Dominique, you did not answer the question. How much will we have to pay?" I insisted.

"Not much," she repeated and carried on with her steps.

"But how much is not much?" I fired back.

"I will tell you," she shouted.

Bang.

The minute she was gone, Ronald hit me on my head and asked why I was being so aggressive. "You should give her a chance to explain what she is doing," he scolded.

"I will give her all the chances she wants Ronald, as long as she tells us how much we have to pay. She is evading the question and I am not feeling good about that. I guess you were right about bringing Dad with us."

"Oh, it is too late to think about that now, Jacky."

"Actually, we still have an out because she already expressed the desire to see our parents. We could always end the meeting right now and tell her we will come back with Dad."

"Well in that case, when she comes out, you let me handle it."

I looked at him and broke up laughing then said, "Do you really want to go to New York?"

"You damn right I want to go."

"Then show me some money." I said laughing.

Dominique walked out, this time with a grin on her face, carrying a purse over her shoulder. She again pulled her chair at an angle looking directly at our faces and sat down.

"All right," she said, "I feel that I need to explain everything, before I can collect any information from you. Obviously, you still have some doubts about how I operate and that is acceptable." She sighed and then continued with great ease in her voice, "I guarantee you one thing, when this is all over, you will be pleased with the result. I have a partner. He has his contacts in Haiti and I have mine in the Bahamas and Miami. You will get to meet him when, and if necessary. We run a very small but extremely well-organized operation. To date, we have yet to run into any problems and we do not expect to come across any, God forbid. We take no chances whatsoever. We even meet you at the airport, clear you through immigration and see you to the door of the airplane. Do you know anybody else who can do this?"

We chose not to answer and just listened attentively to what she was saying.

"Now," she continued, "I think what is important to you is how much you have to pay. Well, the price varies according to how we take you there. It is 3,500 U.S. dollars if we travel with you all the way to Miami or 2,500 U.S. dollars if you decide to go alone and that is per person. Please be aware, we accept no partial payment. It is all or nothing. That is all there is to it. Go home and think about what I said. If you still decide to go, bring the money, and be ready to leave within a week or less from the time I receive your money. I know this sounds unreal," Dominique said with an air of arrogance, "but that is how it works. Once we get your money, we waste no time."

Ronald and I looked at each other for a brief moment and just kept silent. For a second I thought about letting him handle it, as he had requested, but he remained quiet. Dominique stood up, obviously looking to end the meeting. I kept thinking, "Say something, Roro, say something." But,

Roro was still as still water. I changed my mind and jumped in before she called it quits.

"Dominique, let me ensure you we have no doubt in our minds about what you are able to do. First of all, you have proven your work by Thony being in Miami. Second, I find you to be a very intelligent woman who seems to have everything under control. But, given that we are dealing with money and money we will have to pay back even if something were to go wrong, I would like to make sure we understand crystal clear what the plan is and how we are to achieve it. Furthermore, I also want to state our position as precisely and accurately as we can to you."

I looked at her straight in the eyes, cleared my throat and said, "Once we hand over the money, we only look forward to being in Miami and thanking you for a job well done, when we get there. Please bear in mind, no matter the amount, while it might represent a drop in the bucket for you, to us it would be a small fortune. I promise you won't have any problems with us as long as our expectation is met, nor will we have to question your credibility. But, should there be a problem, you will be held accountable."

I didn't know what I said, but my latest statement seemed to add fuel to her fire. She was livid. "Let me explain this to you very clearly, young man. I have already taken about fifty people to Miami and they keep coming every day, by the hour." She opened her purse, pulled out a handful of passports some with money and others without and said angrily, "Take a look at this."

It seemed as though the passports with the money had at least an inch thick stack of bills with both Haitian and U.S dollars. Some looked very crispy as if someone had just withdrawn them from the coffer of a bank. Others were tied with a single rubber band on each end.

"You see, these people are all ready to go. All I have to do is set a date and let them know when I want them to fly."

I chose not to interrupt but watched cautiously for what was to come next. I felt she was about to grab my neck and choke me. I was growing more nervous by the minute thinking, "Is this for real?" She convinced me, but five thousand dollars for both sounded like a huge sum and I did not think Andy had enough to cover both of us.

I contemplated walking away, but instead I gave her a few minutes to cool off and then softly brought the focus back on the price. I said, "Dominique, as far as the price is concerned, I don't think you will have to go with us. That's really asking too much of your time. Why not set aside the $3,500 and deal with the $2,500?"

She sat back down and finally with a smile on her face, she said, "I didn't think I would have to go with you, but since you wanted details, I wanted to give it all as precisely and accurately as I could."

"Thank you again and I appreciate the fact that you are telling us everything. Now, $2,500 is what you usually ask, right?"

She said, without hesitation, "Yes, and that would be $5,000 for you and your brother. Five, Zero, Zero, Zero. That includes your passports, tickets and three days in my house in Florida."

Ronald got up, stretched his legs and back and sat right back down. Every drop of blood in my system was frozen to the point where I had a leg cramp. To me, five thousand sounded more than a small fortune—it would be a miracle.

Somehow Dominique felt the anguish going on between

Ronald and me, so she took the opportunity to deliver yet another blow, as if she wanted to inflict some more pain. "Let me remind you again, we do not accept any partial payment."

"Yes, I remember. It's all or nothing."

"Exactly," she answered.

I was speechless, emotionless, penniless and everything else you could think of with less at the end. There was a huge lump in my throat. I felt as if my tongue had tripled in size. Very heavy!

I opened my mouth and whispered with great courage, "Dominique, since there are two of us, we will offer $3,500 for both. What do you say?"

She started laughing and said, "There is no room for negotiation. I said $5,000 and I mean $5,000. That is the same thing I have been saying for the last five minutes and it seems to me you are not getting the message. I wish I could be more flexible with my price because I am constantly reminded how difficult it is for someone to come up with $2,500 in Haiti let alone $5,000. But I have to force myself to remember that I am running a business, not a charity. No, I can't go any lower."

I didn't recall when I breathed in, but I had to exhale again and it came out as if I had taken the deepest breath of my life.

"Dominique, I understand your position about your time and the money and I must say I agree with you in terms of running a business not a charity. But, I also believe, any deal that does not leave room for negotiation is not a good deal. Plus, if it is closed without proper negotiation, it might turn out to be a very bad deal once it is over."

She looked at me, shook her head and said, "I don't know where you have learned this, but it has never worked before and it is not going to work here today. It is now about 7:00 P.M. and I have been with you guys since 3:00 in the afternoon," she sighed, as if we had exhausted all her patience. "I was supposed to meet with someone, but I cancelled my meeting so I could talk to you. I told you everything there is to know. At this point, if you want to go to the next phase, go home, discuss it with your parents, or whoever is giving you the money, and come back to see me when you think you are ready."

I said, "We are ready to move to the next phase tonight, but I am telling you right now, we won't get there with $5,000. How about $3,500? We would be responsible for our own passports, you get the tickets and we go straight to New York when we get to Miami."

Dominique had a very cold smile on her face. The kind that translates to nice shot but try again. With a piercing look in her eyes, she said furiously, "No one has ever insulted me with such a low price since I have been doing this business and I am not happy. You are crazy if you think I would consider such a low offer. We might as well stop talking right this minute because we are very far apart." She looked at Ronald and said, "You need to take your brother to see a doctor."

I smiled and replied, "Dominique, that was a hundred dollar comment! What about offering you $3,600?"

"No!" she shouted.

"No you said?" I responded gently.

"Yes, that's what I said, no."

"What is the lowest you think you could go?"

"Young man, this is not a game of chance where you hope your number will roll out and draw a profitable return. This is a business. Business is not run by chance. It takes skill and know how to make it profitable."

"With all those passports in your purse Dominique, I am convinced you have been blessed with both the skill and know-how. Actually, looking how tight those dollars are squeezing each other for more space, I can tell business has been highly profitable."

In the heat of the negotiation, Ronald cried out, "OK, Dominique, we will pay you $4,000 for both and that is as far as we will go, but…."

Dominique interrupted, except her sentence was cut short by a light cough and Ronald jumped on the opportunity to squeeze in his last thought.

"We are by no means insulting you and if this is how you feel, I do apologize. You gave us a price and we have given you ours. You don't have to accept it, nor do we have to accept yours. But, if we could come to a mutual agreement that would satisfy all of us, we will go to bed tonight with the inner satisfaction of knowing we have closed a terrific deal."

"Terrific deal to whom?" she asked. "Look, would you be willing to get your passports and tickets?" She said ignoring my second offer.

"Passports yes, tickets, no," Ronald answered back. "Not for $4,000. The only way we would do that is if you keep the price below $4,000." Ronald got up and asked, "How much are the tickets anyway?"

"The price varies everyday," answered Dominique.

"But how much do you usually pay?" Ronald said again pressing for an answer.

"I said it varies," Dominique snapped back.

Ronald said firmly, "We have decided on $4,000. We will get the passports and you take care of the tickets."

She scratched her head for a little while and said, "I do not usually work for that kind of money, but I guess I will have to take a loss."

I kept quiet and let Ronald work his magic. But when I heard the word "loss," I wanted to jump in with a whole new offer. I was biting my tongue and scratching my head, but Roro was behind the deal.

"All right," Dominique said, "you go get your passports and bring them along with the money. Do not waste any time with this because, once I am gone, I might be in Florida for a month before I come back. As soon as I get your passports and money, be ready to leave within a week. I demand that you only take one small bag each, the less the better. Your bare essentials will work just fine. You do not, outside of your parents and close family members, discuss your travel plans with anyone. And also, of paramount importance is that you do not reveal my name to anybody. Is this clear?"

"Very clear," answered Ronald.

"Dominique, I have one more question," said Ronald, "and I hope that will be our last. What happens to our money if anything goes wrong?"

"Your money will be intact until I know for sure you guys are in Miami."

Andy Revisited

"**ANDY, HOW** much money do you have left?"

"Enough to last for a while and still have the bank call me Mr. for a long time," he said with great excitement.

"And, how much are you paying for the car?"

"I have not decided yet, Jacky. In fact, that is the reason I need to talk to you. I want you to be there to help me with the negotiation."

"Andy, I know absolutely nothing about cars. I think you need someone else to advise you on this."

I took a quick look at Ronald to see his reaction. He looked even more confused and nervous. I really don't think he was happy with what he was hearing.

"By the way, Andy, do you have any money on you?" I said.

"How much we are talking about?"

"About 250 U.S. dollars."

"Oh, I guess you need to do some clothes shopping."

"Clothes? No Andy, it is something more pressing than that and it must be done today."

"What is it for?"

"We need to get our passports done."

"Passports? That's big news. I don't know about you, but I am not ready to leave Haiti."

"Why not? I think it would be a very good move for you."

"No, no, you go first then I will follow later."

"Andy, why don't you want to leave now?"

"Jacky, I am having too much of a good time and I would not want to give this up to go to New York right now."

"Well in that case, would you have a problem if Ronald takes your place?"

"No," answered Andy, "it would be great to see the two of you leave together. But does he have any money?"

I smiled, "It's funny you asked. That was my question to him as well. But to answer your question, no, he does not and neither do I. Would you be able to cover both of us?"

"How much and who is getting you the visa?"

"We need $5,000, Andy. The cost for the visas and tickets is actually $4,000, and the rest is for our passports and pocket money."

"Five thousand dollars, are you out of your mind? That is 25,000 *gourdes!*"

"You asked me to think about what I want and you would help me out. This is what I want, Andy."

"Oh no, no, that is way too much. And not only that, you are not even sure if the visa is going to be good."

"I know, Andy. But you told me last week that you would try to work with whatever I decided. I did not ask, you offered. That promise left me with the freedom to choose and I did."

"You could have chosen something less than 25,000 *gourdes.*"

"Yeah, 25,000 *gourdes* seem like a lot. Doesn't it? I see where you are having a problem with this, you are thinking in *gourdes*, but I am talking in dollars. Yes, there is a huge difference between five and twenty-five. Think of the five as the grandbabies we talked about."

Andy smiled as if the interest in his account was blooming like weeds and to get rid of a few thousand was no sweat.

"By the way, Andy" I carried on, "as far as the visa, I had the same concern. But last night after meeting with the person in charge, my fears have all disappeared. So far, she has taken more than fifty people to Miami already and one of them we know."

"Who?"

"Thony."

"What? Thony is in Miami? People. You never know their secrets," he murmured.

"Isn't that the truth? I mean here we are family and I still don't have a clue how much you won. So tell me how much was it?" I teased.

"I don't have to tell you everything, do I?"

"Not the whole thing, but say something for Christ's sake. Is it fifty, sixty or what?"

"Nothing I care to discuss," Andy said giggling.

"I hope I did not offend you by asking for that kind of money."

"No, but I didn't think you would need it so soon."

"I didn't think so either Andy, but now that I realize I do, I chose not to sleep on it."

"I guess I can't turn you guys down. When do you need the money?"

Jokingly I said, "Since we are not in the bank, I won't say now."

"Don't you guys have school today?"

"Yes we do, but we are not going."

Andy rubbed his hands together, remained silent for a minute or two then said, "Let's go get it."

I jumped and screamed at the top of my lungs, "Oh yes!"

By the time I came down, I was moving my legs like I was learning a new dance. Ronald joined me in the dance. I assume it was the dance of change because I heard myself repeating over and over again, "Change is on the way, change is on the way." I was out of control.

Thank God my mother had left the house at 6:30 A.M. to attend an all day prayer so we didn't have to be under her constant surveillance. Although she had no knowledge of what was happening, I believed the way things were happening so smoothly, she must have been praying endlessly. God listened and delivered beyond her expectation. I said silently, "Pray mommy, pray because change is on the way."

"I think I will postpone my plan to buy the car today," Andy said.

"No, Andy, once we get the passports done, I will be all yours, even though I still think someone else might have more knowledge about cars."

"Jacky, I have faith in you regardless of the situation. Let me be the first one to wish you guys luck."

I gave Andy a hug and said, "Thank you Cuz, thank you. God will bless you."

Andy laughed and replied, "He just did Jacky and I am not sure He will so soon again."

In less than an hour, we were posing in front of a camera getting ready to take our passport pictures.

Arnel, the photographer, was no more than thirty years old. But it seemed life's pressure had added quite a few years to his calendar. I asked him to make these shots the best of his career. It was agreed that we would pay him $225 for both passports and pictures and they would be ready within forty-eight hours.

Arnel, or whoever was the owner of that passport business, was collecting mega bucks. For the half an hour we were there, I witnessed the collection of almost thirty passports. Now that we knew the passports were getting ready, I told Andy I was at his disposal.

He surprised me by saying, "Forget about the car. I am seriously thinking about getting my passport done and following you guys to New York within the next couple of months. Once you are gone, the house will never be the same again. I would rather save whatever I have left, so that I can buy a car when I get to New York."

"That is a brilliant idea, Cuz."

New York was only a week away and I really didn't know how to handle it. I was getting scared every minute of the day, yet I refused to let the image of New York out of my mind for a second. I knew even a small second without visualizing ourselves being in New York was strong enough to make a major difference in what we set out to accomplish. If there was one thing I learned about visualization is that it works best when you give it some fuel. In my mind, I took a short trip to New York before Ronald or Andy even noticed that I was gone. I picked up a few pennies and came right back without missing a beat.

The rest of the day was spent window shopping, eating and hanging out in record stores. We listened to some music, which turned out to be a great tranquilizer for the tension I was feeling. We reached home that evening about 6:30 P.M. It was a Tuesday; I did not expect to see my father home so early. He usually got home during the week no earlier than eight. Mom was still out, but was due to arrive soon. With all the pieces now in their proper place, it was time to bring everyone together and put the final touch on our plan.

It was frightening, but for the first time, I felt I was not about to ask my parents for their permission but instead inform them of my decision. Ronald and Andy had gone back out by the time Mom came home. I told my parents I needed to speak with them urgently, but I had to wait for Ronald and Andy to get home before I said anything.

I waited nervously for almost thirty minutes. Ronald and Andy finally walked home together showing no care or concern. I called them in and told Mom and Dad I was now ready to begin.

The pressure was intense. My father moved from his chair and took a seat at the edge of a small table that we used for eating. Mom looked at me as if to say hurry up because I am tired. Ronald began sweating as if someone had chased him. And Andy started to bite his nails one moment and crack his fingers the next. I started to unload our secret.

I went straight to the point. "Mom, Dad, Ronald and I are leaving for New York and it will happen within a week or less from today." I knew I had to back up my statement with some evidence, so I wasted no time. "Here is the receipt for the passports. Andy is lending us the money to go, the person responsible for getting us the visas has already taken over fifty people to Miami and she is getting ready to take some more next week, including Ronald and myself."

Mom laughed and started to walk away saying, "I thought you had something serious to say to me."

Andy stopped her when he shouted, "No, they are serious."

I said, "I know you guys must have been very suspicious about Andy and where he got all the money he's been spending, but he won the lottery and was keeping it a secret."

For a moment there was a shift in the conversation as to why Andy kept things secret, but that was not the goal of the meeting. I intervened and brought the focus back to the table about our trip.

We were bombarded with many questions and fears from both Mom and Dad; however, nothing was strong enough to make me change my mind about leaving. My mother's biggest concern was whether I planned on keeping up with school, once I got to America. I calmly reaffirmed my desire to finish school and told her that was not going to change after I got to New York.

I threw my hand around her shoulders and said softly, "Mommy, you have always placed so much confidence in me when it comes to school. Let me assure you," I continued, "regardless of how things turn out in America, no matter how long it takes or how painful the process, I will someday make something out of my life. And that is my promise to you. Today, I ask that you keep your faith in me."

She started crying, "I am not so worried about you, but I am very concerned about Ronald."

I gently answered, "All I can say is this: as long as he is with me, I will look out for him. He has always protected me; now it will be my turn."

My father was very pleased to hear the good news and supported it a hundred percent. Ronald's breathing finally looked less tense. As much as my mother wanted to put up a fight, she realized we had things under control. In the end, she surrendered and gave us her blessing. We were thrilled.

I had no idea what the future had in store for me, but I was certain if the future and I were ever to meet anywhere, New York was to be our rendezvous point.

Jeda's Decision

I HAD TO go tell Jeda before she heard the news on the street.

She sat quietly and listened to my whole story: how Andy won the lottery, my chance encounter with Yves, the mysterious lady from Miami, and how we were leaving very, very soon.

"How long are you staying in Miami Jacky?"

"I don't know sweetheart."

"Will I see you again…ever?"

"Of course you will Jeda, but I can't say exactly when."

She paced around the room in silence. "I'm going with you," she said raising her eyebrows.

"What?"

"I want to go to America as well. Will you take me to meet Dominique?"

"Shush, Jeda! I wasn't supposed to say her name. Do not mention it again."

She looked around and smiled. "There is no one else here but the two of us."

"Jeda, why do you want to leave Haiti?"

"The same reasons you want to leave."

It was a good answer and one that could not be argued with.

"Besides, I can't stand us being apart. You are my best friend Jacky."

"Where would you get that kind of money?"

"I am not sure. But I do have an uncle who has some money and I have never asked him for anything, so maybe this is a good time to do that. Look, don't worry, I will find the money," Jeda said with finality. "It might take me a few weeks but Roro won't mind if you postpone your trip on my account, will he?"

Dear Jeda. It never occurred to her that Roro would not be the problem if she wanted me to postpone my trip.

"I can't ask him to do that." What a coward I was.

She clapped her hands. "Then I will do the asking. I know Roro. He would never refuse me."

"Jeda, I…"

She jumped up. "Let's find him now. Come. We don't have a moment to spare."

I grabbed her arm and pulled her back down on the sofa. "Stop."

"What is the problem, Jacky?"

I took a deep breath and came clean. "I won't postpone my trip to America, Jeda. Not for anyone. Not even my own mother. Ask me for any other favor and I'll do it for you, immediately. But not that. Please."

"I see."

"No, you don't see. If this chance slips away, I may never have another opportunity. Can't you see that, Jeda?"

"No I can't. If the shoe were on the other foot, you know I would wait for you, Jacky. Isn't that true?"

I started to protest but then closed my lips. Jeda would risk her opportunity by waiting for me.

"Yes, it is true."

"And even knowing that it is true, you still will not wait for me?"

My silence was her answer.

"I tell you what, Jeda. I will take you to meet Dominique, but that is as far as I am willing to go. I suppose you too understand that you have a bright future burning inside of you but it won't shine in Haiti. Come to think of it, you have a genuine talent for dancing. Remember that night at the theater? You had them going. I don't ever recall telling you this, but your kiss sealed the night for me."

"I remember," she said blushing while pulling her hair to the back. "You had such a glow in your eyes Jacky," she moaned affectionately.

"Listen Jeda, our plan is to go New York, but should that change after we get to Miami, you will not have to stay at Dominique's home when you arrive. You can stay with Roro and me for as long as you like. How does that sound?"

"New York? Why I am not surprised? So, it's all about Micheline. Well, go then."

She crossed her arms over her chest and turned away from me. "It was nice knowing you, Jacky."

Jeda was crying.

I felt awful. Jeda had been by my side, doing whatever I needed her to do, for as long as I could remember. She was a true friend and now, the first time she asked me for something, I was saying no.

"Jeda, I cannot postpone the trip. Dominique would kill us! It is bad enough that we will not pay her full price. To go back and ask her to delay our departure may end the deal. How about this? If you decide to close a deal with Dominique and I am still in Miami, I will find out when you are due to arrive and be there to greet you. And don't forget, you can stay with me and Ronald for free."

It was a pretty sweet deal.

Jeda looked at me, long and hard. "Do you really want me to be in America with you?"

I had not thought about my trip in those terms but instinct told me the correct answer. "Yes, I do."

She smiled. "Then I accept your offer."

She said it the way I imagined women accepted proposals of marriage. It made me uncomfortable.

I stood up to leave. "Good! It is all settled."

We hugged and said good night. As soon as I was out the door, my shoulders slumped. I accept your offer. I accept your offer. Why did she put it that way? I groaned aloud and walked home slowly. My hands were jammed in my pockets and I was deep in thought.

Detour

EXACTLY ONE week later, Ronald and I were at the airport waiting for our flight to be called for boarding. According to Dominique, we were supposed to travel to the Bahamas and fly directly to Miami from there. When I asked why we were not taking a nonstop flight to Miami, she explained that ticket was far more expensive and besides, the transit in the Bahamas would only be for one hour.

Meanwhile, Dominique chatted away with all the immigration officers. She seemed to know everyone not only by face, but also by name. Her handling of people was quite amazing. She smiled and hugged just about everyone who crossed her path. I supposed that was a skill she felt necessary for what she was doing. She appeared to have mastered it to the finest detail. On one occasion, I saw her in discussion with my father, but I was not aware of what transpired between the two of them.

Our close friends and family members were at the airport to bid us farewell. All were happy, except Mom. As far as she was concerned, we were taking a giant step and the fact that she was not going to be there to assist us during our transition, kept her tears flowing beyond consolation. Besides, she had no idea if and when she would ever see us again.

About half an hour before the scheduled departure time,

Dominique hurried back and said, "It is time for you to say your final goodbye because I want you to start heading towards the airplane."

There were many hugs, kisses, and handshakes. Almost everyone was in tears and Mom was out of control. My father also had a few drops rolling down his cheeks. I tried my hardest not to establish eye contact with anyone for I knew if I did, I would find myself crying as well.

I kissed and hugged my mom for the last time and switched to my father right away. When I let go of him he said sadly, "Please stay away from alcohol and marijuana."

I thanked him for the advice and, while playing with his hair, I whispered gently, "Papa, if your son is going to get addicted to anything in America it is going to be his books because I know only my books will get me as high as I ever want to get."

By the time we made it to immigration, Dominique had apparently taken care of all the details. She sped us through the line without having to show our passports. I was amazed.

Is this corruption at the highest level or what?

I was finally convinced that when she said they were very organized and things always worked out smoothly, she meant it.

Dominique handed me a closed envelope and said, "Both your passports and tickets are inside. I wish you guys luck and I will see you soon in Miami."

We happily said thank you and walked toward the airplane.

We boarded a Bahamas Air flight scheduled to arrive in Nassau, Bahamas at 11:30 A.M. We took our seats beside each other in the mid-section of the airplane. The reality of sitting inside an airplane for the first time and actually going to Miami had finally hit me.

To my surprise, the first words out of Roro's mouth were, "Jacky, how far away are we from Miami?"

"Much closer than we were yesterday, Roro. But we still have to land in the Bahamas before we get there today."

He teased, "Wake me up when we get to Miami."

We began to joke about everything. The sort of car we would drive in New York, the American girls and how much money we would be making.

"Roro, let's take a look at our passports and once and for all decide who is more handsome."

He laughed and said, "You know I am."

I opened the envelope for the first time since Dominique handed it to us at the airport and started to look at our passport pictures. It was settled within seconds that Ronald was indeed the winner.

As I continued flipping the pages of my passport, I came across something that almost gave me a heart attack. The U.S. visa we paid for turned out to be a Jamaican visa. I closed the passport. I took a deep breath and slowly reopened it just in case my eyes or my imagination were playing tricks on me. Once again, I re-examined the picture bringing it very close to my eyes. Yeah, that's me. So far, so good! I then flipped over very carefully to the visa page. My eyes confirmed it but my mind denied it. It was indeed a Jamaican visa. I opened Ronald's passport again and at this point both my eyes and mind were in complete agreement.

I looked at Ronald and said, "My brother, we are going to jail. Take a look at these passports and tell me what you think."

Calmly he said, "What's going on?"

I said, "Look for yourself."

"What is it Jacky? What is it?"

I said, "Roro, our visas are for Jamaica, not America."

He yanked the passports from my hand. Ronald looked at me and said, "Well, my friend, welcome to Jamaica. I told you that woman should not have been trusted."

I couldn't believe my ears. "Roro, I don't remember when you said that but right now, I don't see how that is going to help."

"I don't know about you, but I am going to Miami."

"Yeah, that was also my destination but now it's not."

"Jacky, I said we are going to Miami."

"Not with this Jamaican visa," I retorted.

Meanwhile, as the airplane began to descend, my blood pressure was going the opposite way. Up, up and rising. I didn't know what to do, think, or expect. I reached into the envelope and pulled out the tickets. They were roundtrip tickets all right, but once again, wrong destination.

I reviewed what happened the whole week. At no time during our conversation was Jamaica ever mentioned as a transit point, much less our final destination. Finally, things started to make sense. Dominique's going through immigration with us and keeping both passports and tickets until the last minute was nothing else but a deliberate move designed to mislead us. I was very angry with myself considering all the things I could have done, should have done, but failed to do. We were like two small rats caught in a bad trap, with nowhere to run.

Ronald started to panic. "What are we going to do?"

"Roro, our tickets are also valid for Jamaica so if it becomes a question of going there, let's not make any fuss about it. Once we touch the ground, let's act as if we know what we are doing." I threw my hand on his shoulder, gave him a couple of squeezes and firmly said, "Everything is going to be all right. Trust me."

"Jacky, we don't know anyone in Jamaica. Besides, you asked me to trust you before and I did, but look what's happening."

"You're right Ronald; I am sorry this is how it turned out. I agree. This is my mistake."

I glanced out the window and saw that we were close to the ground. Though my mind was racing as I tried to figure out exactly where I went wrong, I said to Ronald with full confidence, "We will meet many people in Jamaica and I am sure the little bit of English that I know will come in handy. Now, let me have the passports and I will clear immigration. While we are in line waiting to be checked I will also study the location of the exit. You do the same and also check for security. If there is a way to escape, that's what we will do. Once we get out, we will jump in a cab and figure our next move from there."

"What if we get caught?" asked Ronald.

"For now, all I can say is that whatever happens we will deal with it."

Boom, the airplane touched the ground.

I began to sweat.

It rolled down the runway and slowly began to reduce its speed until it came to a full stop. Minutes later, people stood up and gathered their personal belongings. Since Ronald and I had one bag each, we decided to stay put, let a few people off and then make our way forward like everyone else. We were extremely nervous, but we tried to hide it as best as we could.

"Don't you think we will have to contact Dominique right away, Jacky?"

"Why don't we discuss this later Ronald? Let's get off now."

I felt a ton of strength flowing through my veins. It was like a transfusion straight from God. No more fears, no more worries.

While we stood in the immigration line, I checked out everybody's hand to see what sort of passport they were carrying. I saw all kinds of colors, but the ones that caught my eyes were those that looked like Ronald's and mine. When it was our turn, we were told by the immigration officer to have a good vacation in Jamaica. Vacation? He must be out of his mind.

We were then escorted to the transit lounge along with thirteen other Haitians, all waiting to connect to flights going to Jamaica that evening. The transit lounge was a very small, clean room lined up with multi-colored chairs, fastened to the floor as if they were afraid somebody would steal them.

We both took a seat on the floor and Ronald immediately asked if I could at least pinpoint what went wrong.

I said, "Ronald, it's too early to tell."

"Do you think we will ever find out, Jacky?"

"I am thinking, given time, Dominique may provide us with an explanation, but I won't hold my breath."

"Why is that?"

"Maybe telling us might jeopardize her whole operation. That in turn might prevent her from getting any more clients. Remember what she said. She was running a business and to do that requires skills and know-how. Perhaps what she meant was that she gets to select what to say and when to say it to her clients."

"So you think she might be the problem?"

"No, Roro. The Jamaican visa is, but that's beside the point. However, I am quite confident the problem is not Haiti because we left Haiti. It is not Jamaica because we are scheduled to depart for Jamaica later on today. The missing link is between Bahamas and Miami."

"What do you think will happen when we get to Jamaica?"

"It is hard to say Ronald. We just have to pray and take it one step at a time."

In spite of the intense pressure and the uncertainty about the unknown, Ronald and I still maintained the ability to joke and laugh. This great sense of humor is what kept us so close as we were growing up. It helped us to remain calm. Time was running out and my stomach was starting to feel the impact as well. It was almost three o'clock in the afternoon and the last time I tasted food was almost seventeen hours before.

I was looking around for food, when I noticed the sign for a toilet very close to a glass door leading to the street. I stopped dead in my tracks. I scanned the area for any obstacles that would prevent a successful exit. With the exception of a few security guards, the place was quiet. I immediately worked out a plan in my head. I painstakingly watched the door for a few minutes to see how it opened, to what side and how quickly it closed. If we were going to escape, it had to be done in a timely manner.

As much as I was trying to hide my anxiety, Ronald picked up from my body language that something was not right.

He walked behind me, tapped my shoulder and quietly whispered, "Is everything all right or is there something you need to talk about?"

I turned around, pulled him close and said, "We are getting the hell out. We are not going to Jamaica. Take a look, take a look."

"Take a look at what Jacky?"

"That toilet over there. Do you see it? It is next to the exit door. You go first while I observe. As you get close to it, look back. A thumb's up means keep going and down means stop and return. When you get out, turn right, walk down a few blocks and wait for me there. Do not look back or nervous. Walk with confidence so as not to attract any unnecessary attention. I will try to get to you within thirty minutes at the most. But, if you don't see me, don't panic. Get a cab and ask the driver to take you to a hotel. It is extremely important that you establish contact with Dominique right away. If on the other hand, I have to go to Jamaica, don't you worry, I will be fine and we will meet up later on. That is why it is important to contact Dominique, so we can be in touch either way."

I reached into my pocket and handed over $300 to Ronald and said, "Here, take this and good luck." I hugged him and said, "Go."

But when I let go of him he was in tears. Ronald grabbed me by the shoulder and said, "Jacky, if I can't go with you, I don't want to go at all. We left together and we must remain together regardless of where we are."

I smiled, and then answered, "I am very thirsty; unless you stop crying, I am going to start drinking your tears."

Ronald smiled back and pushed me away affectionately.

"You don't want to split up?" I asked.

"No."

"Then follow me."

"Are you sure we can do this?"

"Ronald, the time to be sure is over. Right now, we just have to play our last card and, whatever happens, we'll deal with it as best as we can."

"If we get caught we might end up in jail."

"That's a real possibility, but we will get out, perhaps in a couple days. We are not going to die there. If it will make you feel any better, at least we will be one step closer to Miami and two to New York. What do you think?"

"I don't feel too good about this."

"Forget what you feel. Listen, enough talking. Let's go. I suggest we leave everything."

"But what are we going to wear?"

"What we have on is more than enough. Wait! Let me double-check the crowd to see if anyone is watching." When I turned around, all except three elderly people were sound asleep. I took a look at them and felt a deep sense of concern.

I began to struggle with my desire to escape and wondered if I should leave them behind, knowing they needed our assistance. I turned back to Ronald and said, "We can't leave those people. I am the only one who speaks English."

"Jacky, you don't know what you want. First, you talk about escaping and now you want to help those people, but I tell you what, I am with you on the helping. I was so worried about your plan. Thank you, Jesus!"

Ronald laughed and hugged me.

We approached an old man and took a seat next to him. At first, he looked a bit suspicious. But when we introduced ourselves and established a connection with him, the conversation began to flow smoothly. We learned from him the rest of the people there were from various places in the country and a few of them were distant relatives. The little girl was traveling with her mom and uncle, and her father was currently living in South Florida. Why they were going to Jamaica was not discussed. Everyone had sealed lips.

I asked the old man whether he was hungry. He nodded yes. The other two ladies also expressed a keen desire to eat. I asked them to wake up everyone while I went to speak to the airport's staff on duty. Within a few minutes, everybody was eating, drinking or burping. They were all very thankful.

In the midst of conversation, I threw myself on the floor, placed my head on Ronald's lap and woke up many hours later facing a young lady who was giving out boarding instructions. We were told to gather our belongings because our flight to Jamaica was leaving in less than an hour.

The flight to Jamaica was very quick. I began to worry, wondering if we had blown our chance. As we disembarked the plane, we said goodbye to our fellow Haitians and wished them well.

The airport in Kingston was crowded. For a brief moment, I thought I had walked straight into a madhouse. I managed to spot the line with the least amount of people and we swung our way into it. While waiting in line, I rehearsed in my mind a list of questions they might ask and how I was going to answer them. Luckily, the immigration officer asked very simple questions. What brought us to Jamaica? How long were we staying? And did we have any money?

When I told him that we were on vacation and had money, he replied cynically, "Lately, we have had so many Haitians come to Jamaica and they all claim to be on vacation, but yet never bring enough money to spend."

I laughed and said, "We have enough to spend for the time we are here."

He looked at us for a minute or so then he stamped our passports and said, "Welcome to Jamaica."

Once outside, we were chased by some very aggressive cab drivers. I examined their faces and saw one that looked like someone we could trust. We walked over to his cab and asked to be taken to a good hotel.

Ronald was silent and I didn't attempt to ask for an explanation. He certainly didn't need to say anything for me to understand he was very upset. To end up in Jamaica with no specific plan was a valid reason to be angry, especially since I talked him into leaving Haiti.

Ronald decided to break his silence in the cab, whispering, "Jacky, this has been a rough and incredible day."

I patted his hand and whispered back, "I am concerned, but not at all disappointed. If nothing else, by leaving Haiti we have set the wheels in motion and we are going to keep them in motion till we reach our destination. I think the outcome could have been a lot worse, Roro. All we need now is a bed, a good night's sleep and another day."

He moved his head to my shoulder and said, "You are absolutely right Jacky. I am very glad we changed our plan about escaping. Maybe, we would be in jail by now."

I smiled and joked, "It might well be where the driver is taking us, Roro."

The fact was, we had no idea where the driver was going. Had it been daytime, we might have felt out of harm's way, but it was almost 10 o'clock at night in a foreign land and away from our parents. I kept looking at the driver to see if he was nervous, but he was very peaceful.

He finally pulled up in front of what seemed to be not just a good hotel, but a very nice one. We followed his instruction and walked straight to what he called the registration desk. A beautiful young woman with a very seductive smile greeted us. It seemed her blouse was a bit too tight, but after a brief look, I concluded something else was responsible for the tight fit. My covert observation led my eyes straight up to her nametag and I took the opportunity to address her by her proper name.

Charmaine was extremely charming. When I called out her name, she smiled and asked softly, "How did you know my name?"

I smiled back and answered, "Secret *d'homme*."

She rolled her innocent, but dangerous tiger-eyes as if to say, *"When it comes to men, we women have the key to all your secrets."*

Maybe some men, but not all of us.

At one point, she let loose the top button of her blouse while saying in a flirtatious voice, "It is very warm outside."

I kept quiet but thought, "Charmaine, right now we share your pain. But if you unbutton the second one, we will feel the pain, so please don't." She smiled probably thinking, I told you.

It turned out the cab fare and the Pegasus hotel took a huge bite of our pocket money. However, given that it was our first night ever in a hotel, we endured the pain gracefully. Once inside the room, we called Haiti.

Thank God Dominique was home and we didn't have to leave a message with anyone. She said hello and started to cry the minute she heard my voice. Hell, we needed to be the ones crying. What's wrong with her? When I asked why she was crying, she complained my parents were over her house trying to find out what happened to us and she didn't appreciate the way they handled the situation once they learned we were in Jamaica.

Her statement clarified what was already too obvious. She knew beforehand if Bahamas failed to deliver, Jamaica was to be the alternative. Since we had no phone at home in Haiti, we were unable to contact our parents directly. I begged her to relay a message letting them know we were safe and well. I knew they were having a fit because they expected us to be in Miami not Jamaica.

Dominique began saying how regretful she was about what happened to us and that she was doing her absolute best to get us back on track without any further delay. She confessed there was a flaw in her so-called smooth operation and she took full responsibility for the outcome.

All I wanted to know was how we ended up with a Jamaican visa in our passports, but no word of it was mentioned.

As much as I wanted an explanation and rightly so, I realized it was senseless to argue with her while we were in Jamaica. If I said the wrong thing that might be the last time we heard from her. So long as we were in Jamaica and she was still in Haiti with our money, she would have no problem with me.

She told us to check out from the Pegasus, gave us the phone number of a new hotel and asked us to contact Ralph, the owner, to get his address. She then promised to call us in his office at 6:00 P.M. the next day with further instructions. She said she was planning to fly to Jamaica within forty-eight to seventy-two hours to get us out. We left it at that, said thank you and good night.

Now that we knew Dominique was aware of our location, we felt we stood a better chance of moving forward. Briefly, Ronald and I went over our discussion with Dominique and finally decided to go to bed and put the day's adventure behind us. We learned that day, when making a major decision every detail, even the minor ones, must be scrutinized to its finest point. Equally important is that if you can embrace your disappointment with a smile, you will muster the courage to move on.

Jamaican Vacation

AFTER A full night of sleep, we woke up highly motivated and prepared to tackle Jamaica and all it had to offer. We packed up our bags, showered, settled our account, and asked the lady checking us out to get the address for Ralph's hotel. She thanked us for our business and invited us to come back again the next time we were in Jamaica. That wasn't likely. Even if we were to take a vacation, the Pegasus was therapeutic to our soul and spirit, but it was downright detrimental to our pocket money.

Ralph laid down the rules of the hotel and told us if we failed to comply he would kick us out without an explanation. He showed us to our room and wished us an agreeable vacation in Jamaica.

When we opened the door, there were two small beds with clean sheets, a small drawer for our belongings and a toilet. It was actually more than necessary and, at $30 per night, it was absolutely beautiful. During our brief conversation with Ralph, he mentioned there were a couple of Haitians who had been there for several days already. The last statement from Ralph raised a red flag in my mind. How many were there? Why? How long had they been stranded in Jamaica? Those were the questions I needed to get answered, but didn't know who was going to volunteer that sort of information.

In less than an hour after we checked in, there was a knock at the door and someone shouted rapidly in Créole, "Open up, open up."

When Ronald opened the door, the guy introduced himself as Josnel. He explained that Ralph told him of our arrival in the hotel, and he wanted us to know should we need his assistance, he was there to help.

We introduced ourselves to Josnel and asked him the most important question. Where do we go for food? Josnel took us to a little restaurant no more than a ten-minute walk from the hotel. We devoured the food.

We found out Josnel had been in Jamaica for almost ten days, waiting anxiously for someone to pick him up to go to Florida. I tried in vain to get the name of the person he was waiting for, but he refused to reveal any information. He did however mention that, according to his contact, a positive outcome was to be expected anytime within the next few days.

He also warned us if we planned on leaving the hotel at night to be extremely vigilant because there had been some sporadic shootings almost every other night. When Ronald inquired about the shootings, he explained that he didn't know any more than we did. We just needed to be mindful of our surroundings.

The food was very delicious and the price was outstanding, well within our budget. They gave us so much food, we could share one meal a day between the two of us to recoup some of the money we spent at the Pegasus.

By 4:00 in the afternoon, we were back in the hotel. Dominique was supposed to call at six. We thanked Josnel for taking us to the restaurant and for his invaluable advice about Jamaica.

We were later introduced to another young Haitian named Patrick. He was in his early twenties, looked very slim and dressed casually in jeans, short-sleeved shirt and sneakers. He was a student at the University of the West Indies and had been attending the school for over a year and a half. After our short conversation, he invited us to his domicile, which was in the vicinity of Ralph's hotel. We informed him that we were waiting for an urgent phone call from Haiti and would not leave the hotel until we received the call. Patrick agreed to wait and we made plans to leave right afterward.

A few minutes past six, Ralph rushed to our room to tell us Dominique was waiting for us on the phone. We hurried to his office to pick up the call. Dominique asked how we were doing and said how happy she was that we moved to Ralph's because of the savings it would mean to us. She stated that she had been working on things throughout the day and she was very confident everything would be back on schedule very soon. We should be out of Jamaica within the next few days. She asked us to call if we had an emergency and promised to remain in contact with us throughout our stay at Ralph's. We thanked her for the call, said goodbye, and hung up.

On our way to Patrick's home we learned a great deal more about him. Patrick's uncle was a prominent businessman in Haiti and had been a diehard opponent of Papa Doc in the late 1960s. As a result, the whole family was expelled from Haiti in the late 1970s by the Baby Doc regime. Some ended up in New York, others in Florida, while he and his sister Lisa settled in Jamaica as students.

When we asked whether there was ever a threat to his

life, Patrick's answer was poignant. "As far as Papa Doc was concerned, there was no safe ground for any opponent, young or old, poor or rich, blind or full sighted. He ruled with an iron fist and if, by misfortune, you got caught in the path of the iron, you got crushed. In no uncertain term was he willing to relinquish power. If anything, he had one goal in mind and that was to strengthen his power base while keeping the country under his firm grip. He did so with the help of his tonton macoute, a paramilitary organization, whose sole purpose was not to clarify his rules but instead to inflict punishment according to his own dictatorial emotions. Anyone who dared to question or disobey had one answer to choose from his multiple-choice punishment: A) death B) prison or C) exile. My family was one of the lucky ones," he concluded.

Patrick had been living in Jamaica for over two years, and he was longing to go back home. He seemed to be very knowledgeable about the ins and outs of Jamaica. Sadly, he expressed his concern about the influx of Haitians into Kingston and kept his remarks going at a fast pace regarding the political situation in Haiti.

He took a special interest in Ronald and me, and like Josnel, volunteered to help with anything we needed.

When we reached his residence, we were introduced to several other Haitians, waiting restlessly to travel to Miami. We also met Patrick's older sister, Lisa. I was very impressed with her elegance, friendliness, and contagious smile. Her glowing eyes struck me as a beacon of hope. Hope for the country we all cherished and left behind. Hope that one day our future generation would live in a more peaceful and progressive Haiti.

Lisa later introduced us to her friend, Andréa, who was

another beautiful and articulate young Haitian studying in Jamaica. As a group, they symbolized the brightest of Haiti's future. But, like the rest of us, they were all living in the mist of Haiti's past and present nightmare. Except for Andréa, none of us knew if and when we would ever get back to Haiti. Nonetheless, we all shared the same agony that our treasure was being destroyed and there was no one to rescue our Falling Star.

When Andréa came near, you had to pay great attention to your environment or you would walk straight into a wall. She was a beautiful woman who knew how to be a woman. She wore her womanhood not by the tight blue jeans or cotton tank top she was wearing, but by the words coming out of her mouth. She chose them carefully and, when she spoke, she did so with such gentleness, you would want to spend all day listening to her sexy voice.

She was extremely confident, smart, and challenging. Even though she was at great ease switching her tongue from Créole to French or vice versa, she much preferred to speak her native tongue. This was a rarity for a young stunning Haitian woman of her caliber. With her sweet brown lips, high cheekbones accentuated by her brilliance and charisma, she fell right into the category that will get your head spinning and screaming at the same time, *Mon Dieu, mon Dieu ayez pitié de moi*, "God, God, please have pity on my soul." In any case, if her tender smiling eyes were a transparent mirror of her heart's desire, I knew Roro was getting ready to stay put in Jamaica. And if she knew how to cook, there was no doubt in my mind we would be having Haitian food delivered to our doorstep very soon.

Everyone welcomed us warmly and we fit right into the crowd. Patrick's residence was a guesthouse owned by an old

Jamaican woman and she rented it out to students and other people. The serenity of the place was its best attraction. We spent about forty-five minutes at Patrick's place, and then we headed for a different hotel to meet some more Haitians. As we were getting ready to leave, we heard bullets singing in the air. Patrick calmed us down and said not to worry because this had been a daily occurrence in Jamaica for the last few months. When I asked why, he explained there was an upcoming election for a new Prime Minister and this was merely a tactic to keep people off the street.

When we arrived at the other hotel, I was amazed at the number of Haitians living there. I wondered if any of them belonged to the fifty people Dominique bragged about back in Haiti. I asked no questions although I eavesdropped to see if her name was mentioned.

My silent observation was fruitless. Everyone was very frustrated because they didn't know how long they might have to stay in Jamaica. But their collective and individual strength were to be admired. Their anticipation for a better tomorrow was the only source of inspiration for another day or what they simply referred to as *la raison d'être*. While they waited indefinitely, some passed the time drinking and smoking. Some played cards or dominoes while others did what most Haitians do in small groups: talk about politics.

About an hour later, I told Patrick we were tired and needed to get back to the hotel. On the way back to Ralph's, Patrick mentioned that he would introduce us to someone he considered to be a good contact who might be able to help us out.

"What sort of help are you talking about Patrick?" asked Ronald.

"Someone who can take you from here and get you to Miami."

"Who is he?" Ronald pressed for details.

"His name is Frantz," he answered. "He is in Jamaica to reassure his clients that he is there for them. You already met some of them tonight," he began to whisper, "but they didn't want to say anything about him."

"Do you know of anybody other than Frantz?" I asked.

Patrick looked at me, said nothing and just skipped to another subject. Since there were other people around, he might not want to discuss certain things, so I left it alone.

When we got in front of Ralph's hotel, I asked Patrick to find out whether there was any vacancy in his place. If so, what would be the cost? He was surprised by my request, but promised to get back to us. He demanded we say nothing to Ralph until he could give us a positive answer. Before shaking hands and parting ways for the night, we made plans to visit downtown Kingston the next morning.

I later explained to Ronald that the reason I asked Patrick to check on any vacancy in his place was to be close to the other guys. I realized there was more than one person involved in the business and all we had gotten so far was bits and pieces of information. I wanted names and details. I presumed the best way to do that was to move with Patrick so that we could listen.

"Jacky, how much time do we want to give Dominique before we start looking at other avenues?"

"Since we don't know what went wrong, I am thinking it might be a few days before Dominique can figure it all out. Let's persist with patience." We left it at that and went to bed, feeling the second day in Jamaica went much better than expected.

We woke up the next day with Patrick pounding on the door and shouting, "What are you still doing in bed?"

In less than forty-five minutes, we were showered, dressed and standing at the bus stop waiting for our transportation to downtown Kingston. The ride was quite amusing and disturbing as well. I sensed I was once again faced with the same mess that pushed me to leave Haiti—no forward movement. One needed not be a sociologist, economist, or a genius to figure out there were some major socioeconomic problems in Jamaica. The disparity was naked. One instant you would see a beautiful house and next to it there was a dump. Some people looked overfed while others near starvation.

It is obvious in any society some degree of inequality is acceptable, sometimes even healthy because it prevents complacency and fuels competition. Competition, if you will, is always at the helm of human evolution or any progressive society. But there is, however, one key question: what is the cost and who must pay for it?

Quite frankly, what I have seen in both Haiti and Jamaica, especially in relation to our young children, went beyond poverty; it was inhumanity. It went beyond inequality; it was a crime. It went beyond gross injustice; it was a shameful blow to the core existence of the human spirit. Sadly, many of us proudly or blindly refer to this as our civilized world. Go figure!

By the time we reached downtown Kingston, I was quite amazed. There were children running up and down the streets, at times looking in the opposite direction of the oncoming traffic, dirty and barefooted begging for money. I was upset that this déjà-vu experience of everyday life in Haiti persisted in other countries as well.

Why the children?

What sort of crime had they committed to deserve such inhumane treatment? They are the future of their country and they ought to be valued.

In my mind I thought, "You are the people Bob Marley sings for, the people of great strength, pride and courage. Don't ever give up fighting. Open your eyes and look beyond, beyond your horizon. Spread your arms and push forward, forward to your destination. Stretch your legs and step ahead, ahead to the finish line."

I listened to myself telling them softly, "Life is a game, like any other game with rules and regulations. Some are visible and others are not. But to succeed in it, there are times you must learn to go above and beyond to create. Create your own set of rules and dictate how the game should be played. Make time to sharpen your mind. It is your best weapon. For when you do, you will pick and choose your battles, but also of paramount importance, you will get to dictate how and when the battle is fought. You will more often than necessary encounter adversities, but learn to master the courage to look at adversity straight in the face and declare with strong conviction: It's either you or me. Keep in mind, it is in adversity's nature to put up a fight, but the remedy is prayer, an unshakable faith in God, patience, persistence, hard work and a definite purpose."

When we got off the bus, I thought I had just walked back into Haiti. We were in an open market, just like the ones I'd left back home. It was cluttered with merchants selling all kinds of goods on wooden or plastic tables, cardboard boxes, colorful baskets or trays. Nothing seemed different except the people were speaking English instead of Créole. I later found out from Patrick that most of them were not speaking

English but Jamaican patois. The merchants did exactly what they felt they had to do—overprice their products. Big or small, I know from experience in Haiti, there were many mouths waiting to be fed from each sale.

The despair and poverty were so easily read on their faces. The pile of wrinkles sitting on the forehead of those old people selling their wares in the market revealed decades of hard labor. But I am sure, if you were to decode the invisible messages hidden under those winkles, you would walk away with a great fountain of wisdom, despite the poverty and misery.

I was convinced my only way of coping with this harsh reality was to be in America. Once I got there, I felt my mind would no longer be preoccupied with poverty or survival. If there was any truth to what Grand Da said about the pennies all over the floor in New York, there should not be any poor people living in the United States.

The record shops were crowded. Everywhere we turned there was another reggae beat in the air. People poured in and out of the stores. Some went in dancing and came out dancing. Just like in Haiti, when music was playing, we didn't dance because we were necessarily happy. Yes, sometimes we were enjoying the music but for the most part it was the best anesthetic to cope with our daily frustrations.

A good example in Haiti was during carnival. We shook our bodies so hard, it seemed we were possessed and trying to shake out a bad spirit. This was about the only time you came close to true freedom. It was like a release of the soul, mind and body. Total madness! But what was interesting is that the bad spirit refused to let go because we kept dancing with the same madness year after year.

The Rastafarians were quite interesting to watch. Their

black, green and gold knitted bonnets displayed the colors of the Jamaican flag, revealing a true sense of their identity. They moved as if they all had shock absorbers or heavy duty springs up their knees. Whether they were dancing or walking, they accentuated every step and never missed a beat. Sometimes when dancing they would bend down so low on one side, I thought they would just collapse to the ground. But instead, they twisted their legs gently, moved their body swiftly the opposite way to perform the same move again with poise. Quite original! There is no question, when it comes to twisting one's step the Jamaican man has no contender.

The day was coming to an end and I kept hoping Dominique would call and ask us to get ready to head to Miami. I was pleased to have gone downtown and seen that part of Jamaica. It somehow rekindled my vision and propelled my drive to keep moving forward because settling in Jamaica was definitely not in our plan.

I stopped daydreaming when someone yelled to get on the bus. It was as unsafely overloaded as the *tap taps* in Haiti. The driver had a hard time maintaining a straight course while avoiding potholes in the road. People swayed left and right with the minivan, but seemed so happy to have conquered another day in the battle of life.

On the way back, I questioned Patrick a little bit more about Frantz to find out why he was so eager for us to meet him.

At first, he said to keep an open mind. But after a minute or so he stated forcefully, "No matter what you guys decide to do, please do not go back to Haiti."

"What's wrong with going back to Haiti if things are not moving according to our plan?" I asked.

"I have seen and heard of too many guys who have chosen that path and lived to regret their decision."

"But why?" I asked again.

"Because they were never able to make it back out," he finally acknowledged.

I looked at him and firmly said, "Patrick, we thank you for the feedback and concern. But we did not leave Haiti to be stranded in Jamaica. Our destination is America. Until we can get there, our quest is not over." I paused, cleared my throat and said, "We will one day wake up in America."

Actually, it was not Patrick I was trying to convince, but myself.

Jamaica was a huge setback and not knowing what was to happen next, I had to prepare my mind for whatever came my way.

Everyone was stunned, including Ronald. But, Patrick responded this time with a more powerful blow. "Jacky, I respect your feelings, but let me warn you, if you go back to Haiti make sure you get a real American visa before you leave. Because if you don't, your butt will be right back in Jamaica."

"I'm not coming back here."

"Well," Patrick replied calmly, "if you think you can get to America with a Jamaican visa, you and a jail cell will become very good friends."

"Whatever will be, will be."

Ronald smiled and said, "That's my little brother. As long as I am with him, I have no need to worry." I received his reinforcement like a gold medal. Just when it seemed I had lost all his confidence, he came in and made me feel that, given time, we would eventually achieve our objective.

The bus ride was getting long and tiring. I asked Patrick

how far we were from the hotel. He joked by saying we were driving back to Haiti. He then smiled and said, "We are less than five minutes away."

A short while later, Patrick told us we were coming to our stop. When we got to the hotel, I walked straight into Ralph's office and asked him to help me place a call to Haiti. A couple minutes later, we had Dominique on the phone. I explained to her we were getting impatient and needed an absolute answer for a time or date when she expected to be in Jamaica to get us out. I also suggested to her that if we couldn't go to Miami, we were ready to go back to Haiti. She listened patiently to what I had to say, but responded with a smile in her voice as if she had already talked to Patrick and knew what he said to us earlier.

"No. Haiti will eliminate all your chances." She then added, "I just found out today that I will be able to come and get you next week. If I realize it is not feasible, I myself will call and ask you to return to Haiti."

I was furious. "What do you mean by next week? First you said between 48–72 hours and now you are talking about a week. No, I don't think we can take it here for one more week. Besides, we are running out of money."

"Jacky," she said kindly, "I have been working on this day and night. Let's be clear on one thing, it bothers me more to have you guys there because I have to answer to you and your parents as well. So please be patient and do not make a move until I tell you to do so."

Dominique made it very difficult to argue with her. Even when you knew she was not sure of what she was saying, she said it with so much kindness and love you had to ease up on her. I made no fuss and just said to Dominique, "Unless something major happens, I will not be calling you anymore."

On that note, I said goodbye and we wished each other a pleasant evening.

Ronald picked up on the nature of my conversation with Dominique and suggested that we speak to Frantz.

"Why not wait until we move in with Patrick? At least that will give us a chance to learn how he operates. If we like what we hear, we'll give him a shot. We can't afford another blow, Ronald."

We stepped outside and invited Patrick to the room. We discussed with him what had transpired between Dominique and ourselves and asked him not to forget to talk to the lady to find out if we could move in. To my surprise, Patrick tried to back out. He said he did not want to introduce anyone else over the house because of what had been going on. When I asked why, he stated that some of those guys get so angry about their present situation that they quarrel amongst themselves often and the lady was not pleased with the drama. She was afraid they would get into a fistfight and that gets her very uptight. "Although I feel she blows things out of proportion, she reserves the right to decide how people live in her house."

"Patrick, that is a very valid concern, but I promise Ronald and I will stick to the rules."

"In that case, I will see what I can do."

We shook hands and parted ways.

Ronald and I started to look at things from all different angles. We covered everything from new alternatives to the real possibility of going back to Haiti in a week.

If we could close a deal to go to Miami with Frantz, we were not sure how much it would cost, and how and when we would pay him. I really didn't think we should have expected any more money from Andy because he had already done enough and to that end we were grateful. Still, we left the door open and remained focused on our long-term goal.

The next day, Patrick showed up with a big smile on his face. "I have good news for you guys," he said, "but there is a small problem."

"What is it Patrick?" Ronald asked.

"Well, there is a vacancy and I managed to get you a good price, but you will have to share the bed."

"How much do we have to pay?" I asked.

"Eighty dollars per week, including one free meal per day."

Ronald asked me what I thought. I didn't answer as my mind went straight into my pocket, subtracting dollars and adding days. If my calculation served me well, we could easily afford two weeks without scratching our heads and still have some money left in our pockets. I said, "Patrick, do you realize how much money you are saving us? If we stayed here for one week we would pay $210. At your place, we only have to pay $160."

"Where did you learn your math? It is $80 for the two of you, not $80 per person."

We packed our bags so quickly. Patrick was thrilled.

We walked into Ralph's office and shocked him with our new plan. He was quite upset with Patrick for taking away his clients and told him to stay away from his hotel. But he did let us use his phone to place one last call to Dominique to provide her with our new contact number. She was pleased to hear things were going fine and happy that we were being so patient and willing to work with her. She also mentioned that she notified our parents of our whereabouts and they sent their love and well wishes. I asked that she give them the number in case they want to get in touch with us.

Within minutes, we were sitting at a small table over Patrick's place discussing with the owner what she expected from us. With a few hundred dollars left in our pocket and a bag full of hope, as they say, *la vie continue,* "life goes on."

Back to Haiti?

WE SPENT the rest of the day listening to what everyone had to say. I asked no questions and revealed no information. If something was mentioned and I felt there was a need for clarification, I simply made a remark that would trigger an answer instead of asking a direct question. By late afternoon, I concluded that Frantz was a middleman, and if he was not working for Dominique, he was her competition. As far as our plan went, there was no room for him. But, there was something I needed to find out and no one but Frantz knew the answer. Who did he work for in Haiti?

One of the principles I had learned back in Haiti was that it is always better to deal directly with God than his subordinates. In other words, when you want to get things done, go directly to the source. Frantz was by no means the masterpiece, but he was a big one indeed. As in any puzzle, sometimes it's best to get the big piece in first because it simplifies the whole thing. Therein lies the beauty of the smaller pieces. They are a lot easier to handle.

There was no question, if we went back to Haiti, we would try again. But we wanted to avoid Frantz or his boss at all costs because their operation resembled our current dilemma. I called Ronald aside and shared my concern with him about Frantz. We instantly devised a plan as to how we wanted the meeting to go and when it should end. Ronald would do the talking, while I agreed to listen.

"I will ask any question I deem necessary no matter how senseless it might sound," said Ronald. "And if he raises a question I don't have the answer to, I will ask him to repeat it. That will be my signal for you to take over and see if you can answer it. Do you have any suggestions?" he asked.

"No, except that when you ask a question, press for details. Do not accept any brief answer. In contrast, when he asks one, keep it short. I am almost positive he will want us to disclose who is responsible for us being here. Make up a name if you must, but by no means should Dominique's name be revealed or her method of operation."

"Why, Jacky? Why?" Ronald asked. "I don't care if he knows."

"Well Roro, as long as she is in Haiti with our money and we are sitting right here in Jamaica, we need to do anything we can to protect her identity because she is currently protecting our money. If Frantz can get her out of business, our money will follow wherever she goes. And make no mistake about it, Jamaica or Haiti would be the wrong place to start looking for her."

The next day went by very fast. According to Patrick, our meeting with Frantz was scheduled for 5:00 P.M., but he was already late by half an hour. A while later, I saw a guy walking in who fit the description Patrick gave to us. I asked Ronald to go get Patrick while I observed Frantz.

Frantz appeared to be in his late thirties or just about to cross forty. He was about 5'10", weighed 200 lbs. or more and had a little belly to go along with his weight. He dressed like a typical Haitian businessman. He wore nice slacks, a long-sleeved shirt tucked inside his pants, well polished black shoes, and carried a small black briefcase. His shirt collar was slightly open exposing his gold necklace with a heavy cross resting right on top of his chest.

He carried himself like a perfect gentleman. By the way he moved, there was no doubt that he had pride, and confidence in what he was doing. As I was going through some mental questioning, Patrick and Ronald walked out.

"Hey Frantz, how are you?" Patrick asked.

"Oh fine, Patrick." He looked at Ronald, looked at me again and said, "These two must be brothers."

"You are not mistaken. Yes indeed, they are brothers," Patrick replied. "Please meet them. This is Ronald and his younger brother, Jacky."

"Pleased to meet you," said Frantz.

"Likewise," answered Ronald.

Patrick reminded Frantz of why we wanted to talk to him.

Before walking away, Patrick said, "If you guys need anything, please come get me."

Frantz had a happy smile on his face and he got straight to the point. "I had heard about you guys and I want you to know, if you can use my help, I am ready to begin with you immediately. I can only imagine how frustrating it is to be here and not having the slightest idea what your next move is. In fact, my sole reason for being here is to reassure my guys that I am concerned about them and also provide some moral support."

He placed his briefcase on the floor and threw his hands in his pockets as if he was searching for his next answer or waiting to see what would be our first question. We offered no clue. He then proceeded, "Tell me, how I can help you."

Ronald took the initiative by saying, "Frantz, if we tell

you that all we want is to go to Florida, what would you say to that?"

"Before I discuss this with you, let me tell you what to expect," he answered politely.

"Then tell us," Ronald said.

"First, you are not my customers. Second, whoever is responsible for you being here might be working very hard to get you out. But having been in the business for almost a year already, I have enough experience to say the unexpected does occur from time to time. However, it does not get solved overnight. For that reason, I would hate for someone to take my clients away from me when I am doing all I can to correct the situation."

"I agree," said Ronald. "But who is responsible for us being here or how hard they might be working is pointless. That will not take us to Miami. What's important is to say what you expect, so this way we can either decide to go along or back out. By the way, do you work with anybody else?"

This was not my soft-spoken brother. He was on fire.

Frantz acted very calm and pretended not to hear the question. He instead was eager to learn more about us. Where in Haiti we were from, how old we were and how did we end up in Jamaica? I wanted to tell him the same way his guys ended up here, but I said nothing and let Ronald handle him as planned. Ronald answered every question without any hesitation.

"All right," said Frantz, "This is how it works. I have my contacts established in the Bahamas and Florida. My partner takes care of Haiti. We charge $2,000 per person from Haiti to Miami. But to go to Miami, you must first stop in the Bahamas. We request half up front and the rest when you get to Florida. But, since you are already in Jamaica, you will only need to pay $2,500 for both. The deal is the same, you pay half here and the balance in Florida."

Everything from his mouth sounded very familiar with the exception of the acceptance of partial payment.

"I will be going back to Haiti in two to three days," Frantz carried on, "If you think I can work with you, I must have an answer before I leave. I am planning on getting a few guys out no later than next week on my next visit. If you are still here upon my return and you have your money ready to go, you too can be well on your way with that group."

"Suppose we can't give you an answer before you leave? Is there a number where we can contact you in Haiti or is there someone else you trust to take a message for you?" Ronald asked.

Ronald's questions seemed to catch him off guard. For a second, he looked very confused, but from the way he placed his index finger on his temple and the intense look in his eyes I could tell his mind was in a thinking mode. Finally he asked, "Why won't you be able to give me an answer?"

Ronald was silent for a second and said to Frantz, "Could you please repeat your question?" I smiled at Ronald and gave Frantz the chance to repeat his question.

Then I said, "Frantz, it is not up to us to decide when and how you get paid. Somebody else is responsible for that and it might take us more than two days to have an exact answer for you."

"Who would be paying me?" he asked with a bit of hesitation.

Ronald eased back in and responded, "The person is in Haiti. That is why it is important for us to know, in your absence, can someone else collect the money for you?"

Very discreetly he pulled a piece of paper and a pen from

his briefcase, wrote something on it and handed it to Ronald. He read it and passed it on to me. Frantz wrote his name, number and right below it, he wrote the name 'Wilson,' with a different number. I questioned Frantz about Wilson. He explained that Wilson was his business partner in Haiti.

"Frantz, can you be a bit more descriptive about Wilson?" Ronald asked, "This way there will be no confusion. There are many Wilsons in Haiti."

"Oh, don't let this be your concern," Frantz answered with a smile. "I know who he is, he knows who he is and you will too when the time is right."

I smiled to signal to Ronald there was no need for any more questions because our objective had been met. He thanked Frantz for meeting with us and said that as soon as we knew something we'd let him know.

Frantz concluded the conversation by saying, "If I don't hear from you, I wish you guys luck."

We shook hands, thanked him again and slowly began to go our separate ways. As we started to walk away, Frantz with briefcase in hand shouted, "If you can't get all the money, let me know what you can come up with because I really would like to help. Please don't let that stop you."

That was a nice thing to say, even if he was the only one to believe in it. Knowing that he was responsible for all those guys being in Jamaica, especially after he too might have promised them Haiti to Miami via Bahamas, he had no chance with us.

"We will keep you posted," Ronald shouted back.

We went inside and explained to Patrick what we had accomplished with Frantz. He told us that he had heard of other people being involved in the business, but Frantz seemed the most reliable.

"He does get them out," Patrick confirmed. "Not as fast as he'd probably like, but he tries very hard."

Ronald continued talking to Patrick and I went to lie down on our bed. I started to think about what Frantz said and what to make of it.

Although there was still some doubt in my mind, in light of Patrick's feedback, Frantz left great latitude for speculation. What would we do if we chose to take him up on his offer? Maybe call Andy and tell him we were trapped in Jamaica and the only way to get out is for him to send us an additional $2,500?

Would he be willing to set us free?

A couple of hours later, I was still struggling with my frustrating thoughts.

Ronald jumped on the bed, "Now that we know of Frantz and his partner in Haiti, what is the next move?"

"Tell me, what are you feeling?"

He turned his back on me and said, "I don't feel like talking about it right now."

"Then let's get some sleep and we will talk about it tomorrow."

It was very clear that Ronald was starting to get depressed. I knew that dealing with him for the next few days would not be easy. He was always so cheerful and forever playful. You knew instantly something had to be truly wrong when Ronald was sad. His sadness brought tears to my eyes. I was glad he was sleeping and did not have to see me cry. It was my firm intention to stick to the plan until we saw the end of it. Yet, the sadness of being away from home was taking its toll. I didn't want to do anything that would beat down Ronald's spirit any more than it was, therefore, I remained flexible, yet determined.

When I woke up the next morning, Ronald was already out of bed. I cleaned myself up and started looking for him. I walked by Patrick's room, but the door was closed. When I stepped outside, I saw Ronald looking around as if he was lost and searching for a new direction.

Slowly, I walked up behind him and affectionately grabbed him by the shoulders and said, "What are you doing here by yourself?"

He turned, flashed one of his big smiles and said, "How was your night?"

"Good. And how was your night?"

"Very good, Jacky, but I hope we won't have to spend many more nights here."

I ignored his remark and asked if he had any plans for the day.

"I don't know what everybody else is doing, but I plan to stay in."

"Good, because I will call Dominique later on today and I want you to be here, Roro."

"Why? You told her the other day you would not contact her unless something major happened."

"That was the plan, but so long as we are in Jamaica with our money in her pocket, nothing we say is final. I'd like us to deal with things day-by-day and hour-by-hour if we have to. After reviewing the conversation we had last night, I feel obligated to call her today to find out whether there has been any progress within the last forty-eight hours. In case she says no, I will let her know we are ready to go back to Haiti."

"Did you say go back to Haiti, Jacky?"

"Yes, Haiti, Ronald, that's what I said. Last night you said you miss home and I began to wonder if going back is not best at this stage."

"We can't leave now. What are we going to do back there?"

"Ronald, Dominique is under no pressure in Haiti. And maybe that's the reason things are not moving as quickly as they should."

"True, but Dad must be talking to her daily, don't you think?"

"We don't know what Dad or Dominique is doing. We hope Dad is talking to her and we also hope that she's listening and doing something about it. We want to go to Miami, not Dad. We borrowed the money from Andy with a promise to pay it back, not Dad. So therefore, let's take things upon ourselves, make our decisions as we see fit and see to it we get the result we expect. This is not something Dad can do for us. Do you agree?"

Ronald said nothing. He paced up and down a few times, and then finally answered, "If this is what you want to do, let's go for it."

"All right, so let's get Patrick."

When we walked inside, Patrick was sitting at the dining table reading a book. We shared our conversation with him and asked for his assistance in placing a call to Haiti. Dominique was not there, but we left a quick message and made it clear it was urgent that she call us back.

Patrick was not thrilled about our plans. He felt we were making a huge mistake by going back to Haiti and jeopardizing our chance of ever getting back out, much less going to America.

Late that afternoon, the call came through. The first thing she wanted to know was what was so urgent.

"What's going on Dominique?" I asked.

"Well, nothing so far, I am still hoping to get you guys out, but it is turning out to be harder than I anticipated."

"You won't have to because we have decided to come back to Haiti."

"You dare not!" she screamed. "Unless I tell you to do so, you will lose your money when you get to Haiti."

Very calmly I said, "Dominique, I don't understand how that will happen, but, if you have other plans, why not discuss them when we get to Haiti. Basically, all I have to say is that we are coming back and we will be there within the next forty-eight hours max."

Dominique started shouting and I just said goodbye and hung up.

"You just hung up the phone on her?" Ronald yelled.

"No I did not. I just finished with what I had to say."

"What was she saying anyway, Jacky?"

"She is talking about losing our money once we get back to Haiti."

"Oh she said that?"

"Of course she did, my friend. But we don't have to buy into it. If we go back to Haiti, she has no choice but to deal with us because we will be under her eyes daily. But by staying in Jamaica she does what she pleases, thinking we just have to accept it. Ronald, this is unacceptable. Not for $4,000. We are going back," I said forcefully.

"Jacky, why don't we think about it?"

"There is nothing to think about, Ronald. The decision is made and we are going to stick to it."

"But what if we lose the money?"

"Ronald, what Dominique said is no more or less than what anyone else would say. I am not too good at playing poker, but I like the idea of calling a bluff. I say we call her bluff and wait for her next trump card. Personally, I don't believe she has any left. That is why I am willing to run the risk."

There was much talk and great confusion, but we finally made the decision we felt was best for us. We got a message to Dominique and, two days later, Patrick accompanied us in a taxi to the airport. We exchanged addresses, thanked Patrick for his help and support, and there began another phase of our incredible journey.

The Homecoming

WHEN WE landed back in Haiti, things went very smoothly clearing both immigration and customs. After all, we were not deported. We chose to go back. Dad was happy to see us, and so were we. Yet, there was something strange about his interaction with us which neither Ronald nor myself was able to pinpoint. He was the only one to meet us at the airport and clearly he had some concerns. But when we asked if everything was okay, he refused to discuss what was bothering him.

A few hours later, my dad, Ronald and I were at Dominique's house trying to set a specific date for us to leave again. After a long evening of negotiation, Dominique said we would have to pay more money and she also needed additional time to work out a new plan. I explained that a Jamaican visa was never a part of our previous negotiation, so therefore we would not renegotiate a new price. She replied that the Jamaican visa was not the source of the problem, Miami was. When we pressed for details, she refused to discuss the issue, claiming that it was best to leave the past in the past. We finally agreed on the time, but not on the money—we refused to spend even one more penny. She asked to keep our passports with a promise to contact us as soon as she could reschedule a new date for our departure. We left her house with an empty promise, yet very hopeful.

My father suggested it was best not to go home because everybody in the neighborhood believed we were already in the United States. He requested that we stay over our cousin Bido's house until we could leave again. He claimed it would be an embarrassment to the family to have us home under suspicious conditions. Finally, we knew he was worried about the repercussions of our failed attempt to make it to the U.S.

Coming back from New York a few weeks after we left was not the problem, even when everyone knew the purpose of our trip was not vacation. But to come back without any suitcases was unacceptable. Knowing my friends, the only excuse they would accept was that we were deported and didn't have time to pack. Since that was not the case, we would have to justify our coming back from New York with not even one suitcase.

No one in his or her right mind who had the privilege to go to New York returned empty handed even after two weeks. If we had been to New York, maybe we would have come back with a truckload of suitcases full of new clothes and gadgets to share with them all. But, we had been in Jamaica, so we brought back what we took plus a "no problem man" attitude. Dad strongly persuaded us Bido's house was the best solution to our problem and we obeyed his command.

In any case, I felt it was our primary responsibility to handle things our way, so staying at Bido's added one more twist to our already complicated drama. We were not able to go to see Dominique or talk to her alone and by Dad's order, we were not permitted to leave the house.

Outside of the family, no one knew we were back in Haiti.

God forbid, to be seen unexpectedly by anyone else would be like committing murder. Under such conditions, it was extremely difficult to evaluate Dominique's progress or what kind of effort she was putting forth to get us back on track. I discussed our predicament with Ronald, but to no avail. All he cared about was when we were leaving.

We ended up spending two weeks in hiding. My mother had always preached about doing the right thing so we could always walk with our heads up. But this time, we even had to cover our heads anytime we wanted to go out. We wore hats and sunglasses even when we were within a few feet from Bido's house at night.

And what had we done wrong?

All along I felt trying to get out of Haiti was the right thing to do, instead I turned out to be an outcast in my own country. I was home but experiencing none of the neighborhood socializing which had been central to my life in Haiti. I felt isolated.

We were now in the first week of March. One evening, about 7:00, I told Ronald that I was ready to go home no matter how Mom and Dad felt about it. He flatly advised me not to go because I would get a whipping.

"Now tell me," I replied, "what do you think is best, having Mom whip me or letting Dominique play her games? She has been telling us from the time we landed in Jamaica that she is doing the best she can. I have heard the same phrase over and over again, too many times. It is old news now. If this is her best, let it be hers, but it should not be ours."

In spite of Ronald's best effort to talk me out of my decision, I jumped on a *tap tap* and headed home to deal with what had to come next.

The street looked very strange. It felt totally different, as if

I was in another world. Haiti was no longer the place I wanted to be and yet I was not in New York. Now that I was caught between two worlds, where did I belong? If you can visualize for a minute a spider being caught in its own web, you can also imagine how confused I was. But having witnessed on numerous instances how a spider could patiently trace its way out from its own trap to achieve its goal, I too believed I would find my way back out.

I started thinking about what Mom would do about my disobedience, the sort of questions my friends would ask, and how I was going to face them. When I reached my stop, I got off the *tap tap* and started to walk in the direction of my house. I was extra careful. Since it was very dark, I was hoping no one would recognize me because I didn't want to answer any premature questions. I now had one last turn before reaching the house.

Suddenly, my father was standing right there talking to one of my friends who also thought I was in New York. I attempted to make a 180-degree turn and run for cover, but it was too late.

From my best recollection, Dad could not see very well during the day, much less at night, because he always asked us to read things to him complaining that the letters were too small. But this particular night, it seemed that the great almighty God had finally answered his prayer for better vision.

He yelled, "Jacky, what are you doing here?"

I was speechless.

He slapped me on my head and said angrily, "You go home and wait for me."

I walked straight in and said, "Hi Mommy, I am home."

"What the hell are you doing here?" she screamed.

I took one look at her face and saw the anger flashing from her eyes. I knew then I was a dead man tonight. But on the other hand, if I survived this, Ronald is going to love hearing about it tomorrow.

After a brief pause, my mother said, "Where is Ronald?"

"He chose to stay, claiming that you would whip me." I answered frightfully.

"Obviously, you didn't believe him because you are here."

"No Mommy, it's not that. I just felt I was in a prison without a cause and I could not take it anymore," I replied nervously.

In that short time, the news had already spread all over the neighborhood. It was big excitement when someone returned from abroad, and people I cared about, friends and family members surrounded the house.

After a few minutes, my mother calmed herself down and asked whether I was embarrassed to face the people who thought I was in New York.

"Mommy, they can start talking from now until they have nothing else to say."

I described to her what happened between Dad and me. How angry he was.

Mom acknowledged, "He has every reason to be angry, but don't worry, I'll take care of it," she promised.

I was delighted.

As expected, when I walked outside, my friends started to ask all sort of questions about why we were back in Haiti. They wanted to know if anything went wrong or if we had been deported, what were our chances of going back and where was Ronald. They also wanted to see if we had any new clothes, shoes or the latest gadgets from New York.

I really didn't have enough answers to go around, so a firm explanation that something was wrong with the visa was enough. I refused to answer any more questions about deportation. Our conversation switched from one subject to another, but the main focus was on girls. When I described Andréa's curves and Charmaine's healthy chest, their imaginations were on fire and that got me off the hook about deportation. What a relief that was!

But all of a sudden, someone asked me about Queens and how long it takes to drive between Miami and New York.

I guessed it was only a few hours by plane.

He said bluntly, "I am not interested in a plane because I want to drive there."

I really felt the guy was going to expose me, so I played it off, "Why not go do it and come back to tell us how long it took."

Quite honestly, Miami didn't matter to me much because the only place in my mind when anyone said America was New York. As far as I was concerned, New York was in America and every place else was in New York. If nothing else, that's where the pennies were and there I belonged.

I was getting a bit tired, so I said, "Does anybody have any more questions?"

"Yes," cried out my friend Youyou, "Did you bring any gifts?"

"Good question," I replied smiling, "but answer me this, Youyou, do you remember giving me any money before I left?"

"No," he said laughing.

"There goes your answer. No money, no gifts."

Everybody roared with laughter. By the time Dad came home, I had done such publicity about New York that even the family dog, who was so happy to see me, was barking in her newly learned New York accent. "Yuk, Yuk. New Yuk."

Dad walked right by me and said nothing. But he did give me a dirty look.

It was hard for me to say a complete sentence without saying a "just," "so" or "my goodness." I had learned those from my cousins, my brother, aunt and friends who had come back for a short visit, so that when I got to New York, I could use them the right way. Such as, "So sir, could you just give me a job. Grand Da, just where are those pennies? I just want to pick them up. My goodness! Why do I have to eat the same food for three days?"

I felt Ronald was missing the best part of it all. Nothing was funnier than playing a tourist in my own land. The only thing I was missing was a camera and a picture album. I had always been amazed that almost every Haitian who went to the United States returned as a photographer. Film or no film, they clicked anything that crossed their path. I wondered if it was a prerequisite to take a class in photography before one returned to Haiti.

The welcome I received from my friends made me think about the whole adventure. My first ever plane ride from Haiti to the Bahamas, the Pegasus Hotel, Charmaine, Andréa, you name it. Despite the setback, those were some fond memories to live by until we left again. I waited nervously to hear what was happening with Dad, but up until that point, he had said nothing. I took it that Mom handled it as she said she would. I tiptoed in slowly to check if Mom gave him a little tranquilizer to calm his nerves down, but surprisingly he was right there talking to her.

I said, "So Dad, how are you?"

He replied angrily, "You had a lot of guts coming back into this neighborhood."

Calmly I explained to him that I shared his concern, but not to worry because we were only in transit in Haiti.

"I hope you are right," my father said. "For your information, I saw Dominique today and, it seems to me, it is going to be a long transit."

"What did she say?"

"She said she did not have an exact date for you guys to go back."

"Is that all?"

"Yes, for now it is."

"Oh, you scared me. I thought you were going to say she's going back to Florida. That would have been a total blow." I smiled then said, "As long as she is in Haiti, we are in transit."

"Well, my son, may your transit time be short," Dad said, sounding a bit discouraged. But then he conceded after a long puff from his cigarette, "As most Haitians would say, if years don't kill you, days and months will not either."

I said nothing and just walked back out, said good night to my friends and went to bed.

The next morning about nine, I was already going back to my cousin's house to tell Ronald everything was ok.

When I got there, he started laughing. His first question was, "How did it go?"

"Well, Roro, other than a slap in my head from Dad, everything went smoother than expected."

"Why did he slap you?"

"It's a long story, my friend, but let's just say he caught me as I was getting ready to make a 180 and run the other way."

"What did he do?"

"I already told you. He slapped me in my head, and very hard too."

Ronald laughed and said, "What about Mom?"

"Nothing."

"You mean my mother did not even touch you?"

"Not even a scratch. I told her this place was like a prison and we could not take it any longer."

"Wow, that's amazing, Jacky. I was expecting her to whip your butt."

"Believe me, that was my expectation too, but it didn't happen."

"Did anyone ask for me?"

"Of course, Ronald, everyone asked about you."

"Did they ask why we are back in Haiti?"

"They asked more than that."

"Like what, Jacky?"

"Gifts."

"Gifts? Are they crazy?"

"Ronald, from now on, we need to see Dominique daily if necessary, to keep tabs on her progress."

"If we do that, we are going to drive her crazy."

"Good, I would rather be the one driving her crazy instead of her driving us crazy. Think about it, Ronald. If we drive her crazy, at least she has enough money to seek treatment in Haiti or the United States. But, if she drives us crazy, we have no money to see a doctor and we will still be in Haiti. Ronald, Haiti is the wrong place to go crazy."

"You need to follow your own advice, because you are getting very close to it."

I said, "You see, you see." Then I started jumping and yelling, "Let's go! Let's go!"

We both had a good laugh and within half an hour were on our way to Dominique's house. Ronald expressed his concern about being seen by someone in the neighborhood and what to say. I reminded him we didn't owe anyone an explanation except Andy who so far had not asked for one, thank God.

Upon reaching Dominique's house, we were met by a young lady who introduced herself as Debbie. We chatted with her for a brief second and then asked to see Dominique.

"She's out for the moment," Debbie answered softly.

"Do you know when she is coming back?" Ronald asked.

"I don't, but usually she stays out very late."

"Then we will wait," Ronald said.

"You might have to wait for a long time because the last few days, she has been getting home very late."

"How late is late?" asked Ronald.

"Not before 6:30 P.M.," she answered.

"That's fine," I said. "If we have to sleep right here tonight, we'll do just that, so long as we get to see her. If you get tired looking at us, we'll move outside and wait there until she comes."

She grinned and walked away.

Ronald looked at me and said, "You are being too demanding."

"Roro, the last time we met with Dominique, Dad was there and I could not say everything I had in mind. Ever since we came back we've kept our tongues tied by Dad's embarrassment and Mom's belt, but as of last night, that's no longer the case. Today it's just you and me. When I start talking to her, please don't laugh and don't say anything."

"Don't you think what we said to her the last time was more than enough?"

"That was cheap talk. I estimate it was worth no more than $100 of our money, which means we still have $3,900 to go. Today, we will talk expensively. I am talking at least a thousand dollars worth," I said laughing. "I want a date, an exact date, Roro."

"Suppose you don't get it, then what, Jacky?"

"Just wait and see."

Ronald just shook his head and started to laugh.

We both knew there was nothing we could have done if Dominique opted to take off with the money. Nonetheless, we were ready and willing to put up a fight till the very end as long as she was still in Haiti.

The clock was ticking and yet there was no sign of Dominique. Ronald was getting impatient and I very hungry, but we decided not to make a move until we saw her. It was almost four in the afternoon and we had not had anything to eat all day. I asked Ronald whether he would mind getting us some food.

To that he answered, "If I take one step from here, it has to be one leading toward home."

The cold expression on Dominique's face reminded me of someone who had been hiding from something and finally got caught yet was confused as to which way to run. Although I felt she was on my most wanted list, I smiled to assure her she would not be handcuffed.

As always, she was calm, confident, and surprisingly she smiled right back at us. "Hi you guys. How are you?"

Ronald and I looked at each other and he answered in a disappointed voice, "Hi Dominique. Besides the fact that we are still in Haiti, we are as good as can be expected." All of a sudden, he rose on his feet and shouted, "Yes, Dominique we are fine. What about you? Are you also fine?"

As hard as I tried not to laugh, I could not stop myself. I said, "Roro, what did I say about sitting down?"

"Let me stand!" He paused for a second then busted out laughing.

Dominique stood there looking as if she had no clue what was going on.

Angrily she yelled, "Listen you two, I told you and your father two weeks ago, all I needed was time. I really feel you are pushing too much. If you have come here to discuss the same thing again, I will not give you the satisfaction or the time. Now, you go home and I will contact you when I am ready to do so."

I looked at her and said, "Dominique, please go inside and ask Debbie how long we have been waiting for you. Must I remind you that you have $4,000 of our money in your pocket? Four, zero, zero and zero."

"Yes," Ronald cried out. "As long as you have that money and we are still in Haiti, our demand of your time and full attention has just begun."

"I am tired and I am going to sleep. Whatever you need to talk about, come back tomorrow and I will answer all your questions."

I said, "Are you inviting us to sleep here tonight? You said tomorrow but we were not planning on leaving, unless we get an exact departure date."

"You two are my worst customers," she shouted.

"On the contrary, we are your best," said Ronald. "In case you forgot, let me remind you once and for all, $4,000 is not just money to us, it is a treasure."

"Come back tomorrow and get your damn money," she screamed loudly.

"We don't want the money back. Take us to America. That's all we want, that's all we are asking for," I replied angrily. "I don't think that's too much to ask for $4,000. Do you?"

"Well, I am not America," she yelled.

"Take us there," Ronald yelled back. "That's all we will accept. Forget the money. You can keep it."

She laughed then said, "You two are crazy."

She started to walk away.

I said, "Dominique. Stop!"

"Now wait, I just got here and I was not expecting to see you here today."

"Well, we are here." I replied.

"I'll be back."

"We shall be here," I answered.

"Jacky, I think she is upset."

"No Roro, she is just playing a game. Do you really think she wants to give us the money back? I hate to surprise you, but if there is $100 left from that money, it's plenty."

"You don't mean she spent it all already?"

"No, she invested it in something else. That's how business people make their money Ronald."

"Watch out, here she comes."

Dominique walked out with a plate full of rice, black beans, and steak. The steak was so thick, if I cut it in the size of a dollar bill, there would be at the very minimum a few hundreds dollars of our money sitting right there on that plate. I thought, "At the very least, you ought to ask us if we cared for some."

After several spoonfuls, it was clear Dominique was not

about to ask that question. The food smelled and looked so tasty every time she lifted the spoon to her mouth, I swallowed before it even got to hers.

Finally, I said, "Dominique will you please stop eating and talk to us?"

"I can't talk when I am hungry," she answered with a full mouth.

"We can't listen, if we are hungry," I replied at once.

"Would you like some?"

"When are we leaving? Any idea?" I smiled.

Dominique took a deep breath, exhaled then said, "Guys, I wish I could say you were leaving tomorrow, but it is not going to be so. I am working day and night to get you out. I have been in this business for almost a year now and I have taken many people to Florida already. So far, no one has ever questioned my credibility as much as you two have."

My mother's guiding principle is, if you want to learn a lesson about pride and dignity, have the poorest Haitian teach you. She often said, it is best to die poor instead of compromising your pride and dignity. I figured if money was going to be the only issue as to whether we would be in America, then it might no longer be a concern. Because Dominique's was talking like a real Haitian, and with the fire in her eyes, it seemed her pride and dignity were now in question and she was ready to take the financial loss, to redeem herself.

I wanted to believe everything she said, but on the other hand, growing up in Haiti, I had also learned not to ever trust the word of a politician. What she said sounded absolutely beautiful, but until she could give us a date to leave Haiti, I was not about to accept that her pride would make her do right.

I said, "Dominique when are you leaving?"

"Not until I can get you guys to Florida."

"Then, can I keep your passport?" I said raising my voice.

Ronald pushed me as if he wanted me to stop talking.

"Why, should I trust you with my passport?" asked Dominique.

"This way we will be certain when you get ready to leave, all three of us will leave together. Besides, we trust you with our money. Right?"

She smiled, shook her head then said, "Please go home and I'll contact you when I have something positive to tell you."

I smiled back and replied, "I still want to keep your passport."

"Jacky, it does not pay to be so pushy," she shouted. "Now for the last time go home because I am exhausted and need to rest."

Ronald and I remained quiet all the way to the house. About ten minutes after we got there, once again the atmosphere in the house was vibrant. Roro received such a warm reception the only thing missing was a red carpet and a band playing "Welcome Back."

Ronald enjoyed every bit of it. In no time, he was either hugging someone, kissing someone else, or shaking hands.

He was extremely happy to be home and see all his friends. I stayed out of his way so he could have his fair share of the tourist moment. A few hours later, I said good night to all and hit the bed.

I had just closed my eyes when I remembered Jeda. I sat up, trembling with fear. Where was Jeda?

Shame

JEDA WAS gone. Her parents would only tell me that she had gone to America and was expecting me to greet her when she got off the plane in Miami. When I questioned Dominique about her, all she would say is, "I will not confirm or deny whether she was my client, but I do remember who you are talking about."

All I could do was worry and avoid the hateful stares of Jeda's parents. When her mother told my mom the story, it was really awful. Mom said until Jeda was discovered alive and well in America she could no longer hold her head up in the streets.

The next two weeks went by very fast. It was already April 1st and we'd had no further word from Dominique. Ronald and I confessed to some of our closest friends what really went wrong, but that didn't stop them from asking questions every now and then. What made the situation even worse was that someone spread a rumor that we were deported and it traveled very fast unfortunately to the wrong ears… Mom and Dad.

Almost everyone had a different opinion about what we should have done or ought to be doing.

I was angry, frustrated and tired of it all. By 1:00 P.M. that day, I resolved to check on Dominique no later than the next day. I consulted with Ronald, but he suggested we give her one more week. If by then, we still had not heard from her, he agreed we would make a move. I was not happy with the suggestion because I wanted to see Dominique right away. But, no matter what I said, Ronald was not convinced.

We had been out of school for two months already and the pressure from my mother to go back was intense.

I guess she was tired of looking at us sitting in the house waiting for news. But for me, my mind had taken a 180-degree turn from the classroom to Miami and then headed for New York. I knew in my head if I ever saw inside another classroom again, it was not going to be in Haiti. I tried to calm Mom down by saying if we were still in Haiti by June, I would go ahead and take the final exam, but to Mom that was not enough. She kept the pressure on and she was firm.

I had not touched a textbook in a while and I was not about to, except for my English books. My recent experience in Jamaica and the Bahamas made it clear how critical it was to learn more of the language, and I did just that. I spent every waking hours polishing what I had learned while adding new words, sentences or phrases at every opportunity.

Later on that day, I was trying to quiet my mind by reading a book when I saw Yves walking toward me at a very fast pace. We had seen him on more than one occasion, but he hardly said a word about the trip, apparently thinking he had something to do with the result. But I felt he had done what I asked and what he knew was in our best interest. I never pressed the issue or made him feel guilty for what happened. He made a fist, threw himself in the air followed by a huge smile. Before he even said one word my mind started to race. God, please let it be good news.

We shook hands and he asked if Ronald was home.

"No, he went out."

"Do you know where he is?"

"Why? Do you have a message from Dominique?" I asked hesitantly.

"Let's go find him because you guys are leaving tomorrow morning." Yves replied with great joy in his voice.

"Yves, I realize today is April 1st, but I think you and I are too old to be playing April Fools' Day. Don't you think?"

"I was not even thinking about that. I should have told you Dominique went back to Miami and then shocked you with the news."

"Yves, for the last time, are you serious or just faking it?"

"I have no reason to play with something so important to you. Dominique wants to see you tonight and she suggests you show up with your father."

I knew then he was serious when he mentioned my father.

I jumped in the air, came down, danced, sang and threw my feet left and right.

"This is the day," I exclaimed with much emotion. "Let's get Ronald now."

As we were walking toward my friend's house where I expected Ronald to be, he saw us and started to meet us halfway. I gave him the thumbs up and he began to run in our direction at full speed.

I threw myself in his arms and said, "We're going."

"When, Jacky?"

"Tomorrow morning, tomorrow, Roro," I sang.

He jumped in the air and screamed, "Yes!" He hit the ground, grabbed Yves by the shoulder and said, "Are you telling the truth?"

Yves did not answer.

I panicked. "Yves, Yves, please tell him what you just told me?"

"He's so excited he didn't even say hello. Let him wait," Yves teased.

"Hello," Ronald said grinning while hugging Yves real tight.

"Yes, you are leaving tomorrow," he answered when Ronald let go of him. "Quite frankly, I was really bothered by the outcome, especially when I knew how much money was involved. And since I was the one to introduce you to Dominique, I felt both obligated and committed to you until I saw the end of it."

"Forget what happened," Ronald said, "we are leaving and that is the most important thing."

He jumped once, twice and I held him down on the third attempt and said, "Ronald, Dominique wants to see us tonight."

"No, let's go now, Jacky."

"She also wants to see Dad. Therefore, we can't leave until he gets home."

After going back and forth we agreed to wait on Dad and go see Dominique as requested.

We could not believe this was actually happening. It was unreal! We thanked Yves for all his support and settled that we would meet by ten over Dominique's.

We rushed home to share the news with Mom.

No one believed us.

There were mixed emotions. Mom didn't think it was a good sign to be notified only hours before we left. I tried to ease her mind by saying that the last time we met with Dominique, she mentioned she was doing all she could to get us out. Mom was still not convinced. All of a sudden she started to pick up vibes. She complained Wednesday was not a good day to travel. When I asked why, she offered no explanation except that it was a bad day. Both Ronald and I kept talking to Mom, but with no luck.

Meanwhile, Dad showed up a few hours later looking all beat up and instantly questioned why everyone was so excited. We were outside chatting with some close friends, so we asked him to see Mom. About ten minutes later, Dad came out and ordered Ronald and I to come in for a moment.

"Your mom explained everything to me, we discussed it at length and we decided you are not going."

I said, "Dad, Dominique wants to see you tonight because we are leaving tomorrow morning."

He glanced at my mother, looked back at me and said, "Jacky, your mom is picking up some bad vibes and I think she's right."

I could not believe what I was hearing.

I kept silent, thinking about what to do. Finally I said, "How could you two make such a decision? Why not go see Dominique, listen to what she has to say and by then you might have a different opinion once we have gathered all the facts."

Dad turned back to Mom whispered something to her and he said, "We don't have any pocket money to give to you."

"Please, please if this is your only concern, don't worry. If we get to Miami by twelve tomorrow, I'll have a job no later than twelve the next day."

"How do you know that?"

"Dad, we are talking about America. I heard some people even have three jobs. Well, come tomorrow, someone will end up with only two because one will be mine. Let's hurry Dad, it's getting late," I said nervously.

"What makes you think you are not going to end up in Jamaica again for a week or two as you did previously?" my mother followed with great concern.

"Jamaica or Miami, we will survive. But no, we are not going to Jamaica. Please stop mentioning it."

"We made friends in Jamaica. Patrick will not let us suffer," Ronald added.

"Ronald, forget about Patrick. We are not going to Jamaica!" I screamed.

Suddenly, I heard, "I am going with them and that's final."

Mind you, my father is no more than 5'3", or maybe 5'4" if we stretch him a bit with our eyes but when I turned to face him, he stood up like a giant with his chest puffed up in the air like a mean rooster getting ready for a cockfight on a Saturday morning. I waited nervously to see what was going to be my mom's reaction.

Surprisingly, she said softly, "Please be careful out there."

Well done, Dad.

My friend had been there with us earlier and had already offered to drive us to Dominique's house no matter what time it was. We walked out, grabbed him and said let's go.

It took us less than twenty minutes to get there. When we reached the house Yves was already outside waiting on us. He had to answer several questions from Dad, but he handled himself extremely well.

We walked in to find Dominique sitting quietly on a small chair sipping a drink. My father took a new approach by thanking her for keeping her promise, but warned her if anything bad happened to us, she would be responsible. Dominique played it very smooth by reassuring my father everything would be fine.

She then switched her focus to us. "I want you to pay close attention to what I say because I have lots of instructions for you."

I began to shake, but regained control of myself. I asked for a pen and paper to write things down, but Dominique claimed it was unnecessary, because someone would meet us in the Bahamas and take over from there.

"Dominique, first of all, what kind of visa do we have this time? If it is a Jamaican visa, I have to write things down even if you tell me you are coming with us."

My father interfered to say a Jamaican visa means you are not leaving.

She ignored that statement and continued providing details about the trip. "Yes, you are again leaving with a Jamaican visa. You will fly to Nassau, Bahamas, then Bimini, and from there," she paused, "you'll have to get on a boat to Miami."

The last part was unexpected by any stretch of the imagination.

There was dead silence.

I must have taken at least ten deep breaths before I gathered the courage to speak again. "Did I hear you right? Did you say boat, Dominique?"

"Yes, it's a powerful boat and the trip should take no more than three hours."

"Please explain to us if you could, Dominique, how this boat thing got into the picture. From our first meeting, you led us to believe, we were to fly directly between Nassau, Bahamas to Miami. Yet, we ended up in Jamaica. Now, you are talking, Bimini, boat and Lord knows what else. What has changed?"

She said nothing and we waited.

Finally, she began to speak very softly. "There has been a major change and I regret that it turned out this way. The person who was supposed to clear you guys through immigration in Miami is presently locked up in jail. As a result, I have no other means of getting you to Florida, but the boat. The choice is now up to you. Go, or, as your father said earlier, no go."

"Yes, that's what I said," my father yelled. "They are not leaving."

Ronald said, "I'm not going."

Dominique opened her purse and showed us the passports and tickets and said, "I have already arranged and paid for your passage from Haiti to Nassau and Bimini to Miami. This time if you don't go, it is not my fault and it's going to take me a while to reimburse you whatever is left from your money."

"Wait! You are talking sheer nonsense right now," Ronald spoke angrily. "If we decide not to go, I will demand that you pay us immediately and in full. You made a choice without consulting us. And worse yet, to slap us in the face with something so crucial only hours before we leave is inexcusable."

What Ronald said must have touched Dad very deeply. He just burst into tears. That was the first time I had seen him cry and so loud. He was unstoppable, no matter what we said.

Ronald was next.

That was too much for me to handle.

I reached into my father's shirt pocket, pulled out a cigarette and lit it up. It was several puffs later that I realized I had the guts to smoke in his presence for the first time.

He started calling Dominique all sorts of names. Thief, inconsiderate, criminal, mafia, you name it and Dad said it.

I asked my friend what his take was on the whole thing. He shook his head and answered sadly, "I am disappointed."

Yves was very quiet and looked puzzled.

I walked outside to finish my cigarette and gave everyone a chance to vent their anger as they saw fit.

It was a beautiful night. The clear sky was decorated by a multitude of shining stars of all sizes flashing like miniature lights on a Christmas tree

I was overwhelmed.

I reviewed in my mind, word-by-word what Dominique had just revealed to us and concluded that a boat and the ocean meant death. I had a vivid flashback to when I almost drowned in the ocean at the age of thirteen. Again, one of those things Ronald and I kept secret from the family. Since then, I had the biggest fear of the ocean and had never learned how to swim. If nothing else, having seen the movie *Jaws* magnified my fear. The vision of sharks swimming away with different parts of my body left me in a state of total fright.

I had been outside for almost five minutes and still had no idea what to do. I struggled with the decision to take the boat and risk death or stay behind and never discover what would have happened. I closed my eyes briefly and said, "God I need you. Here's my problem and I need to make a quick decision before I go back in. What do you say?"

"You go right ahead. I will be with you throughout your journey," He answered softly.

"God, you know I don't swim, so are you sure now?"

"Go already! It's getting late, have no fear," He replied.

I thanked Him for being there and walked back inside. I went straight to Dominique and asked, "At what time is the flight to the Bahamas?"

"Ten o'clock, but I want you to be there no later than 8:30 A.M."

"Do we meet you here or at the airport?"

"The airport is best."

"What are you talking about?" my father screamed.

"Dad, when I went outside, something happened which I won't go into detail about. This might hurt you for the rest of your life, but my mind is made up. I am leaving tomorrow."

"Not if your mother and I say no," he yelled once more.

I gazed right into his eyes and repeated slowly, "I am leaving tomorrow. Now, if Ronald cares to come along, I can only promise that we'll be fine. However, if he chooses not to, I'll notify all of you when I get to Miami."

My father was stunned and so was I. Never before had I spoken to him with such firmness.

"Are you ready to die?"

"Dad, if I die during the journey please know that I love you and Mom dearly. But if I make it, I will see to it that it was well worth taking the risk."

Dominique was now shedding a few tears. "Sir," she began in a very low tone, "being a mother of five kids I understand and share your concern. But for their sake, their future, I'd ask you for one thing tonight and that is, let them go. Let them take their chance. I see no future for them in Haiti."

My father was speechless for almost a minute or two. He then pulled Ronald and me to him and started crying again, louder this time.

He hugged both of us tightly and said, "Remember, I am

not pushing you. I might not always give you all you want, but I always try to give you all that I have." He kissed us both and gently scratched our heads. "Since nobody can stop you, may God be with you," he whispered with tears.

I was trembling and I was cold. I wanted to cry, but there were no tears. I wanted to laugh, but could not. I looked at my father and said, "Papa, you have done enough. It is now time for us to do for ourselves and help you with your load. It is without any doubt, given the circumstances neither you nor Mom would ever encourage us to leave. But tonight, once and for all, let us push not just for ourselves, but everybody else. As a father, the only thing we'll ask is that you pray for us. Pray with faith. Pray that our journey will be safe. We will be all right Papa."

I turned back to Ronald and asked him, "Ready to do it again?"

He buried his face in his palms and remained in that position for some time. Then he let go and said to me, "I only hope we make it there alive."

He walked straight to Dominique, gave her a kiss and said, "We'll see you at the airport at 8:30 A.M."

I tried very hard to hide my emotions, but finally I lost it. I gave Ronald a hug and was in tears. I whispered in his ear "No matter what happens, you coming along will make all the difference and I thank you."

We all said good night to Dominique and headed back home.

At 1:30 A.M., the street was deserted. Although it was final to meet Dominique at 8:30 A.M., my father was still distraught about us taking a boat to Florida. He was saying anything that came to mind to see if he could convince us not to go.

I listened to all that he said, but kept my comments to myself.

Thank God, my friend stepped on the gas pedal and we made it home in no time. The light in the house was still on, so I knew my mother was waiting to hear the details. She was not just another hurdle to jump, but the toughest.

We got out of the car, said goodbye to my friend and Yves with a promise to contact them once we got settled.

Before we went in, I begged my father to explain to my mother that everything would be fine, but he paid me no mind.

If he cried when he found out we were taking a boat, Mom would be screaming. At two o'clock in the morning, the neighbors would want an explanation and rightly so.

A few of them knew we were leaving again, but no one knew how we were supposed to get there. If Mom started to yell at this hour, they would think either a close relative had died and we were just told, or that a robber had entered the house and we were screaming to scare him away.

Mom was still ironing some of our clothes, so I approached her, gave a kiss and said good night. I was trying to avoid any conversation with Mom, but a good night kiss was not enough.

"Is anybody going to tell me what Dominique had to say?"

"Other than we have to meet her at 8:30 in the morning at the airport, there was not much to say," I answered.

"Did she explain why she gave such a short notice?"

"Why don't I let Dad answer this one."

"No, you don't. You and Ronald made your decision no matter what I said, now you explain to your mother why

Dominique gave such short notice," said my father and walked away.

My mother sensed something was wrong, but no one was willing to say what it was. Finally, I mumbled, "We leave in the morning and get there in the evening."

"Did she say at what time in the evening?"

I was a bit surprised Mom was actually handling things better than I expected.

"No Mommy, but I suppose between eight and nine."

"Why so late?" She pressed on looking for an answer.

I remained quiet.

She walked right into my face and yelled, "Is anybody going to tell me what's going on?"

"OK, ok Mom, I'll tell you. According to Dominique, we'll first stop in Nassau, then to another island called Bimini and from there straight to Florida," I said trembling.

I didn't think my father was listening, but he rushed back in shouting angrily, "No, no tell your mother exactly how you're getting to Florida."

"Oh that part . . ."

"Yes, that part," said my father.

"Please, tell her, Dad," I begged him again.

"Hurry up!" my mother shouted.

I turned around to face the wall and said in a low voice, "From Bimini to Florida, we'll be on a boat."

"Boat?"

"Yes Mommy, Dominique said it's a powerful boat and the trip should take no more than three hours."

"Boat?" she yelled again, "I don't care if it's one hour or less. Turn around!" she ordered. When I twisted my head to look at her face, she was fuming. "If Dominique wants to keep the money, let her have it, but you are not taking a boat to Florida."

Thank God Andy is not home to hear the fate of his hard won money.

"Dominique must be crazy if she thinks I would, even in my worst moment, let you get on a boat to Florida," said my mother.

My father joined in and said, "That was exactly how I felt, but they didn't want to listen."

"What is that supposed to mean? The decision to take a boat is not up to them or Dominique. It is up to us. They are not going," my mother said.

Mom's tears began to flow in a slow motion and I braced myself for the worst. I said softly, "Please, Mom, whatever you do, don't scream."

"Don't tell me not to scream. Listen, when I have to go to Jérémie to see my family, I spend many hours on a ferryboat. Don't you remember the time you came with me and vomited all the way going there and back? Do you know how many times I have had to kneel down and pray during rough sea to stay alive so I could come home to all of you? Do you understand how dangerous the ocean is? And today you want me to accept this? Tell me," she addressed my father, "didn't Dominique say she is also a mother? I will have a talk with her," she said angrily.

After listening to everything she had to say, I made one last ditch effort to get her stamp of approval.

I said, "Mommy, I recognize your fear and concern regarding how we are to travel to Florida. But, can you be sure we won't risk death staying here in Haiti? And even if we don't, what will we do with our lives? In spite of the perilous journey and challenges waiting ahead of us, going to America by far represents the best hope for our future."

It was almost four o'clock in the morning.

After much crying, begging, and promises to do well, she and my father gave in and we received their final blessing. We hugged and thanked them both for their love and support one last time and asked them to pray for us.

It was settled. We would leave the house at seven in the morning.

Second Partings

THE ANXIETY about leaving Haiti and taking a boat to Florida added to my fear of what may have happened to Jeda. That mixed in with my jealous imaginings about what Micheline must be up to, made it impossible to rest my mind.

I was counting the remaining hours by the seconds up until six in the morning.

By 6:45 A.M., we were kissing, hugging and asking everyone to pray for us. One of my sisters handed us a small Bible and said to carry it along. There were tears and laughter, but this time it was even more emotional because not only were they not coming to the airport to bid us farewell, they knew, if anything happened, that might be the last time they saw us alive.

By 7:00 sharp, Mom, Dad, Ronald and I left for the airport. On the way, Dad stopped by one of his friend's house to get us some pocket money for the trip. If everything worked out as planned, the 400 U.S. dollars we received from him was more than enough to carry us to our first destination. Miami!

We were at the airport ten minutes ahead of our 8:30 A.M. rendezvous, impatiently waiting for Dominique to arrive. Right after 8:30 A.M., I started to question her lateness and wondered if she was going to show up at all. About 8:45 A.M., I saw her getting out of a car across the street and I waved to get her attention. When you are dealing with a life-threatening situation every second is as precious as your last breath. Therefore, if we could maximize the time we had to talk to her, it might turn out to be the most precious time of our lives during the next twelve hours. I ran across the street and pointed out our location to her.

She placed her hand on my shoulder and said, "You know, I came here to deal with my other clients. Seeing how your father cried last night, I really didn't expect to see you here."

"I told you we were going to be here. Actually, I was worried about you not showing up."

She then took my hand and while crossing the street she said, "I hope you never stop being so persistent."

Persistence? We'll see how much of it is there when I get into the water and some shark starts biting my butt off. I was frightened.

Upon reaching Mom and Dad, Dominique said hello and went straight into some last minute details about the trip. She explained to them how and when she would be notified and once confirmed, she would relay the information right away.

Meanwhile, we learned for the first time, Dominique's older brother Jeb and her cousin Fito would be traveling with us. That was excellent news and everybody was now less worried. We felt she must have confidence in her plan to send her family along. She requested we remain together because she was trying to get us out of the Bahamas at the same time.

We were introduced to our new travel companions. Jeb was probably in his early fifties, but looked twenty years younger. He was tall, fit, and handsome with a dash of silver hair and a twenty-something spirit. From our brief conversation, I was eager to learn more about him.

Fito was just the opposite. He was about thirty-five, but acted as if he could be Jeb's grandfather. He was tall and could have used a few pounds of meat to lift up what resembled a hard, wooden sculptured face. His pants were an inch or two too short and he carried a Bible in his hand that made him look like a typical Haitian pastor without a church or a congregation.

I knew, one way or the other, we were all experiencing some type of fear, but the guy was just too uptight. Nobody was able to get a smile on his face no matter how hard we tried. His bad energy was enough to attract some very angry and hungry sharks. I was praying that he would loosen up by the time we got on the boat.

The clock kept moving forward and as usual Dominique worked her magic. She was all over the place talking to everyone. All her clients were very demanding of her time. They made a few announcements, but she ignored them all.

Mom could not stop telling us to please be very careful. At one point, she moaned, "If you get to New York and you see that you don't like it, please come back home."

I was thinking "Mom, name me one Haitian who has ever gone to New York and chose to come back because they didn't like it." If there was one, I was not aware of that person. I softly kissed her hand and said, "Mom, no matter how difficult it turns out to be, I'll stick it out until I get it to work my way."

When it was time, as before, Dominique walked us to immigration with no sweat and it all seemed normal this time. She waved goodbye and asked us to call when we get to Florida. I sat beside Ronald, while Jeb and Fito took a seat next to each other. About half an hour later, I was once again sitting inside an airplane looking down on my country. It was sad thinking I might never get to see this beautiful land again, but I knew I left behind a country full of culture, tradition and abundant love, not to mention the fine Indian, African, French and Spanish mixed cuisine, our succulent tropical fruits, great music and incredible art that is always a free exhibit on our mobile museum—our *tap tap*.

During the flight we had a chance to chat with Jeb for a short time. His favorite subject was women. And the way he talked about them with such joy and flavor gave us the impression that in his younger days, he was every mother's worst nightmare, every father's worst enemy, but every young woman's best kept secret.

"How did you get to be so smooth?" asked Ronald.

Jeb was quiet for a while, apparently having a flashback of the beauty of his younger days. He was digging, maybe deep into his subconscious, for pleasant memories, painful regrets, anything to rekindle the dim light. "Listen," he said joyfully at last, "the heart is very fragile, especially a woman's heart. So, the next time you think of a woman and love, think of love as the art of massaging her heart. Be kind and tender," he spoke softly.

"If you must talk to her, whisper. When you caress her, close her eyes with kisses. And if you must ever use your hands on a woman, handle her as the most precious creature you will ever touch. You know, more like the way she would handle her newborn baby."

His deep voice resonated that of a father getting ready to pass on the baton to his two young sons. It almost felt as if he sensed at fifty plus years he was burning his last few candles, but wanted to make sure the light stays on. We listened intently and savored every word from his mouth.

The trip went very fast, but this time there was no doubt in mind, even with our Jamaican visa, clearing immigration was going to be a breeze. I made sure Ronald and I remained close to Jeb and Fito as we were instructed before we left Haiti. While we were in line waiting to be checked, I was looking all over for that person Dominique talked about who was supposed to welcome us in the Bahamas like some Haitian diplomats. But it didn't take long to realize we were again heading back to Jamaica. The final word came from the immigration officer, this time a young woman who could not believe how many Haitians she had seen suffering in the Bahamas, yet we had enough money to go to Jamaica for vacation twice in two months.

In her sweet Bahamian accent, she said, "I hope one day, you will visit the Bahamas. Have a safe trip to Jamaica." That lady was insane to think we had money or we were on vacation.

I walked into the transit lounge wondering what were we going to do. There were several people waiting along with us and all were very quiet. How many of them were Dominique's clients? Didn't know and didn't care. I was tired, disappointed and in no mood for conversation. Apart from my brother, I said nothing to anyone in the room. Both Fito and Jeb acted as if what happened was normal procedure because they didn't show even a bit of concern. They apparently were so sure what would happen next, they even napped for several hours. Ronald and I discussed the possibility of trying to escape again, but decided it was best to stay put.

We landed in Jamaica later on that evening with $400 in our pockets and a beat up spirit. Ronald was reluctant about going back to Patrick, but I joked by saying we were just going to say hello before going to Miami.

Fito and Jeb had it all worked out where they were spending the night. Luckily, we ended up not too far from them.

Even though Patrick wasn't expecting us, we decided his place was the most cheerful and affordable.

When we got there, everyone was happy and surprised to see us, and they welcomed us with open arms. They asked many questions, but the one answer they wanted to hear from us, we were not able to give it to them: when will we get to Miami? I came to realize that when you have your destination clearly mapped out, people don't ask where you are going, but instead when will you get there.

We settled in over at Patrick's for almost the same arrangement we had before, eighty dollars per week for both of us. But there was only one drawback, this time we were responsible for our own meals. It was not our intention to show up without prior notice, but everyone understood. It was not yet clear how long we were to spend in Jamaica, but experience is the best teacher. Since we had enough money for at least two full weeks, Ronald and I concluded before going to bed, if it became a question, we would tough it out in Jamaica instead of going back to Haiti.

Thirty-six hours after landing in Jamaica there was still no word from Dominique. She knew Patrick was our first choice of domicile, if all else failed. She also had the number for Jeb and Fito, so we were annoyed that she didn't even call to see how we were.

About two o'clock that day, we walked to a grocery store to buy a few things. When we got back, we had a message to contact Dominique's brother. We dumped the bags and walked straight to Jeb's hotel.

Jeb was so laid back, you never knew what to expect from him. He had a huge smile on his face, so we figured it had to be good news. He kept on smiling, took a puff on his cigarette and simply said, "Dominique called this morning."

"And what else?" Ronald asked.

"She said that she was sorry, but please be patient until she can get us out."

"Did she say when?" asked Ronald again.

"No," Jeb answered, "but I can tell you she's very upset about the whole thing and she's doing her best."

"I have heard this before, so please tell me something new," Ronald said angrily.

Jeb laughed and replied, "You guys have been here before, but this is all new to me. Therefore, I am telling you something new."

We had no choice but to laugh along with him. I accepted everything he said about what Dominique was doing, but I also believed for us to end up in Jamaica twice in a row was either a lack of concern or planning.

Ronald was very upset.

Dominique's promise to get us out was no longer significant to him until it actually happened. We stayed with Jeb for a few more minutes and then said goodbye.

The next few days were both depressing and painful. I felt defeated and ashamed, but I kept saying to myself, as long as the sun rises in the morning and sets in the evening, every day would be a better day. Eventually, a better day will lead to the best day. It is my firm belief even when the daily life is a struggle, if you can get to the end of it and feel that you have fought a good battle, you have lived your best day.

On April 10, 1980, we finally received a call from Dominique telling us to meet her in the Bahamas the next day between 3:00–4:00 P.M.

But, there was a small problem.

She didn't think there was a flight from Kingston that could get us to the Bahamas at that time.

Yet, she asked that we do whatever we could to get there because the person clearing us through immigration could only do so at that time.

We shared the news with Patrick and solicited his help. He was happy for us, but puzzled by our new dilemma. He thought for a quick minute and said he knew someone who could help. He took off with Ronald. Meanwhile, I began to think about the whole thing and tried to sort out our next alternative. We were flying from Jamaica to the Bahamas. If Dominique and her contact were not there to clear us out, it would be a fatal blow. Our options would be limited.

Within an hour, Patrick and Ronald came back with Jeb and Fito's tickets in hand. Patrick got on the phone and made several calls. By the time it was over, the result was superb. We were rebooked on a flight scheduled to land in the Bahamas at three-thirty the next day via Montego Bay, paying a few extra dollars per ticket. How he managed to pull it off was unclear. But I can tell you this for certain, he was not one to take no for an answer. This, to me, is an invaluable quality and one that is absolutely necessary to bypass life's obstacles.

When he hung up the phone, he gave Ronald and me the strongest hug, promising, if necessary, to travel with us all the way to the Bahamas.

He laughed then said, "I wish not to ever see you in Jamaica again."

We didn't know how to thank him. We felt no matter what we said or did, it was not enough. We spent the rest of the evening laughing and joking. Ronald was extremely happy and suggested we all go out to celebrate the good news. During the conversation, we found out that Patrick was coming with us to Montego Bay. We insisted on contributing to pay for his ticket, but he refused to accept any payment. He claimed to have his contact at the airport and plus he had a student ID which made his ticket very inexpensive.

Later that evening, Jeb showed up with a last minute message. He told us that Dominique called to confirm that she would be in the Bahamas in the morning. She wanted us to take our toiletries and no more than one spare set of clothes each. In addition, if there was any significant change that would jeopardize our clearance in the Bahamas, she would notify him with further details. According to Jeb, Dominique will know something by 8:30 A.M., the latest. If by nine o'clock we didn't hear from him or Dominique directly, we were set to go.

I was concerned with this last minute message because it seemed to me, at this late stage of the game, there was still a possibility for something to go wrong. I instantly asked Patrick to find out if there was any flight scheduled to leave for Haiti after we landed.

Everyone wanted an explanation why I was being so paranoid. I don't know if it was paranoia or maybe crisis anticipation, but whatever the case I felt there was no margin for error. I reasoned if there were no more flights leaving to Haiti after we landed, the worse case scenario would be to spend the night either in the transit lounge or someplace outside of the airport. If nothing else, that would buy Dominique some time to maybe rectify the situation, which in turn would increase our chances of moving forward.

Jeb tried to reassure us by saying, given his conversation

with Dominique, it was almost a sure bet we would breeze our way through immigration. But still, I refused to rely on luck and pushed for an answer. After a few minutes on the phone, Patrick confirmed that by the time we landed, there would be no more flights to Haiti. I was relieved.

Ronald and Patrick decided to spend the night out in celebration and I chose to stay behind, thinking of what was ahead of us. As hard as I tried, it was difficult not to experience any sort of fear from one moment to the next. I played out in my mind everything that could go wrong, and how the consequences would affect our plan either short or long-term. First, there was Dominique's inability to get us out of the Bahamas not once but twice already. Second, the likelihood of getting all the way to Miami, be caught and shipped right back to Haiti. Would Dominique try again? I knew we would, but with what money? Third, and worse of all, there was the trauma of the boat collapsing in the middle of the ocean, and facing the risk of dying. A scary scenario to even think about, but a looming threat indeed.

No matter which way I turned things around, there was no inner peace. The critical part for me was the boat and the ocean. I adore being close to the ocean, but when you don't know how to swim there ought to be no confusion in your mind as to where you belong. So long as my brother's life and mine were at stake, the ocean belonged to the ocean and we on the other hand belonged to dry land.

Finally, after all the, "what ifs and buts?" my mind said enough was enough. I talked myself to sleep. I woke up at 7:30 the next morning asking, "What if Dominique calls to say stay in Jamaica until further notice?" A valid question indeed, but there was no answer to it. It occurred to me that Miami might be a big place and that I would need Dominique's help to find Jeda. Meanwhile, my eyes were focused on one thing, the clock, and my ears on the telephone. The loud ticking of the second hand of an old clock, hanging against the wall right in front of my face, made it nearly impossible to ignore the time, even if I wanted to. Every time it went tick, my heart followed with tack. And at the end of each revolution around the twelve o'clock mark I felt the pressure all the way to my bones.

By 8:30 A.M., Ronald was still sleeping. Nine o'clock, no call from Jeb, no call from Dominique; that was it. We were on. I was overjoyed!

Within an hour or less, there was again the same farewell ritual of handshakes, hugs, some comforting words and wishes of good luck. It was clear not all of us would survive the journey, but we knew those of us who made it across safely would be marked by the experience forever.

Connections

WE WERE now in Montego Bay waiting for our connecting flight to the Bahamas. Contrary to Kingston, the airport in Montego Bay was spotless. There were people everywhere, many shops and vendors. One thing that caught my attention was some of the fine women Ronald had talked about earlier. Those beautiful Jamaican women reminded me of my Haitian Queens and Princesses back home. They carried themselves with such pride. For a second I felt like a judge in a smiling contest and could not decide who would be the winner. It seemed as though they all believed no infection is as contagious as the brightness of a genuine smile.

Our transit time in Montego Bay was less than two hours, but Patrick had to catch his flight right back to Kingston. He and Ronald didn't want to part ways. They hugged each other for so long you could tell there was a tremendous amount of love flowing between them.

When it was my time to hug him, I said, "Patrick, I have seen Haitians helping other Haitians on many occasions, but yours was one beyond the call of duty. If I never get the chance to return it to you, I hope to someday return it to your fellow man."

"I hope this time you guys make it to Miami and I'll pray that you have a safe journey," he said in a painful voice. "But if for any reason you don't and you return to Jamaica, I'll do it all over again. It's sad to say, but Haiti just lost two young, wonderful Haitians and I am afraid many more will follow suit," said Patrick kindly.

I thanked him and whispered, "Make it three, with you being the best."

On that note we all said goodbye and he was gone. During our short transit, Jeb passed the time smoking and walking around. Fito kept reading his Bible. Ronald and I took a seat on the floor and joked with each other nonstop. He had me laughing so hard because every time he saw a woman that caught his attention, he would smile and say in a low voice, "Hey baby, me, you, Miami."

After a few times of hearing the same rhyme, I said, "Roro, if they all decide to come, there won't be any space left in the boat for us."

He laughed then replied, "It's okay Jacky, we will only take as many as we can carry."

"Well, if that is the case, let's see how many we can carry. But first remember you don't fly into a woman's heart, you slip into it. That 'me, you,' thing is not going to work."

My statement brought us back sharply to our still uncertain situation.

Just then, Jeb approached us and said we needed to start getting ready because it was time. We gathered our belongings and waited to get on board the airplane.

The flight from Montego Bay to the Bahamas was peaceful. I was just beginning to enjoy the ride when it came to my attention that we were getting close to the Bahamas. I love airplanes and when I was younger I always thought pilots were the most intelligent people on earth because every time an airplane disappeared in the clouds, they got to see God.

But after I saw those fine looking stewardess, I had second thoughts. They light up the sky.

In no time we were on the ground and the pilot managed to make the wheels kiss the ground so softly. I smiled. Any man who could handle such a gigantic machine so smoothly must also know how to kiss his woman very gently. And if he does not, he had no business flying an airplane like that.

My blood pressure was rising, but I tried as best as I could to calm myself down. The second the door opens I will look for one person and one person only—Dominique. I wore my sunglasses to protect my eyes from the glare of the brilliant sunlight, so that I could easily search for Dominique and blend in like a real tourist visiting the Bahamas.

Before we got off the airplane, Fito suggested that we separate to avoid the slightest bit of suspicion. Ronald agreed that it was an excellent idea but requested that Fito goes first. He wavered for a split second, but decided to take the lead and we followed.

As we made our way toward the immigration booths, I whispered to Ronald that I was really nervous. He whispered back that he was as well, but it was best not to show it. I knew there were only two possibilities, jail or the transit lounge until the next day. We made our choice to come back and they were about to make theirs as to where we would spend the night.

My mind was at maximum speed when Ronald said quietly, "Look straight ahead and to the left. Dominique is standing right there."

I fixed my sunglasses and looked exactly where Ronald said to look.

Bingo! Dominique was indeed looking and waving at us.

I have yet to find the words to describe what I felt, but

the only thing that went through my head was, "Thank you, God."

We had no idea how Dominique planned to get us out, but compared to the last two trips to the Bahamas, this was the closest we had ever been to getting out. As we got closer and closer, I kept a watchful eye on her in the event she wanted to send us any message. Facial expression or body language, I was not going to miss anything.

The first sign came and it was the best I had seen from Dominique since we met. A thumb's up followed by a huge smile highlighted by her dark sunglasses.

Well done, well done, Dominique.

To our great surprise, she met us on our way to the immigration officer. It was then I concluded the Bahamas was a done deal. She said hello, instructed us to relax and to follow her through immigration. I looked at the immigration officer to see what would be his reaction. I was amazed.

He stamped the passports and cheerfully said, "Welcome to the Bahamas and enjoy your vacation."

I walked away thinking, "My friend if you ever see us in the Bahamas again, it will be for a real vacation."

Although we were there with Dominique, I wanted to run and get out as fast as we could. Luckily she wasted no time. Once outside, she put Ronald and me in one taxi and the rest of them rode in a different one. Before we left, she gave the driver an address and requested he remain within visible distance from the other taxi.

On the way, the driver started to ask many questions. I understood everything he said, but I tried to discourage any further question by telling him that we didn't speak any English. Apparently, he was not satisfied because he kept asking more and more.

At one point, he said, "Bahamas is beautiful, not like Haiti."

I said, "You know Haiti?"

He answered, "No."

He asked one more question and I again responded, "We don't speak English." That was the end of our conversation.

The Bahamas was really beautiful. Most of the houses looked freshly painted in a multi-colored fashion: white, pink and green. The trees were no exception. Most if not all were painted white at the bottom. The leaves looked so clean and fresh, you would think they had been hand washed one by one. If the Bahamas had a problem, painting was not it. And whoever was supplying the paint was running a moneymaking business.

Bahamas had a very nice flavor to it, but not enough to make me want to spend one more day. We were both very alert and from time to time we would look behind to see if Dominique was still with us. We left the main street and drove into a narrow alley on a dirt road. About five minutes later, we pulled in front of a house. It looked nothing like a hotel. There was debris all over, from tree branches, broken window frames to piles of small pieces of wood tied with electrical wires. So we waited to see what was next. When I looked back, I saw only Dominique getting out and she started to walk toward our taxi. She told us to get out, paid the driver and said thank you.

"This is where you two will be staying tonight," she said pointing to the house. "Fito and Jeb will be someplace else and I am going to be with a friend."

"I will come back later to bring you some food and give you further instructions. Do not say anything to anyone as to why you are here or when you are to leave. Let me walk in with you to make sure everything is all right," she added.

When we walked in, the place was crowded. Almost everyone was speaking Créole, except maybe two or three. The man who met us at the door gave us a sign-in sheet to write our names and signatures. When we returned it to him, he made a sarcastic remark about how well we wrote our names for Haitians.

I felt offended by his remark and responded sharply, "Regardless of what you have been led to believe or heard, don't you ever underestimate the intelligence of a young Haitian."

He shut his mouth instantly and handed over the keys.

Dominique then explained to us that some of the people staying there were assigned six or seven to a room, but only Ronald and I would be occupying our own room. She then repeated that she would be back later to check on us and left. We entered our small room and waited nervously for Dominique to return.

The décor was lines of brown water stains on the walls forming different shapes at various angles, a lifeless wooden nightstand dressed in burnt candle wax on several spots and a faded gray plastic chair looking as if it needed some help to stand on its crooked legs. The room struck me as a perfect setting for a nightmare. The paint on the walls was peeling in different areas. The lighting was dim. When I looked up, there was a single light hanging from a wire. It reminded me of the sort of scheme you will see in Haiti when someone runs a connection directly from their house to a live wire outside on a pole to avoid paying electricity, especially when paying for a full month might only get you power for a few hours daily.

The rooms, separated only by a sheet of plywood, were

so close to each other you could actually hear everything everyone said or the leaking of some Haitian Compas music. At some point, I opened the door and saw at least three men with a small transistor radio glued to their ears as if they were about to listen to one of Baby Doc's famous speeches. They always started and finished with the same line: "My Haitian brothers and sisters" and ended "I am your president for life." I didn't understand why he insisted on calling all of us his brothers, but he was one brother I didn't miss.

Ronald and I were tired, but the anticipation of the next day made us restless. We discussed the idea of walking around the block to get some fresh air, but were afraid to leave the room. As promised, Dominique came back with food and drinks. But, after a few spoonfuls, we lost our appetites and simply sipped the drinks. She instructed us to be ready by 11:30 the next morning and to leave everything except our passports. We talked for a few more minutes and she was gone.

The next morning, we woke up early and waited anxiously for Dominique to show up. About 9:30 A.M. there was a loud knock on our door and we panicked. We remained silent expecting the person to say something.

To our surprise, it turned out to be our cousin Bido.

He too had borrowed some money from Andy, purchased a visa for Miami from a different person, but ended up in the Bahamas just like us. He told us he ran into Dominique late last night and she gave him the address and also let him know we were leaving today, so he rushed to see us. We were extremely happy to see him. He shared with us that he escaped in the Bahamas during his transit to Jamaica and was moving from place to place in hiding. He needed $800 to pay his way across, but he was short $500. He gave us the name and phone number of a woman to contact in Florida to see if she could send him the rest of the money.

Ronald and I were very close to Bido and to know that we were about to leave him behind was painful. We exchanged many words of encouragement and a promise to pray for each other's safety.

At the appointed time, Dominique showed up in a hurry requesting that we leave at once. Bido was so much taller than we were, but Ronald and I each gave him one of our undershirts and ask him to wear it for strength. Dominique took the rest of our belongings and discarded everything. The only thing we had left were the clothes we were wearing, a small Bible in my back pocket, our contact numbers for New York and the rest of our pocket money. Finally, Bido hugged us both and with tears in his eyes, he wished us good luck.

Dominique had a car waiting outside with Jeb and Fito already sitting comfortably in the rear seat. We all jumped in and drove toward the airport.

When we reached the airport, she got out and said she would meet us in about ten to fifteen minutes. The driver drove a short distance to what appeared to be a separate runway from the main airport. I spotted a small airplane parked near where we were.

Yes, if you recall, I said I love airplanes. But I had never said anything about the small ones. So I guess what I meant to say was, I love big airplanes. Very big airplanes! Especially after several trips in the big jet, this small thing looked very dangerous. At the rate things were changing, maybe we were now to fly a small plane instead of getting on a boat. Although I liked the idea of not being on a boat, I still had some suspicions regarding that tiny plane. Could it go up was not the question, but how far could it travel? Could it take us all the way to Miami? I concluded that if this is what was going to fly us to Miami, we were dead.

Finally, Dominique came back and ordered everyone to get out. She said, "If you hear anything, do not look back or act nervous. I am going to be with you, so don't be afraid about anything."

We did as we were told and climbed onboard one by one into the small twin-engine airplane. In less than fifteen minutes, it was up in the air making lots of noise. My heart was pounding, my stomach was boiling, my ears were hurting, and I was sweating. A young white man who appeared to be no more than twenty-five years of age was the pilot-in-command. Every time I looked below, the only thing that kept going to my mind was, "When is this ordeal going to end?"

Luckily, we landed safely almost thirty minutes later in a place that resembled nothing close to an airport. It was a grass runway. I knew we were not in Miami but I remained quiet. As soon as we got off, Dominique said we were now in Bimini and Miami was only three hours away.

"Do we leave for Miami today?" I asked.

"Very possible, but if not, within the next seventy-two hours at the most."

Shortly thereafter, a small boat came out of nowhere and cruised towards us at full speed. Dominique said, "This is it guys."

She can't be serious.

I looked at Ronald, he looked at me and we shook our heads in disbelief. I kept waiting to see whether Dominique was going to say anything else, but she maintained complete silence.

I said, "Dominique, if I recall properly you said we were going to be on a powerful boat, didn't you?"

Angrily she shouted, "Yes, that's what I said. I am in charge, and I'll tell you what to do next."

I lost it. "What else do you have to tell us that you have not said yet?" I yelled back.

"You shut up and let me do my work."

"No, this is incredible. Wrong! My mother would never take your kids and ask them to get on this small boat to cross over to Miami."

She looked fiercely into my eyes and screamed, "This is not the boat that will take you to Miami, but you must get on it if you plan on getting there. Now, let me have your passports so we can get this over with because I have to get back."

"Aren't you coming with us?" Ronald asked.

"No," she answered rapidly. "This is as far as I am coming because the worst is now behind you."

Jeb and Fito were the first to hand over their passports, followed by Ronald and me, but we were still unsure what the end result would be. Meanwhile, the wave was rocking the small boat left and right and Dominique did something that was both strange and frightening. As we watched tensely, she destroyed the passports page by page and threw the remains into the ocean.

She then faced us one by one and firmly stated, "There is no going back. May God be with you and have a safe journey."

In spite of all the inner turmoil, I welcomed her action as a major turning point. Finally, I felt the end was near.

At that moment, I knew for certain Haiti, Bahamas, and Jamaica were the past. Miami and New York were now the present and future.

As we boarded the small boat, Dominique walked back toward the airplane, waving goodbye at the same time. The guy cranked the engine of the boat and slowly began to pull away. He was a middle-aged white man wearing nothing else but short pants and a T-shirt. For a second I was really paranoid, looking for sharks all over. I wanted to tell him to hurry up and get us out of the water, but I was too terrified to speak.

As he battled with the waves, I kept saying to myself, "Oh God, please don't let us die. I promise not to ever take a boat again—except the one Dominique said would take us to Florida."

While I was going through this mental agony, I made myself visualize the beautiful pictures of Florida and New York I had stored in my head. Yes, this was for real. There was no going back. The simple visualization brought a sense of relief. Instead of worrying myself to death looking for sharks, I started looking for pennies, books, beautiful houses, pretty American women, and anything that would intensify the vision and keep my eyes fixed on the finish line.

I felt the ocean breeze caressing my face as if to say the party is about to begin. I smiled and thought, "You get me on dry land, I'd be a much happier man and the party would be endless." Lost in my thoughts, I looked ahead and saw what appeared to be a small dock.

I squeezed next to Ronald and whispered, "We must be getting close."

He was petrified. "I don't know where we are, but I hope we survive."

I looked at Jeb and Fito for comfort, but they seemed to be in worse shape than we were. In the meantime, the guy was gradually pointing the boat toward the dock while decreasing his speed simultaneously. Within a few minutes, he used every bit of skill to safely maneuver the boat in close proximity to the dock and said, "You are here, and I wish all of you good luck."

We jumped off one by one. As we stepped on the dock, I finally admitted that Dominique's business was a multifaceted operation and its success depended on the precise coordination of all involved. I walked away thinking Nassau was the bronze, Bimini is the silver, now comes our defining moment. We're shooting for the Gold. Miami!

Miami!

WE WERE met by three guys this time, all Haitians. I took a quick look around and what I saw was inconceivable. Never before had I seen so many Haitians gathered in one place outside of Haiti and all acting as if they were each other's best friends. The place was crowded with people of all ages, size, and gender. I spotted a few women who looked as if they were ready to give birth at any time, but refused to let go until they got to America. There were but a few small houses in the surrounding area; where do they sleep? How long have they been waiting? And what size boat was going to transfer all of us to Miami?

One of the guys who met us introduced himself only as Alix. He claimed to be the man in charge and should we have any questions, he's the only one who could provide us with the answer. He acted as if he was the Haitian Consul General in Bimini and had the sole authority to decide who got to leave or stay behind. We gave him our names and I left it at that. Jeb and I took the time to exchange a few words about our adventurous boat ride, while Ronald, Fito and Alix kept talking to each other. From time to time, I would listen vaguely to what Alix had to say while trying to frame a picture in my mind as to who he was and how he operated.

He wore no shoes or shirt, but only a pair of pants held

up by a belt that looked very close to his age—well into his mid-forties. His belly was so huge he gave you the impression that he was competing with all the pregnant women. From his conversation, it was easy to detect he didn't have much schooling in Haiti, yet he carried himself like the most powerful man on the island. Amazingly, he referred to everyone he spoke to by their name.

His best quality was his way with children. He would play with them, lift them up and I even saw him feeding two of them. In addition to my younger sisters and brother, I grew up with lots of children around my neighborhood. They taught me so much about the vulnerability of children. When I saw how gently he handled those kids, he scored very big in my book. It was too early to tell if any of them were his, but I could tell he understood a key principle when it comes to children. And that is constantly adjust to their unpredictable personalities instead of hoping that they would adjust to yours. In any event, I prayed that God would look out for them and deliver them to their destination safely.

After almost an hour of close observation, I walked up to him and said, "Alix, you said if we have a question, you are the only one who can answer it. Can you tell me when we get to leave?"

He looked at me and just laughed. "You guys just arrived and already you want to know when you are leaving? I don't want to disappoint you, but it doesn't work that way." After a brief pause he went on to say, "I have people who have been waiting for almost two weeks and to date, they have no idea when they are leaving. The best I can tell you right now is to relax and wait your turn."

I said nothing and just stepped aside. Fito and Jeb had disappeared within the crowd. I went straight back to Ronald who was standing close by, pulled him aside, and said we needed to talk. He was chatting with a few guys he had just met and took the occasion to introduce me. I said hello and kept going.

As we were walking away, we came face to face with a young guy we knew back in Haiti by the name of Daniel. It was quite a surprise to see him because we did not expect to see anyone we knew. Ronald questioned him about how long he had been there. He said almost a week, but he expected to leave very soon.

"Why are you here so long?" Ronald asked.

"Well, if it were up to me alone, I would have been gone long ago," answered Daniel. "But this guy Alix is a real nuisance and loves being with the women. Let me warn you right now, no matter what you have been told or by whom, once you are here he makes the final decision. So, if you want to get anywhere soon, I suggest that you play by his rules." He added in a very emotional voice, "We have been told the Coast Guard are really cracking down because some people died about one and a half months ago."

I said, "Daniel, did you say die?"

"Yeah, I heard about fifteen of them. I feel sad to even talk about it."

"Well, in that case, why don't we talk about something else," I replied.

"No, that's fine," said Daniel.

"Do you know what happened to them?" Ronald persisted.

"We have not been told the whole truth. Everyone has a different version of the story. Some said the boat collapsed, others said the captains forced them to jump into the water at gunpoint. I really don't know what to believe, but I can tell you everyone has been very sad and scared. I think once you step foot on the boat your frame of mind should be kill or be killed."

"Wow! That is very sad. But, we must carry on. Tell me Daniel, did you hear anyone complain about not going?"

"No, not to my knowledge, but some people say they prefer to wait it out before they try and die."

"What about going back to Haiti? Has it ever been mentioned?"

He laughed and replied, "Going back? Where to, Jacky? What I told you about the boat applies here as well; it's kill or be killed. By that I mean, go forward and maybe get killed or stay behind and maybe be killed by starvation, indignation or mosquito bites." Suddenly, the tone of his voice changed from passive to active, he was firm, "I don't care how it turns out, I am definitely going. Staying here is no fun; it is actually sickening. All you do is eat, sleep and wait your turn while you get your blood sucked by starving Bahamian mosquitoes. Here, have some food."

"So, if I hear you right Daniel," Ronald said, "one should expect anything."

"Ronald, frankly, death is the first thing you should expect, and if that does not happen, then anything else is possible."

"Do you have any idea how many people leave here daily?" I asked.

"Not exactly. But for the past two days the traffic has been very slow. One or two days after I got here, there were at least two boats that left the same day. But they were not the same boat or the same captain. I will say about thirty-forty people left that day with fifteen-twenty on each boat. One boat usually leaves about 8:00 or 9:00 P.M., and the other between 10:00 and 11:00 P.M."

"But why are so many people here, if that many leave so frequently?"

"Ronald, people come here daily, just like they leave daily. For instance, many people arrived the same day I did. It is a twenty-four hour business on both ends."

"It seems to me there is a breakdown in the system. Don't you think?"

"Jacky, you can call it whatever you want," answered Daniel. "My only concern is that I get to leave and very soon, I hope."

"I think everyone is wishing for the same thing. But if so many are afraid to leave, it becomes a very complex problem. But there is a solution to it," I said.

"What is that?"

"Daniel, right now you have too many people coming and not enough leaving. The solution is simple. One way is to increase the outflow while decreasing the inflow simultaneously. Or two, stop the inflow all together until you clear out the mess. Anything less is a piecemeal solution. Meanwhile, the number will continue to grow and sooner or later people will get very desperate and start acting real crazy."

Daniel smiled and said softly, "I hope you are right about clearing out the mess because that's exactly what it is. And, as for the people getting crazy, I wish to be long gone before they get to that stage."

We thanked Daniel for his feedback and the offer to share his food, but told him to go enjoy it and we would catch up with him later. When he left, I told Ronald we must find Fito and Jeb and share with them what we just found out about Alix and those captains.

"What's the use Jacky? We can't even get in touch with Dominique."

"Well, at least they will know what to expect in the event we end up in separate boats. Because the way Daniel talked, those captains should not be trusted for any reason. We must talk to this guy Alix."

"Why?"

"You heard what Daniel said. Once we are here, the choice to go or stay is essentially up to Alix. Ronald, so far, we know more about him than he knows about us and that's a plus. We have no idea what sort of deal Dominique has with him, but I think with proper tactic and a bit of luck, we can strike our own deal."

"Jacky, you are always talking about dealing here and dealing there, but so far I don't see where your dealing has gotten us."

"First, from Haiti to Jamaica, twice for an unscheduled vacation. Second, from Jamaica to Nassau and now Bimini where Alix is the decision maker. At this stage of the game, it is critical we move past the obstacles. I mean create new plans and make our decisions according to how things are unfolding."

"We had plans to go to Miami and that is a long shot from here, Jacky."

"I hear you Ronald, but I tell you what. When Dominique threw away our passports, the message was loud and clear. We move forward. Personally, I am not willing to sit here on my rear end twisting my fingers like everyone else and let Alix dictate when we get to go. We came too far to sit on the sideline. Forget how far we have to go, let's talk about where we were yesterday and where we are today. I say we made huge progress. Maybe slow, but progress indeed."

"Jacky, I repeat, we are still a long shot from Miami."

"That's true but think about all those guys we left behind in

Jamaica and the ones we left in Nassau this morning. We are so much closer than they are, don't you think?"

"At least they don't have to think about dying."

"Ronald, whether you think about it or not, it happens. Like most Haitians will tell you, when it is your time to go, no matter where you are hiding, it will come knocking at your door at some unexpected hour, day or night. I am beginning to think it's not death that you are afraid of but change. Remember what I said almost three months ago back in Haiti? When it comes to change, it's either you become a part of it or be a victim of it. As of right now, we know there is a 50/50 chance to die or make it to Miami."

"So what do you think we should do?"

"Roro, if we keep focusing on the risk, we will never take the first step. I say we take the leap regardless of the consequences and, if it works out, we will never have to take the same risk."

"OK, Jacky, what kind of deal do you have in mind, and what about Fito and Jeb?"

"Fito and Jeb are traveling with us, but do remember, they are also Dominique's family, so to each his own."

"Do you think we'll get to go on the same boat with them?"

"I don't know, Ronald. I hope that's what happens. The more we are, the harder they will think about doing anything stupid. But who knows, we just have to wait and see."

"Suppose we get to go before Jeb and Fito? How do we explain it?"

"My friend, the fact is we paid real cash to be here, so we owe no one an explanation. They are not going to be the ones to pay Andy back his money, we will. I am sure if they go before us, they will not even question it. Come to think of it, did they question why Dominique put us in a separate place last night?"

"But we don't know why she did it, Jacky. Do we?"

"I am not questioning the reason Ronald, but did they worry about it?"

"You know, I didn't think about that."

"Roro, it is not that I want us to go without them. We came together but we should not limit our choices or be hesitant with our decisions, based on what they or anybody else will think or say. Here's what I have in mind. And please, no matter the outcome, I want it to remain a secret between us. I am going to speak to Alix in just a little while. We have a bit over $100 left. I was planning to save it for Miami, but the way things are going, I'd like us to consider offering it to him so we can be on the next boat to Miami tonight. What do you think, Roro?"

"What do I think? What do I think? I think you are a fool. A complete fool! That's what I think. I also think it is time for you to give me the rest of this money and let me handle it. No, no Jacky, think about something else. If we had one penny left he would not get it. Not to mention $100. No, no deal."

"Ronald, listen to me carefully. According to Daniel, unless you are a woman, you can't get close to Alix. My friend, any man who wants a lot of women to feel powerful, also needs a lot of money to add to his power."

"Why give him money? Can't you think of something else? I think it's a senseless idea!" he shouted.

"If Alix is ever going to listen to us, we need to address him in the language that he understands best. So far, I can tell you, women or money is the ticket Ronald. But, if you have a better suggestion, I am all for it."

He looked at me and said angrily, "How on earth can you

think of something so stupid? Are you losing your good sense? Frankly, I am beginning to think you never had any to start with because only a fool would think this way. Here we are in Bimini, we have no clue when we will get out, and yet you want to give this guy our last $100. I have some change in my pocket, but it will only feed us for one day or two at the most. Look, next time you have such nonsense to talk about, please spare me the trouble of sharing it." He started to walk away.

"Wait, wait Ronald, come back here," I yelled.

"No," he answered furiously.

"OK, here is the money. Do what you want with it," I yelled again.

He turned back with a smile on his face and replied, "Now we're talking."

"But before I give it to you, I need to ask one simple question?"

"What is it?"

"Do you seriously think I am breaking any rules by wanting to give him the money to get us out tonight?"

"Jacky, I just don't think this is the right thing to do. Up until now, we have already spent almost $5,500 and that's enough."

"And you think another hundred dollars will make a huge difference? Under normal circumstance, I would agree with you without a fight, Ronald, but today our present situation calls for new strategies so we must think and act in new ways as things change. And if I must add, this is no playground. Survival of the fittest is the name of the game."

"Jacky, I don't care what you say, I refuse to pay him any money. First, we don't know how long we are going to be here and second, we have no guarantee, once we give him the money, if he will get us out."

"Again, I agree with you Ronald but since you said guarantee, let's talk about that for a second. When we went back to Haiti, there was no guarantee we would ever make it back out, but we did. When we ended up in Jamaica the second time there was no guarantee we would ever make it to Nassau. We did. Now we are in Bimini there is absolutely no guarantee we will make it to Miami. But regardless, I will continue to trust and believe in the best guarantee we have when everything else seemed to be working against us, and that is our faith in God and in our decision. That's what's going to take us to Miami. Let me tell you, the best guarantee you will ever have in life is life itself, aside from that everything else is fair game."

"Can we think about this and make a decision by tomorrow?"

"No, we can't," I answered firmly. "I refuse to sit here counting the days by the hours or the hours by the minutes not knowing when we are leaving. We must act today because tomorrow might be too late and the day after tomorrow might never come. This is our last step and our best alternative. It's a test. It might be the last one or maybe there are a few more ahead of us. But we must tackle each with the same drive and determination as we have done in the past. So far, we are ahead. I am convinced, if we make it there safely, life will never be the same again."

"If we give him all the $100, what will we eat once we get there, Jacky?"

"We will deal with that later. Although it might seem foolish to still believe in what Dominique said, but for now I will take her up on her offer of three days in her house until we can get in touch with our family in New York. Since she did not specify what was included in those three days, let us assume food is a part of it, which means we will be fed for three days.

By the time we get there, we'll work out a plan for the fourth day."

He pulled me towards him, hugged me very tightly then said, "You win, you've convinced me."

"No, no, Roro, this is not a matter of winning. Throughout this journey, we had to make some very critical decisions and dealt with difficult realities. But the only way we have been able to do all of that is because we supported each other during those tough moments."

"Jacky, are you sure this is not going to be another failure of your so-called carefully planned out deal?" He was quiet for at least a minute then finally he said, "You do what you have to do."

"All right Ronald, this is what I want you to do now. You find Fito, Jeb and Daniel and keep them talking. If anybody asks for me, you don't know where I am. When I come back, if I say I am hungry, it means nothing worked. If I say to you I am full, start counting the hours because we should be in Miami in less than six hours. Time is money. I will be back."

By then, it was already close to 8:30 P.M. If the information Daniel gave us was accurate, there should be a boat leaving for Miami within the next half hour followed by another one about an hour or two later. I knew our chance of catching the first boat was very slim, but I was determined to try it anyway. If not, we should be on the next one. It was clear if anything happened at sea the chance of getting rescued would be nil. But I moved on to my next battle.

I walked over to where I knew Alix would be and when I got there, a very charming young lady named Founa said to me Alix was busy and was not to be disturbed. I kindly asked her to please go inside and tell him there was someone outside who wished to speak to him and he said it was very urgent.

She frowned and replied, "When Alix says he does not want to be disturbed, no one dares challenge that."

"Oh, I see. Well, for now you will have to excuse me because he is going to get disturbed whether he likes it or not."

"Do you know Alix?"

"If you know him as much as I do, you would also know he would be very upset if he found out you did not want me to speak to him."

To my satisfaction, she stepped aside and said, "Just make sure you tell him I didn't want you to go in."

"Not to worry, I will handle it."

The door was closed but I opened it silently and let myself in slowly. As one might have expected, Alix was doing exactly what Daniel said he usually does, getting down with a woman. I stood there trembling, not knowing what to say or do. Then immediately I thought, "Jacky, if she is leaving tonight, it's either you speak up or stay behind."

I threw my hands up in the air while shaking my head left and right and screamed, "Hold it!"

Alix turned his head, opened his eyes and jumped like a frog. For a second, he stared at me like I was talking to myself. I looked at him straight in the eyes while pointing my finger at him and said, "Yes, you, I am talking to you. Stop it."

He screamed, "How did you get in here and what do you want?"

"I came through the door, I let myself in and I want to talk to you."

"I have nothing to say to you, get out!"

"Listen, Alix."

"Listen to what? I said get out! Can't you tell that I am busy?"

"Oh I see that, but I still need to talk to you," I replied with confidence. "Once we are done talking, you will agree that we had plenty to talk about."

He looked at the woman, looked back at me and said, "Go wait outside."

"Any idea how much longer it might take you?"

"If I have to say one more word to you I hope you know...."

"OK, ok don't get angry but please make it quick." When I looked at his face, I literally needed to run for my life. He was not happy.

I left the room thinking, you should never walk away from a closed door because it is closed and assume that it is locked. At the very least, you should attempt to push it open. I tell you, Alix was angry, but if death did not scare me, I was not about to let him frighten me from doing what I needed to do.

When I walked outside, obviously not knowing what had transpired between Alix and I, Founa softly said, "I am sorry."

"Sweetheart, I might have gotten you into lots of troubles with Alix, but we will have to wait and see." Five minutes, no Alix. Ten minutes nothing. I knew this guy might have lost his concentration, but if he had to start all over again, I might even miss the second boat. No, no I am going back in to find out what's taking him so long.

As I was getting near the door, Alix flew out with a huge smile on his face.

I jumped.

He walked right by me pretending I was not even there. He went straight up to Founa and asked, "Didn't I say I did not want to be disturbed?"

"Yes," Founa answered in a low and terrified voice.

"Then why did you let him in?"

"He said you would be very upset when you found out I did not let you speak to him," she answered with her head down.

"And you believed him?"

She chose not to answer.

"Alix, she did try to stop me from going in, but since I wanted to speak to you I let myself in."

He turned to me and asked, "What do you want to talk about?"

"A lot."

"You know for a young man, you have some nerve. Now hurry up. What did you have to say that was so important, so urgent, you could not wait? Say it and make it quick."

"What I have to discuss with you must be done in private. Why don't we walk away from here, so we can talk?"

"Private, private? You caught me in the most private moment of my life. What is your definition of private?"

"You are right, but if I wanted anyone to know what we need to discuss, she would have been the one because she was sharing that private moment with you."

Surprisingly, he led the way to a place where we could talk in private.

"Alix, I know your eyes were closed when I walked in, but I really wish I had a camera to take a picture to show you that woman's face. I must say, based upon what I saw, you were doing an outstanding job."

He was grinning all over, "How did she look?"

"Man, if I didn't know better, she could have fooled me. She acted as if you were her best and only heaven at that moment of her life."

Alix laughed his tail off. "Tell me more, tell me more, what else did you see?"

"When she heard my voice, she opened her eyes, then

closed them again and just grabbed you. I was so surprised to see how fast you jumped. Man, are you fast."

He kept laughing, "You saw everything, didn't you?"

"I tell you something else, when you asked me what I wanted, she opened her eyes again and just waved for me to go."

"She did?"

"I don't know what you were doing to her my friend, but whatever it was it worked. I guess you were performing at your best and she did not want to miss an iota."

"You are very funny you know?" Alix said laughing.

The moment he mentioned the word funny, I knew it was time to change the subject. "Alix, what is the chance of leaving tonight?"

"Tonight? Where are you going?"

"To Miami. Where else is there my friend?"

"What is your name again?"

"Jacky."

"Jacky, there is no boat leaving tonight."

"I heard some of those guys talking about leaving tonight."

"Those guys don't know anything. That woman was supposed to leave next week, but I am going to try to get her out tomorrow night. Things have been so bad we can no longer afford to have a boat or two every day as we did in the past. So now we have one or two, three times a week with fewer people in each."

"Oh, so you do have a boat leaving tomorrow?"

"If I get lucky, I might even have two."

"This woman you are trying to get out tomorrow, are you going to give her some cash so she can at least have some spending money?"

"Money? Are you kidding me? I don't have any money to give her."

"Alix, how come a man of your caliber does not have money to give a woman? I want to cut you a deal." I reached into my pocket, pulled out the money and said, "This is $100. If you say to me you will get my brother and I a space on one of those two boats tomorrow night, and I prefer the first one, I'll pay you $100."

His eyes were lit like a fireball and his face was saying to me, don't just tell me, convince me.

While I was waiting for an answer, I started counting the money. Twenty, Forty, Sixty. "So, Alix, what do you think?" Seventy. Eighty. Ninety. He remained silent. "Did I say anything wrong?"

"No, no Jacky, I am thinking."

"Take your time." Now that I knew there was no boat leaving, there was no need to rush him.

"OK, you give me the money and I will see what I can do."

"No Alix. Not so quick. I want to hear a yes or a no. What do you say?"

"You are asking for too much, you know that?"

"Look, I just counted $100. Now tell me which boat do you want us to take tomorrow, first or second?"

"I can't promise anything for tomorrow, Jacky, but I will get you guys out soon."

I folded the money, put it back in my pocket and said, "I was hoping that we would leave tonight. But since there is nothing happening, tomorrow is as close as we'll get to soon. Anything else, no deal."

"All right, the second one is best," he said in a hurry.

"Why is that?"

"It leaves later and it carries more people. But the real

benefit is this, there is less surveillance at that hour of the night."

"Is this a closed deal?"

He happily answered, "It is so closed, I don't want anybody to know about it."

I pulled the money out of my pocket and repeated, "Tomorrow, second boat." Then I handed over the money.

He grinned and said, "Thank you."

"Alix, can I tell anyone about your private moment?"

"Jacky, do you really think I did a good job?"

"I would call it an excellent job, not just a good one. But, since you asked for my opinion, I do have one suggestion."

"What is it?"

"I know it was not planned for you to jump as fast as you did, but next time you ought to be more careful because you are not a young man anymore."

"Next time, have the common courtesy to knock instead of just walking in, so this way I won't have to be so concerned about my age," he replied with a grin.

"On certain occasions I forget my good manners Alix, and tonight was one of those occasions. Please forgive me."

We had a good laugh, shook hands and said good night. I learned that day when you are afraid to ask for what you want, you might end up walking away with what you don't want.

The American Dream

I COULD NOT wait to share the news with Roro. When he saw me coming, he rushed to meet me and asked, "Are you hungry?"

"For real food, Roro."

"No, no, Jacky. How did it go?"

"Smoother than expected!"

"Yes! So, when are we leaving?"

"That I don't know yet Ronald. According to Alix, there is no boat leaving this week, but he promised to get us out on the first one next week."

"Next week? Is he crazy? I hope you didn't give him any money."

I turned my pocket inside out and said, "He has it all."

He went berserk. "You are sick, senseless. No, you are a total idiot. Now what are we going to eat for a whole week?"

"Talking about food, did you get some food for me to eat yet?"

"Yes, I did. I left some for you."

"Well, where is it Ronald? Go get it."

"No forget it," he said furiously. "You go get your own food or starve."

I broke up laughing and said, "Ronald, calm down, we are

leaving tomorrow night between ten and eleven on the second boat."

"Are we Jacky?"

"With no problems, we should be in Miami no later than 2:00 A.M. Best time to get there. We can still go to sleep and dream the American Dream," I laughed.

"Are you serious about this? You play so much sometimes I can't even tell when you are serious. But I know you wouldn't be laughing unless it was good news."

"Ronald, let's get the food because I am starving. By the way, did anyone question my absence?"

"No."

"Did Alix ask any questions about Fito and Jeb?"

"Actually their names were not even mentioned in our conversation. But, I do plan to talk to him again tomorrow. I will see if we all can leave together."

"Do you think you will succeed?"

"I am not sure of that, but Daniel was right. He loves to talk about his women, so I will stick with what is working for now."

"Anything else?"

"There is nothing else, Ronald. Come on, I am hungry."

"OK, ok, let's go."

When we got to our little area, people were lying all over the ground. Some were on pieces of cardboard, some on sheets and others on mattresses. Even though Alix said there was no boat leaving for the night, my philosophy was anything illegal is unpredictable and timeless. Therefore, anytime is the best time. Those guys could choose to come at no specific time, load and take off. The more people asleep, the greater our chances. If one boat comes by mistake, those of us who are awake will also leave by mistake.

Other than a few lights along the Bimini coast, the place was completely dark. I took a seat on a rock and Ronald handed me a brown bag and a cup full of lemonade. I opened the bag, pulled out an aluminum container and started devouring the food like I had not eaten in years. While I was eating, I was thinking about anything that would prevent us from leaving tomorrow and, if so, what our next course of action would be. Daniel interrupted when he asked why I was being so distant.

"I am just too hungry to talk right now."

"Oh, I thought something was wrong." He reached into my plate, took a piece of meat and started to walk away.

"Daniel, don't leave yet. I need to talk to you."

"Are you sure everything is all right?" I ignored his question and kept on eating.

I took a sip of my lemonade and asked him to give me a few minutes.

My eyes were wide open looking for any lights coming from the ocean and my ears listening for any unusual sounds. I was observing everyone's movement very discreetly. Besides the beautiful and unique language of those big waves, the place was very quiet. In spite of my dreadful experience in the past when I almost drowned, I sometimes wish I had the ability to communicate with those waves to let them know what immense pleasure and sensation they bring into my life.

As soon as I was done eating, Daniel and I went for a walk. I asked whether he would have any objections about leaving tomorrow, if he had the chance.

His answer proved beyond any doubt that his patience was running very short. "If an opportunity is not given to me very soon, I am going to create one for myself." He spoke with great determination in his voice.

I shook his hand and said, "Daniel, I am happy to hear it. This is the only way to think around this place."

"Unfortunately, I have learned this too late. But why did you ask the question about leaving tomorrow? Do you know something?"

I threw my hand on his shoulder and started to walk back. "Daniel, I have learned from a recent experience in Haiti that money can create opportunities where at times we think there are none. But, to get the full benefit you must also learn to play your part."

As we were getting close to our little spot, I pulled away from him and said, "I'm not going to sleep tonight but should you choose to, I'd like you to reflect on this for a while: human miracle is almost nonexistent, but God's power should never be questioned."

Daniel kept staring at me for a few seconds and then said, "'This trip has been nothing else but a huge puzzle."

"Yeah, that it is. But do remember there is a huge difference between the puzzle and a piece of the puzzle. The day you forget that—you become the puzzle."

He smiled, said nothing and we split. I walked to where Ronald was and Daniel went to speak to some other people he knew.

"Anything new?" was the first question out of Ronald's mouth.

"I already told you everything that was necessary, Roro."

Meanwhile, Fito, Jeb and so many others were in deep sleep already. It was quite obvious they were tired, but why they chose to sleep was beyond my grasp. Suppose the boat showed up and the captain said he only had five minutes to load and take off, then what? Sleep? I would wait until I got to Florida.

A few minutes later, Daniel came back with a few other guys and we all started to joke. I was however, desperately looking toward the ocean for a sign of a boat, but there was none. It must have been around 2:00 A.M., when Ronald said he wanted to close his eyes for a few hours. I was exhausted and needed to rest as well, but I kept saying to myself, the moment you choose to close your eyes, a boat is going to come by and take off without you. I would rather be awake and nothing happens instead of rest and miss the boat. That fear kept me going until about 7:00 A.M. I woke up Ronald and asked him to take over but to please wake me up at about 11:00 A.M.

"I can't believe you spent the whole night without sleeping," Ronald said.

What happened next I don't know because when he woke me up it was already past noon.

I was upset with him. "Why did you wake me up so late? Didn't I say eleven o'clock?"

"Jacky, why are you so tense? If anything is going to happen it is not going to be until tonight, so, relax."

"Did Alix come by?"

"No, Jacky."

"How did you wash your face?"

He walked a few feet and came back with water and food.

"You said we only have money for one day or two at the most, Ronald. We can't afford three meals a day."

"I didn't buy it, someone else did."

"Who?"

"Does it matter? As long as we eat, forget who pays for it."

I looked at him and pondered, "How would I cope without him?" He was strong where I was weak and we provided such a good balance for each other. To me, food was the least thing on my mind, but Ronald always made sure that I got something to eat.

I reached over, gave him a hug and said, "Let's hang in there. It will be just a few more hours."

"Here, Ronald, have some more food. I need to see Alix."

"What for?"

"I need to talk to him, Ronald. Better yet, forget the food and come with me, please."

"No, you go. I will wait here."

"I feel something is not going right. I have to see him now."

"What is it, Jacky?"

"I will see you shortly."

When I got to Alix's apartment, Founa was standing right there as if she was guarding a treasure. She told me Alix was out. I left him a message to contact me when he gets back. By the time I returned, everyone was chatting away.

About 2:00 in the afternoon, I spotted Alix from a distance and I rushed to get his attention. "Alix, what's going on?"

"Not much Jacky. What's going on with you?"

"Did you find out anything about tonight? I mean how many boats are leaving?"

"No, not yet," he answered.

"When will you know?"

"You see that small boat you came over in yesterday? They gave me a message directly from the Bahamas. That's how I was notified no boat was leaving last night."

"In other words, when I see the small boat today, you will know whether we are leaving tonight."

"That is exactly right, Jacky. They will also tell me how

many boats to expect for the day and I will decide how many people are leaving."

"So, if I understand you, by 3:00 P.M. today, you will definitely get a message from the Bahamas."

"As long as they come, good or bad, I'll get a message."

"Does that mean they don't come sometimes?"

"Yes, sometimes we have none. Based upon what happened recently, we became very concerned. We can't stop people from leaving once they get here, but we also don't want them to die. It always depends on what's happening in Florida."

"If it depends so much on Florida, why not get a message directly from Florida?"

"The boats are positioned in Florida, but the command post is in Bahamas. Florida notifies Bahamas what to expect and in turn they decide what to do."

"How do you decide who gets to leave and how many people you want to leave?"

"It depends on the size of the boat. I have more people here than I ever had before and yet the traffic is slower than it has ever been."

"Would you say that is why so many people end up in Jamaica for weeks at a time?"

"Jacky, let's just say when it's bad in Florida nothing else works and that's as much as I am willing to tell you."

"Wow! You really surprise me, Alix."

"What do you mean?"

"We'll talk about it some other time. By the way, any new girl tonight?"

"No. If I have all my boats, I will be very busy."

"How much do you get paid for doing this?"

"Not enough."

"Alix, I have a small request."

"What is it now?"

"Besides the two guys who came along with us yesterday there is also someone else. Do you think you can try to get all five of us out together?"

"Do they have money?"

"I can find out. If they do, can you get them out?"

"I can only try. I have people here who have been waiting for a while. To have you guys leave one day after you get here is a bit too obvious."

"It's not your fault if people choose not to leave because of their fear."

"That's true. Since that accident many of them said they would rather wait."

"That's my point. Those guys don't want to wait. They are ready. While on the subject, any idea how the accident happened?"

"Jacky, no one will ever find out all the details, except those who were present. I must say we were all saddened and traumatized by the loss. Oh, oh, I have to let you go now."

As I looked on the other side, the small boat was indeed getting near the dock.

"Alix, do you want me to see you later or will you come to see me?"

He was walking very fast to the dock.

"What do you want me to tell them?"

"Just tell them to be on guard tonight. And see if they have any money."

"If they don't, will you still give them a shot?"

"We will talk later," he shouted as he continued to walk away.

I glanced over to see what was happening with Alix. I

knew he didn't speak very much English, but I hoped he was able to piece together the message relayed to him and come back with favorable news. A short while later, I saw the boat leaving and he headed directly towards us, along with two other fellows who came on the boat. Not knowing what to expect, I was very apprehensive.

He kept coming and I kept watching his steps. I knew something was about to happen, and the way Alix was smiling, I interpreted it as a positive sign. I looked at Ronald and smiled. When he got to us he ordered the two guys to go wait for him someplace else and said, he needed to see me.

I approached him with a heart full of emotions and a mind loaded with questions. I was saying inside, "God, whatever it is, let it be about leaving today."

"Jacky, I have got good news."

I said nothing and waited eagerly for the news.

"Did you hear me?"

"Yes I did, Alix, but you have not said anything yet."

"Did you ask if those guys have any money?"

"No, I have not discussed anything with them yet. I was waiting for you to tell me something before I said anything."

"Well, they will not need any."

"What are you talking about? Are you saying without any money they will have to wait for much longer?"

"No, far from that," he answered calmly.

"So, what's going on?" I could no longer hide my nervousness.

"I wish you luck." I started to shake as if he had given me the worst news of my life. I felt I was going to collapse. I took a deep breath, slowly exhaling until I regained my self-control.

Courageously I said, "Alix, at what time tonight?"

"Much sooner than you would have expected. In about three hours from now, you guys will be on your way. I have just been informed there is a special boat coming for all four of you. I might also have as many as three boats tonight, but I am not going to count on all of them."

"Are you serious?" I asked, still a bit shaken.

"Jacky, do you think I am playing?"

"Yes, because if you were serious, you will start counting my money back to me."

"What money?"

"What I gave to you last night. The $100, do you remember? Could I please have it back? Even if...."

"It is all gone," he interjected quickly.

"OK Alix, no time to argue. Do you at least have some left?"

"Jacky, I am totally broke. The only reason I accepted the money from you was because I needed some cash and didn't know where it was coming from." He laughed then said, "Do you have some more? I can use it, if you do."

"Alix, let's get back to business. You said we have to leave in about two to three hours, right?"

"Yes."

"Do you know the size of the boat?"

"No, in fact I am really surprised. I never have just four people in one boat, especially at five o'clock in the afternoon."

"I am asking you one more time, are you serious about this?"

"Listen, you have to tell the other guys what's going on. Once the boat gets here, you will have less than ten minutes to say your goodbyes."

"OK, concerning the money. Here is what I want you to

do for me. You see that old man over there and Daniel, the one next to my brother, I want you to use it to get them out tonight. Please, please, especially the old man. Do whatever you can do to get him out."

There was a drop or two rolling down my cheeks. I guess it was happiness. Finally my journey to America would come to an end.

"I really want to thank you Alix," I said fighting back my tears.

He pulled me to him and said, "Everything will be fine."

Eventually, Alix judged that it was best to deliver the message himself.

He called everyone over and briefly explained what was to take place and what to do once the boat arrived. Their reactions were memorable.

Fito couldn't stop dancing.

Ronald was on the floor doing some push-ups.

I couldn't stop laughing.

When I questioned him about what he was doing, he shocked me with his answer. "I am trying to build some muscles. In case they mess with us, I will be prepared."

Jeb was puffing his lungs out and kept saying, "I'm ready. I'm ready."

It was truly remarkable to see the joy and happiness on everyone's face. I was thinking, "What will I do with my first pay check? Will I ever see Micheline again? When will I get my alien card? Is Jeda in Miami? When will I start school?" And tons of other questions. I concluded by tomorrow at this time, I would have answers for some of my overdue questions.

Alix was quite satisfied with everyone's reaction. He said, "Guys, just remember to remain as a group. Do not use force if those guys decide to do anything because they all carry some sort of weapon. As soon as the boat gets here, walk straight to the dock. Wait for the captain to give you instructions on where he wants you to be. It's a daunting voyage, but many have survived. And you too will. Good luck and be safe."

He started to walk away. I went right behind him. "Jacky, what's the matter now? You know everything you need to know, don't you?"

"Yes Alix, but there is something else I want to say to you. Yesterday when I came here I was under the impression you were someone very mean. But based on our conversations last night and today, and seeing how you handled those kids, I am glad I had the chance to see the better side of you."

"Thank you for saying that. But let me say this. To do this kind of business, you need to have more than one personality. Once people get here, after two or three days, they start going crazy. Unless you show them you can be crazier, they will walk all over you for no reason."

"I can see how easy that could happen. In any case, thanks again. Alix, when you get ready to send those kids away, will you please see to it they are in good hands?"

"They will leave when I get ready to leave. I am sure you heard what happened to one of them."

"So, it is the truth?"

He nodded and gently replied, "I'll see you in a few minutes."

By the time I walked back everyone had a different opinion about what might happen and what we would do if indeed something did happen. It was a chilling moment, but the reality was that's the only way we would get to Florida.

Jump or Die

THE CLOUDLESS sky and the calm waves set the stage for a perfect day to be on the ocean, for someone who enjoys being there. The butterflies in my stomach kept reminding me how quickly I wanted the trip to be over. It was almost 4:30 P.M. and I was counting the last thirty minutes in my head by the second. My eyes constantly scanned the horizon for the boat that was going to take us to America. I was glad I didn't have a watch because I would have gone blind. I was asking for the time every other minute. Finally, when it was five minutes to five, I headed for the dock. I wanted to have a good look at the captain and pay very close attention to his moves.

In less than fifteen minutes, I saw a boat making waves, directly toward us. Oh God, thank you; it's finally coming. Yes, here it comes. I was going crazy. If I knew how to swim I would have jumped in the water and start swimming to meet the boat. As it got closer, I saw the U.S. flag flying on top. Yes, that's it, an American flag. I looked back to see where Ronald was. He was jumping up and down.

I yelled, "Roro, Roro, hurry up. Come here."

Every second brought the boat closer and closer until it was finally at the dock. Everyone watched with keen interest. Meanwhile, Alix, Fito, and Jeb started to walk slowly toward the dock. Personally, I was dumbfounded by the size of the boat. It was nothing like the small one we were on the day before. It was huge and beautiful. There were two guys at the command. A big tall white guy wearing boots, jeans, and the kind of shirt you see in western movies. He had long hair and wore it in a ponytail. The other one was Hispanic looking, shorter, and very slim. He was wearing sneakers, jeans, a sleeveless v-neck t-shirt and a gold chain with a cross hanging on his hairy chest. As far as I could tell, neither of them carried a gun, but the Hispanic fellow carried on his side what appeared to be a Swiss knife.

The white guy got off the boat while the Hispanic one remained on board. Ronald and I positioned ourselves right in front of the dock. I asked Ronald discreetly to keep an eye on the guy on board while I tried to listen and understand everything the other one was about to say to Alix.

He proceeded directly to Alix. They seemed to recognize each other instantly. I took it as a positive sign. He shook hands with Alix and asked where were the four he was taking. Alix pointed us out one by one.

Alix translated in Créole what the white man wanted us to do and reminded us to cooperate fully once we got on board. Although I understood everything he said, I kept my knowledge of English a secret. He thanked Alix and they both walked slowly to the boat. I was right behind them with my ears glued to their lips in case they decided to discuss anything significant at the last minute. Of course, the captain's last words were the best, "Let's go to America and hope we will have a safe trip."

He then gave us the order to get onboard and to wait for instructions. I moved close to Ronald and asked him secretly whether he had detected anything unusual.

Sadly, he said, "No Jacky, but I am very afraid."

I was feeling worse than Ronald but I pretended everything was just terrific. I took his hand and said, "Roro, from here on everything should be a breeze. Let's go."

Fito and Jeb were the first ones to board.

I looked back and waved goodbye to everyone watching. I shook hands with Alix and wished him a safe passage when it came time for him to leave.

He asked us to pray, as he too would be praying for all of us. Ronald jumped in and I followed immediately. The captain shook hands with Alix again, said goodbye and came on board. We all sat nervously on the floor and waited patiently for valuable instructions. The two exchanged a few words and the Hispanic fellow walked a few feet away, lifted a trapdoor that brought to view a ladder and asked us to follow him downstairs. I was apprehensive because I didn't know what was down there. We looked at each other, but decided to follow his lead.

Fito and Jeb were assigned to one cabin and Ronald and I to another. What we thought was a cabin turned out to be a small cage. I understood for the first time how excruciating it had been for those pigeons my dad owned when they were kept in a small cage most of the time. No wonder why, once the door was opened, some of them flew away to never return. I now wished I had their wings so I too could fly away.

We were told the trip would be anywhere from two and a half to three hours, depending on the roughness of the sea.

Before he shut the door, he opened a small drawer, pulled out some crackers in a plastic bag, threw it on the floor and said, "Eat these if you get hungry."

At the time, had I known how to say "Up yours," I would

have told him just that because all I felt like doing was grabbing him by the neck and saying, "Eat it yourself." Luckily, I knew enough to tell him, "No eating, only America." The tone of my voice and the anger cruising from my eyes were enough to get my message across.

He slowly bent down while looking at us, picked up the crackers and said, "Excuse me." He then added, "If you hear any noise, do not make any move, do not scream or try to get out."

I said, "Señor, por favor America, America *vaya, vaya.*" I caught him by surprise because he didn't know I also spoke a little Spanish.

He smiled then asked, "Hablas Español?"

"No, *ahora,* yo hablo solo America. Por favor *vaya.*"

He broke up laughing, shut the door, locked it from the outside and then climbed back upstairs.

Ronald asked what I said to make him laugh.

"Roro, I told him my brother wanted to know if he could sit on the deck with them."

He knocked me with his elbow and once more asked what I really said.

"All I told him was please let's go to America. He asked if I spoke Spanish and I repeated no, I only speak America so please let's go."

"Jacky, you made him laugh. Maybe they will be good to us."

"It's moving, it's moving! We are on our way, Roro."

"Wow Jacky, I hope nothing happens to us."

"Roro, I am sweating like hell."

"I am too. It's very hot in here."

The boat started to move at full speed, up and down, left and right. There was a long silence between Ronald and me.

Although I was very much aware of the possibility of being thrown in the water or the likelihood of getting caught by the Coast Guard, I refused to dwell on those possibilities for even a brief moment. All my concentration and vision were focused on getting to Florida. The sound of the powerful waves hitting against the structure of the boat grew louder and more intense as it sped away.

"Roro, are you ok?"

"Yes Jacky, but I feel nauseated."

"I do too, but just hang in there. This should be over soon."

About fifteen minutes later, he said, "Jacky, I feel like throwing up."

When I looked at him, his face was pale and lifeless. His eyes were popping out like a frog posing for a scaring contest.

I panicked because I hate frogs. Under normal circumstances, I would have run away.

"Hold on Roro, hold on, let me try something."

I started to knock on the door to see if any of those guys would come down and open the damn thing. If there were any windows we would at least catch a little breeze from the ocean. The first couple of knocks were quite unsuccessful but when I took my shoes off and started to hit real hard, it didn't take very long before I heard someone walking down toward our cage. The person spoke in a very low voice asking if everything was ok and if we needed anything.

I replied, "My brother is sick and he wants to have some air."

Immediately, he opened the door. It was the white man. Again he said, "Are you ok?"

"My brother is sick."

He went back up and returned with a gallon of water, cups, candy and what looked like an Alka Seltzer tablet. He poured some water into a cup, dropped the pill in it then asked my brother to drink it.

I grabbed the cup from Ronald and asked him to wait. I said, "Mister, how long more to Florida?"

"Another two hours."

Nervously I said, "Please to drink first, my brother second."

"Where did you learn English?" he asked.

"In school."

He took the cup from my hand, sipped from it, swallowed and handed it back to Ronald. I signaled to Ronald it was okay to go ahead and drink the rest.

They were capable of doing anything. I had been aggressive and demanding, but my brother's life was at stake.

I asked him for some paper or anything that could be used to wipe our face since we were both sweating heavily.

He walked a few steps, opened a cabinet, came back with a clean piece of rag and said, "Here, use this."

We stepped out, I poured some water into Ronald's hand and asked him to wash his face and wet his hair. A few minutes later we went back in and he ordered us to remain silent until we got there. He closed the door again and went about his business. Ronald was doing much better. Thank God!

"Jacky."

"Yes Roro."

"Thanks, I really felt I was about to faint."

"You might have gotten seasick, Ronald. I heard this is very common on a boat ride. Luckily, we only have two more hours before we get there."

"Jacky, if I knew this is how it would turn out, I would have stayed home."

"I agree. I thought about the same thing on many occasions, especially when we went back to Haiti. I tell you it is painful and frustrating, but it's coming to an end or better yet to a very fresh start."

"Are you scared?"

"Of what?"

"Death. What else?"

"Of course I am Ronald."

"Jacky, why don't you ever give up? I wonder sometimes if you know what you are doing. For instance, the $100; that was poor judgment." He laughed, "Now, we have no money."

"It was bad judgment on my part, but I never insist on being right all the time, Roro."

"I understand, but don't think you are getting out of this. When we get to Miami, you better make sure you pay me back half of that money."

"I will."

"You know Jacky, I have been wondering if the people we left behind understood the danger, would they still be willing to take the risk?"

"I really can't tell you Ronald. I think all of us make our decisions for different reasons. Honestly, I believe our unwillingness to take risks or embrace change is what keeps many of us from moving forward. Yes, those we left behind are safe. And here we are on the rough ocean, but the fact remains, they are behind and we are pressing forward."

Our conversation went on and on until I felt a sudden decrease in the speed of the boat and a sharp turn to the right.

"Be quiet Roro," I whispered, "Something must be going on."

"Maybe we got caught," he whispered back.

"Shhh, hold your breath as long as you can."

I started to sweat all over again. I was trembling. My heart was racing, my ears in tune with the outside noise and my eyes wide open. The boat was losing power. It was getting slower and slower by the minute. I didn't know what to expect; my mind went wild.

The boat stopped and the engine cut off. Moments later, I heard steps coming downstairs. With a very strong and confident voice I said, "Hello, please open door."

"Stop!" Ronald said.

I ignored him and continued.

"Hello, hello, there are people here."

I heard a voice say, "Yes."

I asked, "Miami?"

The voice said, "Yes."

"Please open door," I said again.

"Wait," answered the voice.

"Roro that's it, we are in Miami, man. It is not the Coast Guard. Trust me on this. It's not the Coast Guard."

"Jacky, don't be so sure."

"Roro, listen to Jeb and Fito talking. They don't sound like anyone in danger."

"Thank God," he said.

The door opened and the white guy asked us to step out. I had a leg cramp and, it was difficult for me to walk. I limped slowly and shook hands with Jeb and Fito.

They both asked whether I was ok and why I was limping. I asked them to take a look at the small cage we were in and that would answer all their questions.

They took a look and started to laugh.

Fito said, "I'm surprised you made it alive. We had a big cabin."

The guy asked us to come up with him so he could explain what was happening.

When we reached the deck, I was stunned. We were nowhere near Miami, but rather on the ocean floating next to what looked like the foundation of a burned down house, sitting on four poles right in the middle of the water.

I was filled with uncertainty and despair. You never know what those guys would do if faced with trouble from the authorities. Swimming was not an option for me. I was afraid. The agony of the moment numbed me, but I tried to listen with an open mind.

They explained slowly but nervously that because of heavy patrolling along the coast of Florida, it was impossible to take us all the way across to the shoreline. If they got caught, not only would they lose their boat but also be thrown in jail.

And we would be subject to deportation.

I quickly tried to think of an alternative.

I remembered my conversation with Daniel the previous day: kill or be killed. Given the current reality, the chance of being killed by those guys was far greater than us killing them. So far I hadn't seen any guns, but they could be hidden anywhere. I kept repeating to myself over and over again, "We are safe and we will survive."

"What are we going to do?" Fito shouted at me, frustrated by his meager English.

"We have a problem, but nothing that can't be solved. How fast we react will dictate how much longer we stay alive." I rapidly explained to him why they didn't want to proceed at this time.

"What do they want us to do, or better yet, what do they want to do with us? Ask them," he yelled angrily.

"All right let me speak to them, but I want you to get ready for anything. Whatever they say, we must decide promptly. The goal is to stay alive and nothing else. While I am talking to them, I want all three of you to think of any possibilities to save our lives. Think individually, but decide collectively. I repeat, the goal is to stay alive and, that said, whatever you decide, count me in."

When I turned my head to talk to the fellows, I could see tension on their faces and extremely defensive postures. My question was addressed directly to the white man since he had done most of the talking. I supposed he would also be the one to make the final decision as to whether we die or stay alive.

"If you are not going to take us to Florida, what do you want us to do?"

Meanwhile, I was looking deeply into his blue eyes, bluer than the ocean surrounding us, searching for life or death in the deep ocean of his conscience. I kept saying silently, "You can't do that, you won't do it."

From time to time, I glanced all over looking for anything that could be used as a weapon if they chose to shoot us or asked us to jump in the water at gun point. The place was spotless, not even a bottle or a can of beer.

My legs were starting to get numb again.

The Hispanic guy glanced at his watch and said to his partner that they had to get going. They moved a few feet and discussed something in a very low voice. Not knowing what they had planned, I looked at the water and thought, "If we have to go, one of you is coming along."

I could hear my mother's voice screaming in my head, "*If this is your last day my son, die with pride and dignity.*" The little boy inside of me screamed back for her help, but I tried to calm him down.

If this must be my introduction to manhood, it is a harsh one, but so be it. If I survive this, I will forever be a man. Yes mommy, if I must go, I'd see to it that the sweat on my brow and the blood of my soul would serve as my dignity blanket to cover my body, just as you would have done. My eyes focused on the Hispanic fellow. Even if I took a couple bullets, he was an easy target because of his weight. I was sure that Ronald and the others would take care of the white guy.

"OK. This is what I want you to do," said the white guy. "It's about 7:30 P.M. We are going to leave you here," he said pointing toward the top of the structure anchored in the water. "We will come back to get you in about an hour or two. Miami is only forty-five minutes away from here."

I took a look at the structure and I was relieved.

"We will be bringing a smaller and slower boat, so please remain calm even if you don't see us after two hours." He then secured the boat very close to the place and said, "Now go."

Again, Fito requested that I ask why we can't go all the way to Miami.

I said, "Fito, if you have another question go ahead, ask your question. But I have one suggestion, jump or die."

I made no inquiry as to why and when they were coming back. Whatever the reason, it was better than seeming like a threat to them.

I looked at Ronald.

He looked at me.

I said, "Roro, let's go now."

I can't describe how fast we were out of that boat. We flew.

Bits of Wood

THE FIRST thing I did was say, "God, thank you for saving our lives. That was a close call."

I turned to Fito and Jeb and shook hands with them. I didn't see when or how they made it there, but I was pleased to see them next to us. It was too early to tell if this was going to be the end of a rough journey in search of a better world or the sweet beginning of a whole new life. But whatever the case, we were grateful to be alive.

I pulled Ronald to me and hugged him real tight. Tears were rolling down my face.

"Jacky, Jacky, are you all right?" he asked tensely.

I let go of him and buried my face in the palm of my hands. All I wanted to do was scream. I uncovered my face with my eyes still filled with tears. I looked at the sky and happily whispered, "We are in America, Roro."

He looked at me like I had lost my mind. He turned his head in all directions, and then he said, "Jacky, I don't know what you are seeing that I am not. But I can tell you this for sure, we are on the water in the middle of nowhere and I don't have a clue when we will get out of here."

"Roro, I don't care which way you look, North, South, East or West, this can be no place else but America."

Two hours later, the reflection of multi-colored lights was

shining over the ocean; the clear and pretty sky was filled with all sizes of stars dancing around the moon, some as close as couples madly in love.

The light breeze coming from the ocean caressed my tired eyes. The closeness of Miami made this one of the best days in the last two months.

Meanwhile, Fito and Jeb were talking to each other. They caught my attention when Jeb said he was getting impatient. I turned back to him and asked for the time.

"About 9:30 P.M. They should have been here already. They said no later than nine."

"Well, let's give them some more time, Jeb. Maybe something unforeseeable happened. I am sure they will be here soon. If not tonight, sometime tomorrow."

My calmness about the whole situation seemed to have soothed his panic because he went back to his conversation with Fito.

I closed my eyes and made a call to my best man. I said, "God, I know you didn't leave us here because you wanted us to die. Yes, I am very hungry and thirsty, but I am not worrying about the time. I truly feel you have been there for us and I want to thank you for everything. Please let my family know we are fine and I love you."

It didn't take long to realize we would be spending the night on the water. With no food, no drinking water and no place to sleep, I did start to wonder if life would always be so agonizing.

We were all growing more impatient by the minute. But I remembered that when there was heavy patrolling, no one dared take a chance. My eyes could not take the constant scanning for boat activity anymore. They were too tired to stay open and my brain was too restless to think.

I laid my head on Ronald's lap and was soon in deep sleep.

The sound of Fito banging on rusty nails and a few pieces of wood woke me up several hours later.

"What are you doing?"

He answered in a voice filled with emotion, "I am making a little canoe from pieces of wood to take us to Miami."

I thought he was going insane. "Can I help with something?"

Jeb made his position clear, "I am not getting on that floating board."

Fito kept on banging.

The area started to get noisy. Aircrafts were flying overhead and there was buzzing of boat engines, way on the other side. We were nervous but did what we could to attract attention. Since I was wearing a white shirt, I took it off, got a piece of wood and tied it to make a white flag. Anytime I saw a boat or a helicopter, I waved it while all four of us cried, "HELP" at the top of our lungs.

No matter how loud we screamed, our voices were too weak to be heard. I gathered several pieces of wood and asked Jeb to use his lighter to start a small fire. It took a good ten minutes before I started seeing any smoke and even with my 20/20 vision, I had a hard time detecting it. Jeb's smoke from his cigarette was far more visible than the fire; that was not going to work. Besides, it was the wrong place to take a chance with fire. One mistake and the only place to run for cover would be the ocean.

From time to time, Fito would take a breather, but he was convinced he had put something together that would get at least one of us out. His thinking was that if the Coast Guard caught him, they would know where to find the rest of us.

Jeb was the first to tell him to get a grip on reality and to stop talking foolishness.

Roro looked fiercely into my eyes and said, "I am only here because you didn't want to leave me behind. You are not going. It is too dangerous."

The temptation was strong. When I looked at where we were in relation to where we wanted to be, I imagined it wasn't a long distance. I rolled up my pants, removed the piece of paper with all my contact numbers and placed it in my back pocket along with my little Bible. But after minutes of agonizing, I decided I wouldn't leave my brother behind.

Fito was upset about the whole thing. He really wanted to go and was very impatient. After I changed my mind and sided with Jeb and Ronald, we all tried to convince him that his plan was not viable.

Minutes later, Jeb screamed, "Guys, look!"

All we saw was this big thing splashing in the water. We could not tell whether it was a fish, a shark or a dolphin, but it sure did make Fito reconsider.

We started talking and joking again as if it everything was back to normal. We kept scanning the area for a boat or helicopter to rescue us. The possibility of spending another night loomed over us, but I had a strong feeling something would happen.

Every now and then someone cursed God, often asking, "Why have you been so unfair to us?"

At about 11:15 A.M., something very strange happened. My eyes were closed and I felt a strong sensation.

A soft voice inside whispered to me, *"Read Psalm 91, read Psalm 91, read Psalm 91 and everything will be fine."*

I am not in the habit of opening up the Bible and just

reading passages. I grew up Catholic and had gone to church regularly, but I was not a good Bible reader. As far as I could recall, I had never read Psalm 91.

I opened my eyes and started to shake. But a voice urged me to do as I was told. I reached into my back pocket, pulled out my little Bible and looked up Psalm 91. Of immediate relevance to me in the Psalm were the lines: *"He shall cover thee with his feathers, and under his wings shalt thou trust."* It went further on to say, *"For he shall give his angels charge over thee, to keep thee in all thy ways.... Because he hath set his love upon me, therefore will I deliver him...."*

I read it very loud, three times. Everyone thought I was crazy. But since I am so used to people calling me crazy it didn't bother me a bit. I then closed my eyes and prayed silently. I said, "God, I have done what I was asked to do, anything else is up to you."

I was thirsty, hungry, and dehydrated but my yearning to reach my destination was refueled by the Bible verse. I felt renewed. Instantly, I had this great desire to tell others it's not that I don't love my country, but the dictatorship that was created and maintained for so long made it impossible for young people like me and countless others to dream or hope. Yes, I decided to run away because I didn't see any change in the making.

It must have been about twenty minutes after my inexplicable experience, that I first became alarmed by the buzzing sound of a boat's engine.

I turned my attention in the direction of the sound and, to my great surprise, the boat was pointing its nose directly at us. We quickly formulated a plan by counting one, two, three, then calling out, "Help, Help!"

Our cries for help came out like a single chorus with my voice being the weakest. I was totally worn out.

I kept repeating softly, "Yes baby, yes baby, come here."

It kept coming straight to us. The operator was an older white man in his sixties. Next to him was a young man who looked no more than twenty. As soon as he was close enough to speak, he turned off the engine and asked, "Are you Haitians?"

Everybody nodded and, at the same time, answered, "Yes."

"Miami? You want to go to Miami?"

We all said yes again.

He switched his attention to the young man and spoke quietly.

Soon after, he moved the boat very close until it was safe enough and with a huge smile on his face he said, "Let's go."

He gave us orders to jump one by one while he and the young man helped to ensure we got down safely.

We were all mesmerized. But I did learn one powerful lesson—faith is inexplicable. It must be lived and experienced. And that is a solo mission.

Almost immediately we were all in the back of the boat, moving things around to make sure everyone was comfortable. The old man was quite impressed to see how fast everyone took their place and how well the boat was balanced.

He yelled, "Ready?"

"Ready," we yelled back.

"OK, let's go to America."

I said to myself, "Yes, yes, yes, yes! America, America here I come." The old man put on quite an exhibition. He slowly moved the boat away then performed a complete 360. This signaled to me, our journey was finally over.

The old man asked whether we were hungry or needed something to drink. Before we even had a chance to answer, the young man was already passing out sandwiches and drinks.

What a beautiful human being!

It was hard for me to even imagine how just last night someone else had left us in the middle of the ocean with no food or drink without having the least bit of concern whether we would survive or die. And now another being was putting his life and his boat in jeopardy. He treated us with decency, pure human kindness, compassion and love. Again, it is hard to explain this beautiful part of the human spirit, but I can tell you, it always feels good when it is shared.

I remembered what Mom always said, *"Never hesitate to do good even when someone has done you wrong."*

I closed my eyes and thanked God for coming to our rescue and asked Him to forgive those guys who had done us wrong the night before.

When I looked back to see how far we had traveled, to my surprise, nothing seemed familiar. All I saw was my past waving goodbye behind the roaring speed of the boat. Ahead of us was a brand new sky, new ocean, new horizon and a bright sun, all merging to form what I interpreted as a brand new world full of promises and boundless opportunities.

I had a Coke in my hand, popped it open and made a silent toast. I took a toast to the unforgettable past, one to the incredible present and lastly, one to the great mysterious journey of life.

When I turned back to Ronald, Fito and Jeb, I was met with glowing eyes, victorious smiles, happy faces, and captivating looks as if to say, "Finally, this ordeal has come to an end."

I started to see cars, trees and buildings.

"Roro, we must be getting very close."

The old man kept going. I felt he was speeding faster and faster.

I was tempted to say, "Don't drop us off yet because I am having too much fun."

Suddenly, the boat slowed down. I closed my eyes to fine-tune my vision. I looked for anything—penny, book, woman, dollar, you name it I saw it.

My thought was interrupted by the old man's voice when he softly said, "Gentlemen, welcome to America."

When I opened my eyes, I knew this was no longer a dream. The houses were getting bigger and bigger. The cars were moving faster and faster. The trees were getting taller and taller. I started to see people. I mean live people. I thought, "No sir, this is not America, this is Heaven."

"You are now in Miami," the old man said in a lively voice. "Do you know where you will be staying?"

With much excitement, I said, "Florida."

Both he and the young man smiled, and then he asked again slowly, "Where in Florida?"

Jeb picked up on it and answered rapidly. "Fort Lauderdale."

He reached into his pocket, pulled out a roll of quarters and said, "Take this and use it for phone calls. Fort Lauderdale is about thirty minutes from here. Jump out and don't look suspicious. If a cop stops you, don't be afraid, they will not kill you."

We all jumped out, one by one.

I was speechless.

Everyone was saying thank you, not just once, but many times.

When I opened my mouth, the only thing I was able to say was, "God bless you."

"Go, go, hurry! Go make your phone call. Get out of here now."

As he was instructing us to leave, I was looking deeply into his eyes and his face. What I saw were both sadness and happiness. Sadness because he was probably concerned about what would happen to us if we were caught by a police officer. Happiness because he knew if nothing happened we were home free.

I sadly waved goodbye, for the last time, and threw a kiss to both of them.

Why did he come to our rescue?

How did he get to us?

Was it planned?

To this day, I still have no idea.

It is said that some questions in life must be left unanswered.

I looked at my brother. He looked at me. He smiled. I smiled.

We hugged each other and whispered with silent tears, "We made it."

Looking Back

I LOOKED UP and down, left and right and said, "America, here I am. As of yesterday, to be here was just another dream like so many I dreamed back in Haiti."

This trip had taken me a long time, more than I had expected. It had caused me a great deal of pain, more than I supposed I would be able to sustain. It took me away from the people I loved the most, my family.

I had no passport or green card, but I will tell you what I had. I had a pocket full of goals, a plan, determination, strong commitment and willingness to work my plan until the very end. I believe how I tackle my dreams, cope with my challenges, obstacles and setbacks, will determine how my life turns out.

I knew that to prepare a better future for my unborn children, and myself I had to face and deal with painful realities.

I knew I would get it done.

Looking back at the great challenges we had to deal with along the journey, I said, "If life was not called life, challenge would be a better name for it."

I was grateful and felt exceptionally blessed that our journey, unlike many others, was quite successful. I know many have left behind wives, kids, parents, friends and other family members in search of a better world, a safe haven and yet never accomplished their dreams. Consequently, those they left behind with greater hope for a brighter future, their dreams were also shattered. Their hopes vanished. Their futures?

Alas, some were interdicted at sea and sent back to the same monstrous regime they were trying to escape. Others, including my own cousin Bido, were caught and thrown in jail in the Krome Detention Center in Florida without due process because they were labeled as economic not political refugees. Still countless more perished.

How many of their innocent souls are lying silent below the bottomless ocean, one will never know. But what I do know for certain is that they didn't go down without a fight. For Haitians, it is well within their nature to fight for their freedom as proven from their legendary heroism in 1804.

In fact, their very act of embarking on such a death-defying journey to break free from a long, ferocious and well-established oppressive system speaks volumes about their desire for change; they valued freedom, not oppression.

That said, if taking a boat and risking death in the treacherous waters of South Florida or the Bahamas was not a loud enough testimony of their political opinion, we must ask, "What is?"

It was their horror, their struggle to survive, their drowning souls that kept me afloat, captivated my existence and gave me the vigor to carry on so I can exemplify their tremendous courage. It was their long-lasting cry for help, waging their last battle to plead their cause while gasping in desperation for their parting breath that kept me breathing so I could tell their children and grandchildren that they were not criminals as they have been characterized to be.

It was their tears of joy as they went down in dignity, with honor, instead of succumbing to the horrific machine of dictatorship that kept my eyes dry days after days, nights after nights, years after years to keep plugging so I can illustrate their true strength, give them a face and share their story.

According to The Universal Declaration of Human Rights adopted by the General Assembly of the United Nations on December 10, 1948, the Haitian government and their bed partners violated every article of this declaration and beyond. Article 14 in the same Human Rights Declaration stated: Everyone has the right to seek and enjoy in other countries asylum from persecution. Yet in light of this, the Haitians were still not protected in the very same country that was so instrumental in drafting this colossal declaration in 1948. We must ask why.

America is the symbol of liberty and freedom. However, failure to adhere to her own principles, even when contrary to her heart and soul echoes a very disturbing message to tyrants all over the world including those in her own backyard.

You, my boat people, my Haitian Boat People, I salute your incredible courage, your contagious resilience, bravery, defiance and fighting spirits.

Consider these words from the brilliant thinker, Rev. Martin Luther King, Jr.: "Rarely do we find men who willingly engage in hard, solid thinking. There is an almost universal quest for easy answers and half-baked solutions. Nothing pains some people more than having to think."

To the leaders of Haiti both present and future, set aside your power struggles, think of Haiti—our children. Give them the chance to dream!

Epilogue

ALMOST TWO weeks after reaching Miami, we woke up to a beautiful surprise. Jeda arrived safely. I hugged her tightly, releasing the burden and anguish of not knowing if she were dead or alive. Finally, I was able put to rest the heavy weight of guilt and worry that have been dragging way too long into my conscience.

She was very happy to see us and we were even happier, especially in light of our experience. It seemed as though the journey had taken a toll on her as well; she had aged a little and sounded more mature.

She was surprised to see that we were still living over Dominique, but we explained to her that we felt compelled to wait and hear of her fate. We owed that much to her parents and even more so to her. We spent the whole day recalling and sharing tales of our survival stories. We laughed and teased each other about our fears and horrors and yet cheered joyfully for having the courage to persist and thrust forward even on our twisted paths. We listened to some music, danced and surrendered to each step as a way to embrace life with all its tribulations, sadness and joy. It was a blissful moment! We were humbled by the experience and we gave heartfelt thanks to God for a safe ending.

Given the ongoing chaos, struggles and gloom that reigned

in Haiti, we knew the journey toward the ocean would be irresistible for many, so we prayed ceaselessly for their safe passage. But above all, our greatest hope and aspiration was of course, a better Haiti. One that reflects the beauty and love burgeoning silently in the hearts of her sons and daughters.

As for Micheline, out of curiosity, I found out her number by calling Haiti. When I spoke to her she was madly in love and expressed no desire to hear from me anymore. Jeda toasted to the news.

About a week later, we boarded a flight from Fort Lauderdale to New York's LaGuardia airport. Ronald and I went to live with my aunt where Grand Da lived as well. Jeda, on the other hand, went to live with her Mom's cousin.

Eventually, I lost myself in her arms…the woman whom I should have known had always loved me.

About the Author

JEAN-ERVÉ TONICO was born in Haiti in 1961. In 1980, he reached the shore of Miami on a boat, illegally. Today, a U.S. citizen, he resides in Georgia with his wife and son. He is the father of two, and grandfather of one.

Five years after reaching the United States, Jean decided to spread his wings across the world. He worked for Pan American World Airways and currently Delta Air Lines as a Flight Attendant. He is also a licensed Commercial Pilot with an instrument and multi-engine rating. His favorite destinations are Miami, Florida, Dakar, Senegal, Rio De Janeiro, Brazil and Nice, France.

Jean is an avid reader who is also very passionate about the stock market. He is fluent in Créole and French, and speaks basic Spanish. He's currently working on his second book, *Eye on the Threshold*.